Gail Hamilton

First Love is Best

A Sentimental Sketch

Gail Hamilton

First Love is Best
A Sentimental Sketch

ISBN/EAN: 9783337009731

Printed in Europe, USA, Canada, Australia, Japan

Cover: Foto ©Andreas Hilbeck / pixelio.de

More available books at **www.hansebooks.com**

A Sentimental Sketch.

By GAIL HAMILTON.

"What is it all? an ancient rhyme,
Ten thousand times besung;
That part of Paradise which man
Without the portal knows —
Which hath been since the world began,
And shall be till its close."

BOSTON:
ESTES AND LAURIAT.
1877.

Stereotyped at the Boston Stereotype Foundry,
No. 19 Spring Lane.

PREFACE.

I DESIRE to present to the novelists — of whom I am a constant reader and ardent admirer — the most abject apology for poaching on their manor.

But it is their own fault! The hard-heartedness displayed of late years by novelists towards their own creations is such as to demand the establishment of a Society for the Prevention of Cruelty to Heroes and Heroines. There is nothing left for a reader of sensibility but to follow the track of these luckless yet often excellent young men and women, and lay out for them a happier fate than the unnatural authors of their being have provided. I give the novelists fair warning that without assuming ability to write even their poorest novel, I assert my right to rebel against their best and rescue their helpless victims. Nor let any writer fancy himself to have secured immunity from me by throwing a final gleam of joy over previous reams of wretchedness. Years of misunderstanding, misrepresentation, and misery are hardly atoned for by the brief formula: "She leaned her lovely head upon his lordly shoulder and sweetly sighed, ' My Frederic ! '
The End."

I confess that many otherwise idle moments have been spent in these works of necessity and mercy. But the present is the first one I have ever so much as thought of committing to paper ; and the only excuse I have to offer is the unusually aggravated, not to say impious, woes heaped upon the heads of some very worthy persons at a time when I happened to be spending winter weeks in a climate so wooing and winning that the devout church-goer had to dig through five feet of snow at his own garden-gate on his way to the sanctuary, and then have the snow-shovel pitched over at him when he got back, that he might dig his way in through another snowbank on the same spot, as exactly like the first as two peas in a pod ! If any one thinks that, under similar circumstances, he can get more enjoyment out of less mischief, I should like to see him try it.

In further apology — though no apology can lower me so deep into the Valley of Humiliation as I wish to burrow — I will only add that my wildest aspirations originally touched no more than a single chapter in some gasping Magazine ; but

> "Who can contend with his lords ?"

and ladies ? I thought I was but letting a few fancies stray into a snowbank ; and — there came out this calf!

As there is now, on this 13th April, only a foot of snow under the north wall, I have no further use for him. I therefore deck him with ribbons and lead him forth to sacrifice — a free-will offering to all who are tolerant of veal.

G. H.

FIRST LOVE IS BEST.

I.

KATHERINE HAVILAND emerged from her school-days as strong as a young moose. If she had lived a little later she would have had more regard for the exigencies of science; but, as it was, she never in her ignorance suspected that anything ailed her, and was therefore practically as well off as if nothing had ailed her. This was not at all because she did not violate every rule of mental and physical health which the wisest experience has established. She took six "studies" and held them all well in hand, and read Butler's "Hudibras" hidden under her "Corinne," while the rest of the class were stumbling through their translation, — always keeping sufficiently on the watch to be ready when her own turn should come. She learned no art and no science thoroughly except the art of concentrated attention, and that she mastered by learning each lesson perfectly, and that she did not from principle but from instinct.

Because she was an ignoramus, she got up at three o'clock in the morning to study; but because, with all her ignorance, she had common sense, she soon saw that nothing was to be gained by this, and gave it up of her own accord, instead of having it put into her obituary like a simpleton, or prohibited her by written law. She ate cake and candy and mince-pie, — not inordinately, but whenever it came in her way, — and, if she thought of it in season on Saturday night, always laid in sufficient store of nuts and figs to carry her over Sunday; and whenever a box was expected from home, was careful to enjoin the senders by mail to BE SURE and put in a jar of PICKLES. For a day or two afterwards, half a dozen girls might be seen through silent study hours hunting up Latin definitions in a big dictionary with one hand, and brandishing a cracker and pickle in the other. She took no regular exercise whatever, except possibly jumping down stairs five at a time when no teacher was by, and running off blushing and shamefaced if she were caught in the act. Gymnastics there were none in the school, and calisthenics she could not abide, and begged off on the most barefaced pretext; but sometimes, when the mood took her, she would wander away with two or three friends over the hills, and across the rocks, and into the swamps, on the wildest ten-mile tramp, without path or guide, declaiming Byron, and conjecturing all sorts of astronomical fancies and mid-earth myths, and come home late to supper, and assure her alarmed teachers that she had not the least idea it was so late, nor how far or where she had been, but she had had a glorious time! and then would she fall to on her bread and butter, or brown brewis, with the appetite of a Wantley dragon. She did not hate her teachers or play tricks upon them, but for the most part loved them devotedly, admired them with enthusiasm, and had no higher ambition than to become a teacher herself. Flirtation never entered her heart or mind; the butcher's boy, and the green-grocer's son, and the slim, trim little dry-goods clerk, and similar available beaux, she no more thought of as belonging to her world, or as human beings, than she did of the rampant, painted Indian that stood forever proffering his huge bunch of wooden cigars at the druggist's door. She had indeed her dreams of a future, in which love and knighthood loomed heroic and alluring, but these dreams were vague and far off. For the present, she had a grand passion for Macaulay. She took sides strongly against successful and selfish Æneas, and gave all her sympathy to war-worn and love-lorn, brave, beaten Turnus. She was alive and alert in all great causes, in all warring nations, though they had been dead for centuries. She browsed in the library among all the old English Reviews and all the cloudy German poetry. She read "Jane Eyre," and was led captive, and saw no badness in it; and lay on the bed and talked it over with her most intimate friend, who had read it with her, chapter after chapter; and entered into a mutual vow that she never would read it with any other person except the man she should be engaged to marry, — believing that to be the deepest mark of confidence it would be possible to show that remote and contingent, but unparalleled hero.

So, then, as I have intimated, my Katherine left school, knowing nothing of any consequence, endowed only with the much-deprecated smattering of many sciences and many tongues, but with a power of close and continued application, with an ability and a will to accomplish results, with a knowledge of the difference between mastery and feeble attempt, with an enthusiasm for letters and science, with an eager love of life and activity, fearless, careless, honest, high-hearted, — and of exuberant health!

Have I lingered too long? That is because I love her so. And I love the class to which she belongs; and I do not gladly see them spoiled, by over-much interfering, into self-inspection and self-absorption. Katherine came out of her school-room brave and buoyant, not because she had done the wisest thing, still less because she had done many unwise ones; but because she was of sturdy stock that never meddled with its functions and never knew it had any; that seldom talked or thought of duty or principle, but simply did the thing that ought to be done, through an upright instinct developed by generations of honorable ancestry; because she had lived a free, natural life, in which inclination alone compelled exercise, and health and happiness wrought unconsciousness, and left ample room and verge enough for all the mistakes a well-brought-up girl of good family is likely to make.

And if the new gospel of girlhood is to prevail; if the reticence, the delicacy, and the dignity of nature are to be coldly and coarsely violated in the name of science; if girls are to be held up before the public gaze to be discussed, and dissected, and vivisected, analyzed and anatomized, cosseted and coddled to keep breath in their lungs and blood in their veins, the puny wretches might as well die out altogether and make an end of it.

At least, this is what Katherine says, glancing around with careless pride upon her own romping girl and lusty boys, and aglow with the unmarred, mantling modesty of her own pure maidenhood and matronhood.

But this is later.

Thus it befell Katherine in the days of her novitiate. She was filled with great thoughts, and meant to do great things. Chiefly her aspiration took the rather unromantic, the decidedly prosaic form of establishing a school. It should be a school founded on a unique system; a school in which mere continuance should be a certificate equal to the diploma in other schools. Fresh from the impatience of her own enforced delaying, she decreed that in her school, stupid girls, dull girls, girls who were slow and stumbling in recitation, who made ridiculous, literal translations, and blundered and cried over problems, and professed a profound indifference as to whether or not the stars were inhabited, — these girls should be turned out of school instantly, though they were saints, and models of demeanor. There should be no rules and no punishments, but the bright, alert, conquering girls should stay, and the dull girls should go, on the first symptom of dulness, and then we should see what girls could do!

"But, Katy," would meekly murmur Mr. Haviland, venturing a mild remonstrance to this brilliant young priestess of the future, "is not this rather branding a weakness as a disgrace? Is it not punishing a trait?"

"It is only following the 'Vestiges of Creation,'" would Kate reply, airily. "I do not make them stupid. I only recognize stupidity, and accommodate myself to it."

"By turning it out, neck and heels."

"Just as you would do, father, if your life had been worn out of you, hearing girls try to remember a theorem instead of getting hold of it."

"Are not they the very ones who need teaching? Those who can get hold of it may be let alone."

"O, there are plenty of schools for them already; and there is not one where a girl can go ahead as fast as she wishes to; and there won't be till I set it up."

"And when will that be?"

"O, when my trunks are unpacked, and the garret is sorted, and I have made a visit or two, and have had a mound built in the garden, and been to Niagara and the Mammoth Cave. One wants some experience before starting a school."

"I hope you mean to start it in the neighborhood, Katy."

"Not at all. I should never be anything here but Kitty Haviland. Every one would prophesy failure, and I should not be able to impose upon people enough to make them think me dignified. I must go far away, where I have never been heard of. Then I shall be stately. I shall be Miss Haviland. I wish it could be Madame Haviland. I am sure that would strike awe into the beholder. But I suppose Madame would not do;" with a little sigh.

"I think Madame would do beautifully," says a chance, and, it is needless to add, a male interlocutor; "but I question if the Haviland would be equally acceptable."

"If I were Katherine Haviland, I should lay out something else than a school for my course in life," Martha Midkins would say, in response to Katherine's enthusiastic educational plots. Martha was the daughter of Mr. Haviland's good old housekeeper, and a few years older than Katherine. She had been an industrious and faithful pupil of the district school, and had made the most of her opportunities. She was an affectionate creature, with a taste for poetry and melancholy, foredoomed to martyrdom. She had mind and education enough to be unhappy in her lowly circumstances, but not enough to lift her out of them. She was sufficiently accomplished to talk with considerable correctness and a certain precision, but the courage of her grammar she never attained.

"Why should not I school it, I should like to know?" cried Katherine, mounting her high horse instantly on suspicion that her ability was called in question.

"Because the dreams of ambition can never give such lasting happiness as the sweets of domestic life."

"Well," said Kate, rather descending from her altitude, and quite unaware that she had been cherishing dreams of ambition, "I don't intend to murder all my relations before getting out my prospectus."

"I am hardly adequate to criticise your syntax, but is it not a provincialism to preface a remark with 'well'?"

"Very likely. But I am a provincial myself, so it is all in character."

"But ought not one to assist in erasing little superfluities of that sort rather than aggravate them?"

"I don't consider 'well' a superfluity. It is an expression of acquiescence in the existing order of things — means that you don't fly out against fate. All is well. You had better say it yourself, Martha, and stand by it, and not flout at my school."

"I should not flout at it if it were necessary to enable you to obtain a livelihood. But with a parent ever ready to respond to your slightest wish, you will need only to accept happiness, and where will you find it so rich and inexhaustible as in the 'sweet, safe corner of the household fire, behind the heads of children'?"

"Yes, a hundred and fifty of them. *We* had a hundred and twenty-five at school, but I expect there will be a rush when I show the true capabilities of girls, Miss Midkins!"

"The true capability of a girl is to give her hand with her heart in it to a noble, true man, who will sympathize with her in joy and sorrow, and protect her in all the storms of life."

"Horribly tame, Martha. Storms are fun if you don't have on your best clothes.   I like them."

"And no doubt your strong woman's heart would be a staff of strength to the object of your devoted love.   That is your present and highest mission, I am sure."

"Don't you believe it, Martha Midkins.   My woman's heart is not going to hobble along after a man who can't go alone."

"Ah, Kate, you laugh; but you will yet find yourself under the strong necessity of loving. And then your school will be but a bruised reed to lean on."

"But *don't* I love fifty people already?   I am tired to death of loving now, and long for somebody to hate.   You could not recommend anybody, could you, that wants to be soundly drubbed?"

"Ah, Kate, youth and beauty are defiant; but the time will come when you will want a loving breast to lean on, and a strong arm to encircle you, and then you will learn that general love can never satisfy a void and aching heart."

But Martha went away from Katherine to sprinkle and fold the clothes, which she did carefully and cheerfully.   It was the gay and happy

Kate who sat down in the sunshine and emitted the following dismal

WAIL.

" Moaning, sobbing, howling, shrieking,
  Sweeps the night-wind by;
Fearful wailings, fierce contendings
  In the wrathful sky.
But within, the fire-light reckless
  Of the wreathing snow,
Flickereth, danceth, leapeth, setteth
  All the room aglow.

" Yet in vain the airy prancing
  Of the rosy light;
Vain to keep the brooding shadows
  Off my heart to-night;
Heeding nevermore the beauty
  Which it loveth best,
But the writhings of the storm-god
  In his wild unrest.

" So my soul takes up the dirge,
  And my eyes are dimmed,
Thinking of the hopes that flourished
  When life's cup was brimmed;
Thinking of the dew-wet garlands
  That entwined my brow;
Thinking of the desolation
  That enshrouds it now.

" O, the bliss, the thrill, the madness,
  Of my early dreaming!
O, the brilliance of that sunshine,
  O'er my pathway streaming!
O, the weary, hopeless aching,
  O, the dull, hard sorrow,
Shrouding the relentless present,
  Shadowing the morrow!

" In yon village churchyard resteth
  Many a weary sleeper,

2

> But my heart outnumbereth all,
> And its graves are deeper.
> They shall yet with life immortal
> Up to glory soar, —
> Glide my buried through death's portal,
> Never, never more.

> " And on, still on the great world goeth,
> Sparing not my pain ;
> Trampling on my quivering heart-strings
> With a calm disdain.:
> Mocking all my fairy fancies,
> Scorning my appealing ;
> Heartless to my agony,
> For its stern revealing.

> " And is this life ? O God in heaven,
> Hear my earnest prayer,
> In the darkness lost, bewildered,
> Groping every — "

How long this howl would have lasted, we can only conjecture, for at this moment Kate was startled by the alarm-cry of her favorite hen, mother and foster-mother to a brood of fifteen tiny chicks ; and Katherine, with a premonition of hawks, rushed down into the yard, brandishing her arms, and uttering high-pitched trills, to scare away that bird of prey ; and her poem was consigned to the limbo of Lost Arts, where it remains to this day. But even from its fragmentary, though long drawn-out bitterness, we can see to what straits the happy heart is reduced in order to exercise its power of suffering, and what very bad verses a girl may write without being a very bad girl.

II.

AS time went on, Katherine's school retreated
farther and farther into the future, and the
farther it went the less persistently and win-
somely it beckoned to her. Her life was so full,
calls upon her time, her ingenuity, her sympathy,
were so many, that she seemed to have neither
space nor leisure for a plan. Even her Latin
and German studies slipped away from her, and
the stars and the under-world were left very
much to themselves, while she became absorbed
in the concerns of this world.

So much absorbed that a footstep on the
threshold quite startled her. She looked up,
however, to behold only the very honest face
of a neighbor, Mr. Glynn. To be sure, Kitty
would quite as soon have been left alone to her
own busy, happy thoughts; but Mr. Glynn's
look was so hearty and cheery that she flung
open the wire doors and welcomed him in, at
first with politeness, and then with real hospitality.

"Have you just come from the city, Mr. Glynn?"

"Yes; I have not even been home."

"Did not my father come down in the train with you?"

"No; I saw him half an hour before I left, and he begged me to call and say to you that he should not be able to come until the late train, and then he would like you to send Donald to the station for him."

"You may say to the gentleman that you delivered his message faithfully, but that I declined to comply, and insisted on going myself."

"But I shall add that, foreseeing this insurrection, I forestalled it on the way up by determining to take Miss Katherine for a drive, and bringing her father from the station at the end of it."

"O," replied Katherine, joyfully, "that would be delightful. Go immediately home. Go at once, and get your supper, that we may lose no time."

"Does it not occur to you, Miss Haviland, that it would be more hospitable in you, and more comfortable for me, to invite me cordially to stop and take tea with you?"

"There is no tea to take, Mr. Glynn. There is only coffee and cold meat, which my father likes after a day in town. And as for the biscuit, they are a sight to behold; I made them myself."

" The biscuit, I doubt not, are a great success."

" No; but they are a very brilliant failure. Because there is absolutely no doubt about them. You do not labor under the disadvantage of eating them with misgiving. You cannot eat them at all. Even Towser howled at beholding them."

" But you have a cracker or two in the house?"

" I cannot deny that."

" And you will make me one little cup of tea?"

" Why, yes, I suppose if I must I must. But I wanted you to go home and get the ponies. It does not suit me to drive with one horse."

" I have often seen you driving with one horse."

" That is my own. But what is the good of having rich neighbors if you cannot drive all their horses at once? Let me hereafter only associate with paupers."

" Heaven forbid! I will tell Andrew to drive home and bring the ponies."

A little later, Mr. Glynn glowered about him savagely as he was invited out to tea on the back piazza.

" Is this what my friend Haviland is daily doomed to?"

" No," said Katherine. " In snow-storms we always eat in the house."

" Is not the sky a little threatening? Or suppose we sup at my house on our return. I shall be sure to upset these little tables, and not a chair here is strong enough to hold me."

"Of all forms of pride," observed Katherine, pouring tea from an odd and ugly little Japanese teapot into an equally odd and ugly little flat Chinese teacup, — "of all forms of pride, I have ever observed that pride of wealth is most offensive. Pride of birth presupposes merit in your ancestors. Pride of power implies merit in yourself. But pride of *money!*" And Katy handed the tea with an air of ineffable disdain, but with a smile that took all the sting out of it.

Mr. Glynn received the tea in one hand, and tested the stoutest chair with the other. "It is tempting fate," he said, seating himself dubiously; "but they do very well for you."

Indeed they did. The tables were anything but safe, for the slightest push would have sent them over; but they were small and bright with their dainty burdens, and the honeysuckle and roses, and the soft sky, and the gay, green garden, and the smiling, fresh, happy, young girl were certainly very winsome. Mr. Glynn might bemoan himself for pitfalls which beset him, but he took in the loveliness of it all the same.

"If only you would stay just as you are, with all this trumpery, and let me go in and eat like a Christian off the dining-room table, and look at you through the window, it would be perfect."

"It is perfect as it is," said Kitty, composedly. "You cannot help being a man."

"Why, what has that to do with it?" replied Mr. Glynn.

"Only that being a man prevents you from adding to the picturesqueness. Being a man, you can have no lines and no colors. Being a man"—and she scanned him circumspectly—"you must be gray and grewsome. You do not blend. There is always a certain immovability about a man, a sort of obstinate, protruding selfhood that makes it difficult to harmonize him with a landscape. Still, it is an estate not without its advantages."

"Thank you, ma'am," said Mr. Glynn, humbly. "If you would be good enough to pass me your table, I would like another of your minute bits of chicken. If I were a humming-bird, I think your carving would suit me exactly. But of all forms of pride, pride of beauty seems to me the most—"

"There are the ponies!" cried Kitty. "O, the beauties! O, who would not be proud of such beauty? Mr. Glynn, there are a great many chickens in the larder; you will have time to eat them all while I am putting on my boots. If you will excuse me"—and she left him unceremoniously to feel his way as best he could among the uncertain toy tables and the doll morsels. He contrived, however, to make a very substantial repast; and when he finally arose, behold, Miss Katherine was safely bestowed in the wagon, awaiting his advent, and chatting learnedly on horses with Andrew. Mr. Glynn smilingly took his seat, gathered the lines into his grasp, and away they flew over the hard, winding roads, under the greenwood trees and out again into the brilliant western sunshine.

"Well," said Mr. Glynn, when they had bowled along some two or three miles without uttering a word, "what have you to say?"

"Nothing—just nothing," said Katy, with sparkling eyes and glowing cheeks, and clasped hands of intense enjoyment.

"Nothing? Then I shall pull up to a soberer gait. I want to hear you talk."

"O, one can talk any time; but this is just scorning the earth. It is power. It is trampling all things under your feet. O, Mr. Glynn, does it not make you feel strong and brave and —and—overpowering? Does it not seem to you now that you could do anything?"

"No, Miss Kitty, it does not. At this moment I feel myself the most arrant coward upon earth."

"That is because you have come down from that splendid, all-conquering gait, and are just trotting mildly along in a subdued sort of way."

"Which you do not like?"

"O, yes; this, too, is charming, but in a different way. It is delicious and tranquil. See how loosely the lines lie. The ponies go of themselves. All the evening softness sinks into me. Those workmen in the fields yonder are a part of the dream of tree and sky. We are all alone in the world. And this is the whole world, and all the universe. Mr. Glynn, are you so very, very rich?"

"Why — yes — no," said Mr. Glynn, laughing at the rapid transition ; "rich perhaps, very rich, possibly; but when it comes to the 'very, very rich,' I think I must draw back."

"Is it not delightful, Mr. Glynn?"

"It is very comfortable, Miss Katherine. I never did have a taste for crusts and curb-stones."

"No, I do not mean that; but the command it gives you over time, and space, and earth, and air. Now, we are rich enough for comfort and independence, — my father and I. We do not have anxiety for the morrow, and we do not have hard, grinding, disagreeable work to do. But we have not had a new, nice, out-and-out carpet since I can remember; and the house is only painted once in a generation; and my turn has not come yet; and the horses stiffen their bones with working; and such a pair of horses and carriage as this would take a very generous slice out of our income, — if not the income itself, — and are not to be dreamed of, even in a delirium. Not that I am complaining, you understand," said Kitty, arching her neck as indignantly as if she had been suddenly accused.

"Not at all," Mr. Glynn hastened to assure her, being forewarned.

" It is only that I was thinking how powerful money is — a great deal of money. I am very happy as it is, but to have oceans of money, that would be brilliant! Still, I really do not care."

" No, indeed, Miss Kitty. Money is extremely convenient. I am not the man to speak ill of it; but there is so much that it cannot bring, that sometimes it seems worse than worthless, a mockery."

" And, after all," continued Katherine, bent on self-consolation, " what it brings is not the best things."

" Very far from it."

" But if you have the best things, then money comes in very handsomely for the setting."

" What do you mean by best things?"

" O, I mean strength, and nerve, and will, the power to be grand. I don't mean simply to be good, though of course that is in it; but commanding goodness."

" Nothing else? Friends, for instance?"

" Yes, indeed; but we always have friends. Besides, friends are not really necessary."

" Is that flattering?"

" Very pleasant, but not absolutely essential.

You can fancy that it would be possible to be very happy, inwardly and exultantly happy, though you had estranged all your friends, if you could feel that you had done it for some great and adequate cause. But no love of friends could give you the least satisfaction, if you felt that you had sacrificed to it your integrity, your heroism. So I say that friends are pleasant, but not necessary."

" Katy, you are a friend not only pleasant, but necessary."

The words were nothing. Katherine could have returned fire a hundred times, but there was a pause preceding them, and they were uttered in a constrained and muffled voice that gave them an intensity which silenced and shocked her. She sat still in a cold tremor of wonder and waiting.

" What my money will not give me, Katy, is you. Will anything give me you?"

And still Katy was stunned into throbbing speechlessness.

" Katy," he went on, a little more clearly, since she was clearly not mistress of the situation, " all that I have I would give to be able to tell you how I love you. Because, if I could tell you that, if I could make you see it, I think you would love me a little in return, I think you could not turn wholly away from me."

" O, please don't, Mr. Glynn! Pray, pray

don't!" cried Katy, wildly, as soon as her voice could find way.

"Must I not?"

"No, indeed!"

"Am I then so disagreeable?"

"No, indeed. Not at all. But it is so un-natural. I never thought of such a thing."

"Why is it unnatural?"

"O, I cannot tell. It turns the world upside down. I do not like to think of it. Please let us forget all about it."

"Miss Kitty," said Mr. Glynn, after a pause, "I do not mean to distress you, and if you will let me say a few words more, perhaps we can then forget all about it. But if you force me to stop here, it will be impossible to forget. Will you not trust me enough, have you not friendship enough for me, to hear me?"

Katy moaned a feeble assent.

"Will you not, then, Katy," sweeping into her assent a little more than his question contained, "will you not tell me just how you feel towards me?"

"I don't feel at all," said Katy, with uncomplimentary frankness; but she was too much startled to disguise the truth. "I never thought about you at all, that way."

"But now that you do think of it, do you hate me, and despise me, and shudder away from me?"

"No—not if you will never mention this again."

"But suppose I will not promise never to mention it again? Suppose I will not mention it for six months? Will you promise to think it over?"

"O, no, no, no, no. I never can think of it. It never must be thought of. It would spoil all my happiness and pleasure. O, Mr. Glynn, we have liked you so much, and it has all been so pleasant. It was perfect. You were just as nice as nobody. And now it will spoil all. O, why did you spoil everything?" cried Katy, towering out of her amazement into wrath at this unlooked-for invasion of her domestic tranquillity, this unparalleled outrage upon her most sacred rights.

Poor Mr. Glynn had thought that he had made up his mind for every form of rejection, and was fortified at all points; yet, after all, he found himself taken by surprise, for he had not expected to be scolded. And indeed, it must be admitted that, though a proposal of marriage from a respectable and responsible gentleman may be declined by a young woman, it is not usually considered a flagrant offence against propriety.

"But, Katy," said Mr. Glynn, gently, "nothing need be spoiled. If it was nice and pleasant before, it can still be pleasant, even if it never

can be anything more. You will not shut the
door against me?"

"But it never will be the same again. You
will be thinking something. I know you will
be thinking something," said Kate, viciously.

"And, Katy, if I really have been nice and
pleasant to you, why—"

"You are thinking it *now!* after what I
said. O, Mr. Glynn, I have lost you. There is
no use. Let us go home."

"Let me talk to you a little, Katy. I will not
tease you about this. I will not urge you or
worry you ; but let me speak as if it were some
other persons than you and I. This all comes
suddenly to you, Katy. I suppose I have made
a very awkward bungle of it all. Perhaps that
made no difference. But there has never been a
day since I first knew you, when you were a
little toddling baby, and I a great lonely, bash-
ful, awkward boy, that you have not been the
dearest and sweetest and —heavenliest thing in
my life."

A great pang tore Katherine's heart, but she
said nothing.

"Can't you tell me what it is that makes me
repugnant to you?"

"O, you are not repugnant at all," groaned
Katy, in despair at being able ever to make him
understand. "You are not repugnant, only —
indifferent."

The poor man may have winced inwardly, but he gave no sign.

"You mean that you do not care about me one way or the other?"

"In the way that you mean — yes. I have always liked you as you are — well enough — a good deal."

"Why, then, does it seem so impossible to you that your liking should ever grow into anything else? You have never — O, Katy, forgive me — but I have so much at stake. *Do* you love any one else?"

"No, indeed!" said Katherine, as energetically as if she were repelling an unjust accusation. "I have never seen any one;" dismissing with a superb, unconscious scorn, a tolerably large circle of male acquaintances.

"You have seen a good many people?"

"None of any account," said Katy, tranquilly; "no one that was worth while. Still, I know exactly what he would be." Then she blushed, and that somehow encouraged her lover.

"And you think I never could become that?"

"O, no; you are —"

"What?"

"Nothing bad at all; only —"

"Only what?"

"O, *why* do you make me say things I don't want to say, and ought not to say, and it is brutal to say?"

"Because, Katy, I want to know everything that is in your mind. What am I that you cannot get over?"

Katy looked up into his face, and away across the fields, and down upon her helpless hands, and wished sorely that the horses would run away, or the wagon break down; but nothing of the sort happened, and still he waited for an answer, and in a sort of remorseful desperation she faltered out, —

" Only — just — *commonplace.*"

He stared at her.

"Not for a neighbor, you know," pursued Katy, rather incoherently; "or your father's friend — or — or — a husband — somebody else's — but, — O, just think of giving up all your dreams for — a — banker — that you have known as long as you can remember ! "

The response to this dreadful revelation was a downright hearty laugh — very inappropriate to a discarded lover; but what can you expect in a banker ?

" You dear little puss," said that commonplace, good-natured man.

"Why ! " ejaculated Katherine, somewhat amazed and discomfited, " I thought you would feel badly."

" Not at all. I am a banker. Why should I try to blink it out of sight. If you had disapproved of a burglar, now, perhaps I should have had something to say."

" You are laughing at me," said Katy, ruefully.

" Partly, perhaps, but partly also because I am glad it is no worse."

"It is just as bad as it can be, now. It would not be any worse if it were worse," said Katy, lucidly.

"Katy," he continued, when they had gone on for some time in silence, "you don't want to be teased, and I have promised not to tease you. Let me speak this once and make an end of it. I love you. That is the beginning, and the middle, and the end, and that never can be changed. But I cannot dragoon you into loving me. Let everything be just as it was before. Do not be embarrassed. Do not be afraid to be just as free and friendly as you have always been. I will not misunderstand you. I promise you to take no advantage of it. Order me, use me, scold me, be kind to me as you have always been; but let me stay near you, and be still your neighbor and friend. And by friend, Katy, I mean such a friend as never was — a friend who will give you everything, more than friendship, and will ask for nothing again. Will you remember, Katy, that here is a man who loves you, and to whom, since you cannot love him, the greatest happiness you can give is the opportunity of serving you? Count just as confidently on me as if I were to you all that you are to me. Will you do that, Katy?"

"Why — if I can — yes, Mr. Glynn; but you are very generous."

"I am not generous at all, only selfish. I want to save myself from an utterly dreary life, that is all. Don't say, If you can, Katy. Say that you will. I have great faith in your word."

"I don't know that I quite understand."

"If you and your father were in any trouble, had been before to-day, would you not have come to me first?"

"Yes, certainly. That is, he would."

"Do just the same now. And when you are not in trouble — always — be just the same as you have been. Forget all that I have said, and let us be on the same footing as yesterday, except that you know now — what you did not know then — that all my life and soul are in you, and that my happiness is in your friendship. Friendship, mind, is all I ask."

And Katy so little appreciated, and so little deserved the generous love of a sincere, if somewhat limited nature, that she could go home and tear his passion to tatters this way: —

"ANSWERED.

"Gold, and gear, and princely birthright, — take the gilded trumpery up!
    Life may bring me gall and wormwood, but I scorn your honeyed cup.
Meekness lends its graceful semblance as you come with bended knee,
But I read your inmost soul, and I know its mockery.

"Ha! your white hand, diamond-flashing, it would clasp my hand,
    forsooth!
You would condescend to give your name in barter for my youth.
At your footstool I should grateful lay my eager spirit down,
You would stoop and place the jewel somewhat kindly in your
    crown!

"Long the doubt has been, and bitter was the trial to your pride.
  Should you through those grand old portals lead a nameless,
    dowerless bride?
Should the blood to you transmitted in a pure, untainted flow,
Through a thousand generations, now a base admixture know?

"Up rose love and showed the maiden, as you saw her day by day,
  How the magic of her presence wrought red gold of coarsest clay,
  How her grateful love would halo with its warmth your calm,
    cold life,
And her gracious service be the guerdon that you called her wife!

"So you breathed a *requiescat* to the dead within their graves.
  'Blood is strong, but love is stronger; blood claims service, love
    makes slaves.'
Thus with smiling self-excuse far flung back my garden-gate,
Soothing Pride's Cerberean mouths with the home-made sop
    of Fate.

"Listen! When we stood last evening underneath the apple-tree,
  And you, in your self-complacence, dared to speak those words
    to me, —
Dared invade my tropic summer with your pale and nerveless cold,
Dared to set your tawdry tinsel off against my beaten gold;

"Though my heart flamed out in passion fit to scathe you where
    you stood,
Flinging up your puny soul blindly to my womanhood, —
Yet I spared you, for the past's sake, thinking it were better so,
Bade my white lips hide their scorning, and breathe back a
    kindly No.

"Fool! that would not be enlightened by the simple words I spoke,
  For the threefold brazen armor of your pride turned back the
    stroke,

But must goad my slender patience with your weak essays to win,
Though I stab you to the heart, shall my soul be free of sin!

"Listen! Were you humblest ploughboy, horny hands em-
      browned with toil,
Scanty life for soul and body wresting from a surly soil,
And an honest heart had proffered, with its holy deeps all stirred,
Baby-breath had not been softer than my sorely smiting word.

"Wherefore prate of summer mornings, musical with laugh and
      song ?
Do not airs from *Trovatore* make a summer day less long ?
Rippling laughter in the pauses — was it never heard before ?
Did I blush and smile for you, sir ?   So I did for twenty more!

"But in singing, did I ever sing my mother's songs to you ?
Did a silver silence ever fall upon us with the dew ?
Did we ever wander vaguely from the common ways of speech,
Or the soul scale higher summits than the lips essayed to reach ?

"If I frolic in the garden with my keen-eyed pointer here,
Does it justify his claiming to be recognized my peer ?
On the banners of my jesting, to all common eyes unfurled,
Shall be read the Open Sesame to my divinest world ?

"Faith, born of self-adulation, holds in store but inward smart,
You could move me, but not sway me — while my time, not touch
      my heart.
If, in your blind ego-worship, some dim phantom passed before you,
Must I vindicate my womanhood by kneeling to adore you ?

"Go your way.   The world is wider than that you and I should tend
With unequal steps discordant, down one pathway to the end.
Leave me, if so be the silence soothe me to a calmer state ;
Leave me, lest, with petty urgence, my indifference change to hate.

"June's fresh roses, bloom above me!   Bud and blossom, hide my
      pain !
Murmuring music, lull my senses!   Subtile odors, pierce my brain
O, to sleep a hundred cycles, if the guerdon they should bring
Were a thrill along my pulses at the coming of The King!"

All of which was not only very haughty and disagreeable, but unjust and misrepresenting; since Mr. Glynn, though richer than Miss Haviland, was not, and never claimed to be, better born, was the farthest in the world from purse-proud, never wore nor owned a diamond in his life, and had wooed her with all modesty, devotion, and deference. But Katy, like all immortal poets, only needed a picket-point of fact to start her fancies from, and away they flew, out of sight and sound and earthly recognition. Quoting from memory, I believe I have left out some of the stanzas; but here are enough. I should apologize rather for giving so many than for not giving all. It is appalling to reflect that at this moment there are probably ten thousand girls in our beloved country wreaking their emotions in just such verse. Sad stuff as it all was, Kate thought it was good, and on a sudden audacious impulse sent it off to "Harper's Monthly," walking five miles to the next village to deposit it in a post-office not familiar with her handwriting. Thereupon was she instantly panic-struck lest Mr. Glynn should see and know the poem, and experienced a strong reaction in his favor as being most unfairly treated. Luckily, "Harper's Monthly" had an editor who knew that it would never do to make up his moon of such green cheese as this, and sent it back to her with a respectful intimation that she had read Elizabeth Barrett Browning to some purpose. Kate's relief at having the offending verses under her own control again completely extinguished her literary mortification at their rejection, and she felt greatly elated at the thought that she had got near enough to Mrs. Browning to be suspected of attempting to imitate her. So, on the whole, she came off much more handsomely than she deserved.

III.

AS for Mr. Glynn, the most casual observer cannot fail to see that he was no expert in affairs of the heart. All the experience he had ever had was the very simple one of loving Katy out and out, boy and man, straight along for about eighteen years. That he was a rather slow-going, stupid sort of man, this single fact is enough to indicate. Nevertheless, in this particular case, I think he was as wise, and his uneducated instinct and unpractised heart led him to as true a course, as if he had flirted with a dozen women in the course of the eighteen years. For, in spite of all his magnificent renunciation of love and love-talk, there was the one fact securely lodged in Katy's mind, and thence easily transmissible to her heart — that he loved her; and in spite of himself, all his old kindness and friendliness and home ways would take on a new tenderness, would have for Katy a new meaning; and as Mr. Glynn was, and knew himself to be, an honest man, albeit no hero, a man of principle and intelligence, of honorable fame and gentle manners, Katy's ideal knight was in imminent danger of being gradually dethroned, and of finding a—banker—reigning in his stead. Of course, this might never happen; but if it ever could happen, surely he took the right way to make it happen. Katy's suspicions and apprehensions being lulled to sleep,—and perhaps the enemy's too,—there was nothing for the enemy to do but noiselessly march in and take possession, without any especial consciousness or design on either side.

Whether Mr. Glynn deliberately thought this out with malice prepense, or whether he simply acted from the impulse of the moment, I do not know. The latter, most likely; but it would not have been so very bad a thought if he had thought it.

But it seemed otherwise to the gods. Down upon the scene, down into Katherine's life, down upon Mr. Glynn's hopes and plans, to his infinite discomposure, swooped Mr. Walter Laballe, tall, dark, gay, rather handsome, frank, careless, with impressive eyes that could be pensive, and with a certain devotedness of manner that was quite natural to him and became him wonderfully. He was born to the patronymic Ball, and christened Samuel Walters, and had been tossed up through his childhood as simple Sam Ball,—all of which he told Katherine with a laughing grace that quite robbed the fact of what otherwise might have been considered finical. But when he grew old enough to pursue historical investigations, he discovered, or decided that he discovered, descent from an old Huguenot family exiled for principle, La Balle by name; and solely out of compliment to them — he assured Katherine — he had reinvested the somewhat demoralized and curtailed name with its ancient dignity. For the discarded Samuel he had no better excuse than a distaste for the *Sam* into which it usually degenerated, and he merely sent the final letter of his middle name to keep it company. He had lived in different cities, he had been abroad, he knew a great deal of the world — at least, so it seemed to Katherine, who knew very little of it. He could ride, and row, and play croquet, and, better than all, he could sit under the trees the long, shimmering summer mornings through, and recite poetry, and talk eloquently of all things in heaven and earth. And sometimes there came into his eyes a dreamy sadness, and into his voice a patient pathos — the lingering echo of a half forgotten sorrow, — that won for him Katy's young and ready sympathy or ever he had so much as bespoken it.

He was spending his vacation with family connections in Katherine's vicinity, though of his occupation when he was not taking a vacation Katherine had but a vague idea. His cousins he found rather dull, which did not surprise Katherine, as she had found them rather dull herself, though she did not say so. And so it got to be that the mornings were very few in which he did not saunter in on his way from the post-office, and sit down to read his letters and papers on the shady piazza; and the evenings were few that did not find them together: at first playing croquet on the grassy slope that served for a lawn, then resting on their mallets as they discussed earnestly some interesting theme; and then gradually croquet and mallets were left behind, and they strolled slowly through the orchard, or down by the brook, till the evening dew lay heavy on the earth and the happy stars sparkled in the perfumed sky.

And Mr. Glynn looked on with bitter pain. He had borne that Kitty had said him no, for he looked forward to long companionship, and tender waiting, and ever present friendliness, and she was so dear to him that that was almost happiness enough; and at the end was hope, unspoken, perhaps unacknowledged, but vivid and vital. And now this man had come in and changed the aspect of all things. Katherine was preoccupied. She was always kind and gentle and polite to him, never saucy and tyrannical as in the old days. But he could have borne that, because with the change had come also a half timidity, the least little touch of shyness, that was infinitely sweet to him. How he would have loved to watch it, and caress it, and conquer it! How he fed his fancy with the delight of living all outside of Katy as it were, yet bringing all his force of will and love to her subjugation! She should imagine herself free. She should suppose her decision final. She should fancy him to have relinquished all intention in any other direction than that of friendship. But he knew now that he had made no such relinquishment. He had not even mentally framed the resolution; but he meant, if there was any strength in him, to draw her to himself. He meant to enchain her in the same bonds which he found so dear. By self-suppression and self-assertion, by patient waiting and eager devotion, by ministering to her intellect and to her heart, by gratifying her taste and her frank, girlish, innocent pride, by every outlay of love and power, he meant to fasten upon her life, to take possession of her, as she had long ago taken him in thrall; and he meant it none the less because he made no ado about it, because he never even formulated the resolve to himself in words, but only silently lived his purpose, as he went to and fro in his commonplace banking-house days.

As for Katherine, something new had come into her life. The young men around her were only "the boys." They had grown up with her, and while she had a friendly comradeship with them, she had not a particle of sentiment about them. Bearing herself towards them with a sincere though superficial cordiality, they had no existence in the world of dreams which was to her as real, as absorbing, and as satisfactory as the visible universe. But this man had come in from the great old-new world beyond her horizon. He was to her all novel and mysterious. He was not a growth of her every-day hills, not tied down by hours and cares, not a creature of duties and days' works. He had a past, fruitful of story, a future big with promise. Something of the atmosphere of poetry clung about him. All his walks might have been down the paths that bloom in romance. He was gay and graceful, bright and brave, cavalier and debonair. He was never moody; he was too deferential to be moody; but sometimes he seemed to brush away unshed tears from the depths of some divine despair, and Katy mused and marvelled whether into that arcana her trivial feet should ever be permitted to tread. And with the deepening summer their companionship and confidence took on a deepening color, and Katy's question was gradually answering itself.

Walter Laballe told her of his past life something more than the half jesting story of his name. He told her in many a pleasant, pensive hour, of his father's early death and the loss of his mother's fortune, of his own disappointments and struggles, of his hope and resolve to win name and place; and Katherine listened with her heart in her eyes, and gave him that sweetest of all flattery, utter belief and sympathy; nor withdrew it when he remarked one morning, in the course of conversation, that this had been so very much the happiest summer of his life, that it should not even stand at the head of the list. It could only have a place by itself. It was *the* summer of all his life.

Whereat Katherine, inwardly tremulous, but outwardly bold, remarked carelessly that the summer was not half through yet. Why be retrospective? And there is the Indian summer, too.

"O! but I was not thinking of the weather exclusively. I believe I am under a spell of enchantment. The whole summer seems like a dream, and you and I have been wandering through it together. Miss Kitty, I wish it might never stop."

"Do you?" said Katy, stupidly, frightened out of her senses, but not shocked or chagrined, as she had once before been.

"It never *shall* stop if I can help it, Katy; there is nobody in the world like you!"

And then it all came out — the old, old story

— when the language of flattery ceases to be flattery, and became the all-inadequate expression of feeling that never can be spoken ; when youth, and expectancy, and aspiration meet and recognize their own; and Katherine, with new and novel humility, marvelled within herself what strange fate it was that should have brought so rich an experience to her. " My hero," she said softly, " whom I hardly thought to see, and yet I always knew I should see him, and he walks in through my own garden-gate."

An idea which Walter always combated fervently, albeit not altogether sorry to stand as a hero before the eyes that looked into his so soft and clear. " I am no hero, my Katy. I am a sad humbug. My only safety is in making you so much in love with me that you will never find me out."

" Ah, stupid!" would Kate respond, with pretty petulance, " he thinks because he wears no helmet and bears no sword, he is no hero. It is only that the fashion is changed."

" But I love pleasant things. It just suits me to sit here and talk with you, and look at you. It is peace after the long storm of my turbulent life. Your hair is really brown, but just as the sun lights it up under the leaves, it is all sparkling with little gold stars."

" Because it is your vacation. If the trumpet should sound, you would leave all my gold stars instantly and take up arms. It is not unheroic to be comfortable, but it is heroic not to mind comfort, or think of it when a grand thing is to be done."

"But it would not be a grand thing to leave you, Katy; and I will not do it for any war or battle sound that is to be heard the world around. So you must make up your mind to it." And the dark, handsome eyes looked into Katherine's with such a careless arrogance, such a laughing confidence of love, that Katherine bent to the love and the arrogance, and held the carelessness and self-scorn to be only raillery, as they were, and dreamed her dreams of heaven all the same.

And as the happy summer droned on, honey-sweet with bee and bird and blossom, heavy-scented and vocal, opening all the world to the heavens by day and by night, the little hamlet was thronged with summer guests; and in the round of garden parties, and boating parties, berry parties, and bug-huntings, and picnics, and amusements of all sorts, Walter Laballe took a prominent part. Katherine had no especial knack at organizing or executing amusements — simply, perhaps, that she found life so exceedingly interesting that she felt no need of amusements herself, or that she really lacked the devising faculty; but she made an excellent audience. Without the ability to be a leader, she was singularly successful as rank and file. It tired her merely to think of the paraphernalia of preparation, but when there was a call for sympathetic enjoyment and admiration, Katherine came to the front. Mr. Laballe, on the contrary, was first and foremost in every plan. If it was drama or tableau, he was the cleverest of all obdurate fathers, or knightly warriors, or princely suitors. If it was Shaker-singing, the sheet was wrapped about him with the forlornest asperity, his countenance was marked with the deepest gloom, his voice intoned the drollest, the most lugubrious cadences. If it was charades, he found the best words and made the wittiest of conversation. In rowing, in croquet, in anagram, in the Virginia reel, in clam-chowder, and fried potatoes on the rocks, in every form of fun, he was ready, fertile, indefatigable. Kate was invaluable when it came to inspiring the actors with " inextinguishable laughter," or sitting in the stern of the boat with speechless delight in the molten water and glowing sky. She could even bear a respectable hand in croquet if she were allowed to shove and cheat when necessary, to take a mallet's length with or without reason, and quietly lift her ball to the desired side of the wicket. But she really found far more pleasure in looking on — admiring Mr. Laballe's splendid split-shots, the easy sweep of his oars, his vigorous and vigilant ladling of hot soup — than in any more personal share in whatever was going on. "Happy me!" would Katy muse. "He does everything well. How came all this to me when it is just what I wanted? His lightest touch is grace and vigor. How strong he must be in real things? He who is so admirable in trifles, how all-commanding when he takes hold on life! Wretched me! I can do nothing well. I can do almost nothing in any way. I am not good enough for him. O, I am not fit for him. He should have fallen in love with a royal woman — tall, and statuesque, and fascinating — a superb woman who could sing the wild woods into hush, and walk sister and wife of the gods, and — " By that time a new scene had opened, and Katherine was called on to admire Mr. Laballe anew, as he stooped, in the character of Leicester, over some pretty imploring Amy Robsart, — and so never quite gave him up to the superb Juno, to whom the fascinating creature really belonged.

Mr. Glynn seldom mingled in these gay companies. As Mr. Laballe rose above the horizon, Mr. Glynn sunk out of sight. His visits to Kate's father, even, diminished, to that gentleman's consciousness and dissatisfaction. Whenever Kate met him she was almost over-kind. At home she could never quite free herself from embarrassment; but in company she talked to him, she deferred to him, she showed him every sign of regard, respect, and even honor, so

that he felt in his deepest heart that there was
no hope for him, that his cause was lost. Katy
was trying to make up to him in what he did not
want for what she could not give.

When the summer festivities broke up and
the summer sojourners began to go, Katherine
was not sorry. She lapsed again into the life
that she loved best. Light, pleasant household
work, tidy, thrifty housewifely cares, replenish-
ing, rearranging, freshening, brightening; overlooking stores of spotless, sweet-smelling napery,
redding and refilling ample closets, devising little
plans for kitchen convenience and kitchen pleasure; darning the flour-sieve with a fine wire
thread, greatly to Tishy's astonishment and
admiration; and changing the outworn of the
old red sandstone period, as Katy used to say,
into the bright and new of the alluvial age; in
short, making all common things snug, comfortable, and agreeable, — such was Katy's ignoble
but interesting work; and from the depths of
the camphor-chest, and the inmost recesses of the
china closet, her voice rang out as blithe and
free as if she had been singing to the listening
spheres. Then the solid delight of reading —
novels, history, essays, poetry — torn copies of
Godey's Lady's Book, and the American Tract
Society's stirring Appeals to the Sinner in convenient barrels "up garret;" Whelpley's Bacon,
and Burton's "Anatomy of Melancholy;" and

poor old Charlotte Temple, in their own, not over-stocked library, — everything that she could buy, borrow, or otherwise lay hands on, good, bad and indifferent, that was Katherine's solace and society. And O, the exquisite rapture of long, solitary walks through the wild, wet woods, cushioned with heavy moss, alive with every grace of springing vine and drooping spray; over the dry, crisp hills pungent with the breath of the Indian summer, delicious with the melancholy of departing bloom and the languor of reposing growth! Beyond the encircling line of dense, blue sea, Katy's thought was wont to penetrate into the romance and mystery of the wise old world, and sometimes, by some mirage, the far sea swept its white beach inland, and lay in a lovely amethystine haze over against the still, low-lying fields that stretched at the maiden's feet. All this had been rapture when only an atmosphere of dreams enveloped her. Now the soft skies bent over her as of old, and the smoky hills rose warm around her, and the yellow sunshine trembled into her most secret heart; but the banner over all was love. So, for Katy's happiness, there was no speech nor language.

IV.

THE only drawback was a lack of warmth in her father's liking for her lover. He did not oppose him. He seldom thought of opposing Katy in anything. Nor is it to be conjectured that he was in the least degree chagrined that Mr. Glynn and Katy could not make up their minds to each other. Katherine had never lisped to her father a syllable of Mr. Glynn's wish, and Mr. Haviland was an innocent, straightforward, royal old gentleman, who had seen little Kate and big Richard Glynn growing up together, the latter having the start by a respectable and disarming number of years, and he never any more thought of a marriage between them than between the two rose-bushes hob-a-nobbing at the garden-gate. In fact, it was a good deal of a shock to him to come all of a sudden upon Kate as a grown-up girl. It never disturbed him in the least that Mr. Glynn should come to his house. Mr. Glynn had always been coming to his house. The various young men and maidens who pulled his latch-string were but the boys and girls who had grown up with Katy. A woman might have enlightened him. But the one woman of his life had gone out of his sight long years before, and, alone as he was, it was probably for his happiness that there was no one else to ravage the late-lingering bliss of his ignorance. But when Walter Laballe came, there was no misunderstanding the situation longer. This was no old schoolmate chatting with a girl about old times, but a man grown, come out of the great world, wooing Kate as a woman; and Mr. Haviland sorrowfully tried to comprehend it, and adjust himself to it. What he would have liked, what he, perhaps, unconsciously hoped for, was a continuance of things exactly as they had been. Katy, home from school, Katy about the house, cheerful, courageous, energetic, if sometimes a little dreamy and impracticable on the one side, a little impatient, impetuous, and imperious on the other — striking out occasionally into the border-lands of home, but never overstepping their boundary-line; gone only long enough to give the zest of return, and coming back with fresh store of pleasant girl-gossip of church and state, of science and society, and every living thing under the sun, — Katy, the bright link between his past and his future, the rosy, radiant medium through which the world looked in upon him, and he out upon the world, — this was what he

"Says he is waiting for a summons from his partner, I suppose."

"Lays it all to me. Says he should have gone to town a month ago but for me. Did you ever hear the like of that, when I have a fresh surprise every day at seeing him?"

"But, my dear, he is a young man, and without money, and he has made no real start in life yet."

"Yes, dear, I know he is poor. He has no money. That is the only point on which we are really equal — "

"No, Katherine, you are not equal there. It is not right to say you have no money. You are not rich, but I have provided for your comfort and independence as long as you live."

"That you have, you dear old daddy! I could not be a happier girl if you had earned millions. So I can't be frightened at poverty, or be worried because Walter is not rich."

"Nor I either, Katy. It is not poverty I am thinking of, though you know nothing about poverty, and I hope you never will. But the habits that prevent poverty are the thing."

"Habits! Walter's habits! O, my dear, what are you thinking of?"

"Of you, Katy. Always and only of you, my child."

"That is a wicked story, now; for I know you are thinking of poor Walter, whose habits are perfect. That is, he does smoke; I wish he did not; I admit I wish he did not. But, as he says, very truly, 'What else do I do? Tolerate this one little wickedness.' And I confess, papa, that with the closest scrutiny, and after a long and intimate acquaintance, there is not another single thing that I want him not to do. Now, dear, admit yourself that I have made a pretty narrow escape."

A laugh met Katherine's quaint defence, but Mr. Haviland was not satisfied.

"Don't be fretted, lovey; but what I want to see is that Laballe is a man —"

"Pap must not call names. It is not civil."

"Call names?"

"Certainly. Pap says 'Laballe.' Don't say 'Laballe.' It sounds hard and cold, as if he were only — anybody — and not Walter. Walter, Walter, Walter, — is it not a lovely name? Even 'Mr. Laballe' sounds more as if he were to be respected. Won't you say '*Mr.* Laballe,' when you don't feel equal to saying 'Walter'?"

"Mr. Laballe — Lord Laballe — anything you like."

"O, I like that amazingly! Why, gentle shepherd, tell me why I was not born in marble halls, and christened Lady Katherine? Instead of Tishy calling after me 'Kath-er-*rine*, you'll get your death o' cold; come back, and put on your shawl;' it would be, 'Will your ladyship

wrap your ladyship in your ladyship's diamond-dew velvet, or in your ladyship's sultana shawl?' What does your ducal highness think of that?"

"That you are a silly chatterbox, and will stay so to the end," said Mr. Haviland, with a smile.

"Dear old duck!" cried Kate, encouraged. Then, more softly, "Say you love Walter."

"Love Walter! Bless your heart, *I* am not going to marry him. Why should I love him?"

"Because I — I care for him, papa, and he cares for me."

"Yes, dear, he is very fond of you. I am not worried about that —" And down would go Kate's fingers, over — not to say into — his eyes, with a shy, laughing, chiding, "What business have these meddlesome eyes to be seeing what does not belong to them?"

"But, Katy, I should feel easier about you if I could see him showing a sense of responsibil-ity, — taking hold of things with any sort of grip. I don't see that he is up and astir. In my day, we used to call it dawdling."

"O, papa dear," cried Kate, shocked. "Just because he stays a week or two into September. That is not fair. That is not like you. Why, he is studying all the time."

"But his business is in Branch & Hale's law-office in town, and he cannot transact it fifty miles away. Besides, he is seven-and-twenty, and his studying ought to be in connection with cases, and on the spot; at least, so it seems to me."

"And it is, a good deal of the time, you know, father. It is only just now—just this little, lovely fall, that he takes a longer vacation than usual. And you know, dear, you must go shares with me in being to blame for that. But this is not really the whole reason. I assure you, Walter has thought very seriously of—everything. And many things which he seems to do simply for amusement, from self-indulgence, he does from a really high and noble motive. You see, papa, I have talked about this myself. We have talked it all over. Indeed, we talk over most things," added Kate, simply.

"And what is the high and noble motive here, Katy?"

"Don't be sarcastic, there's a love! It is a dear old daddy when it is simple and docile; but when it is sarcastic, I really must have recourse to discipline. Promise? Yes. Well, then, Walter says—and I think it is very true, and so do you—that the great trouble with our country is, that every one does everything. We are eager and hurried. We are not restful. Now, it is necessary to do things, but it is just as necessary to the country's dignity to have a class that shall not be over-eager to do, but that shall be tranquil to judge. We need to take account of stock, just as much as to accumulate stock. We want not only geniuses to make discoveries, and invent machines, and write books, but we want a cultivated, discriminating, and appreciative people, to create the receptive atmosphere that stimulates genius."

"So Mr. Laballe is going to act the part of atmosphere to other people's genius."

"There, you are at it again, papa! But I forgive you, in consideration of your benighted ignorance. No, Mr. Haviland, Mr. Laballe is not going to limit himself to being atmosphere. On the contrary, I shall be much surprised if he does not before long, and in many ways, appear in the rôle of genius. In fact I think he has already done so. But don't you see, dear, that it keeps him from over-eagerness, from that fierce restlessness which makes life such a hurry, such a race and a wrestle, and precludes all leisurely and rational enjoyment? Would you not,—now, papa, tell me 'honest, true,'—would you not rather live with — people who are quiet, and take pleasure as it goes, than with people who are in a frenzy of hurry to work from morning till night?"

"That may be, lovey; but when a young man has his fortune to make, and his burdens to take from other people's shoulders, I should rather see him hurry too much than take it too easy."

"I don't understand you, papa."

"Why, dear, for instance : Laballe's — excuse me, *Mr.* Laballe's mother lives with her brother, and is maintained by him. Now, if I were a young fellow, with two hands of my own, I could not stand that for a day. I should let atmospheres slide, and look out for my mother. It is a humiliation for a woman to depend upon her brother when she has a son."

"I — do — not know anything about that," faltered Katherine, the painful blood crimsoning her cheeks; but her father did not see it. It was a rude transition, that must be admitted; from high purposes of fashioning your life on broad, patriotic, and philosophic principles, down to this petty, prudential, domestic arrangement.

"It is all very well," Mr. Haviland meandered on, not knowing how sharp was the wound he had inflicted; "it is all well enough for a young man to think how he would like to live if things were to his mind; but it is another thing to live in that way when things are not to his mind. I am not finding fault, Kitty, but I can't exactly like the lay of the land. Laballe may be only thoughtless, but thoughtlessness is as bad in its results as malice, when it is well rooted down. I can't trust my girl gladly to any one who would not rather be rough-shod and honest, than tiptoe fine and make somebody else pay the bills. Don't be blind, Katherine. Don't be too sure."

This was a great deal for Mr. Haviland to

say — a violent opposition for him to set up against Kate. Kate felt it, but she could not go to Walter Laballe, and remark, casually, "Do you come here and set up for a leisure class, and talk about being the judgment-seat before which the workers are to present themselves, while you allow your mother — you, who have been a grown man and a voter for six years, allow your mother to be dependent upon her brother; allow another man to perform the duty which should be your highest pleasure ; allow her to be subordinate to one on whom she has but an inferior claim, instead of being mistress of your house, on whom she has the supreme claim?" That, of course, would be a lecture, and an insult to Walter. Neither could Katy go to work clandestinely to find out something against her Walter. She was very sure that the case, if known, would not count up against him. She was sure that in some way unknown to common observation he was bearing himself as became a son towards his mother. If she had had doubts of him herself, she felt that she could speak them boldly, or boldly wait the issue. But she only believed that some one had given her father wrong impressions, — he, in the anxiety of his great love for her, being naturally open to wrong impressions. She wanted to be able to convince her father, without Walter's suffering the distress or the shame of being aware that he was misunderstood by her own father. So she led him, at the earliest opportunity, to speak of his mother, which he did with great frankness and great affection, — to Kate's unbounded delight.

"She must miss you so much," said Katherine, when a niche came for her to interpose that little remark. "It is such a pity that you cannot live together, when you are both free."

"Only that the dear dame is so much happier with Uncle Ned and Aunt Eva, and the children, and the open country life, than she could be cooped up in such a home as I should be able to give her in the city. Katy, I have one dream, by day and by night — to live with the two women that I love, my mother, and — my wife."

Of course, Katy had nothing to say to this, and Walter went on, — " to give them, I mean, such a home as is worthy of them. I confess it would be no pleasure to me to see them restricted, hampered, economizing, — bringing all their minds to bear on making both ends meet. None of that for me, if you please. But when I can see them dispensing a liberal and elegant hospitality, living in the state that befits them, — 'Fly swiftly round, ye wheels of time!'"

"But," said Kate, running the risk of seeming to argue her own case in unmaidenly fashion, in her eagerness to argue the mother's case, "to be with you is the main thing, after all. Your mother would rather be with you in ever so small a house, than away from you in a large one."

"Don't be too sure of that, Katy. My lady-mother is not one of the kind that takes gracefully to poverty. She has always been used to wealth and she becomes wealth; and I would not be the one to use her to anything else. Bless my soul, Kate, I can't think of anything more comical than to see my mother pottering about in an economical way. You ought to see her."

"I know she must be tall, and stately, and handsome. I shall be afraid of her."

"She is, and you won't. She will take you straight into her heart. She will patronize you a little at first, but you must put up with that. She would patronize the king on his throne. When she enters heaven she will make a gracious courtesy to all the angels standing around, and will consider in her heart that good society there has received a valuable accession."

"Then I should like to know why I am not going to be afraid of her."

"O, she is very amiable, — thoroughly good-natured. And she has the weakness of being a devout believer in your humble servant; so if you had no other charm for her, you would have the charm of being one of my little belongings, and that would secure her allegiance at once."

"It is so vexatious that she should not be able to live with you, when she loves you so."

"Vexatious! It is — condemnable! There never was anything so unreasonable as the way things are divided in this world. There is old Glynn, with nobody on earth to care for, and not a thought beyond note-shaving, leading his dog-trot life, solid-stiff with money that he does not know how to dispose of; and here am I, with everything under heaven to bless myself with except money. I declare, Kate, I feel sometimes as if I could rob a bank. If Glynn is found some morning under his window, bound, gagged, and plundered, don't you report this conversation, will you?"

Kate did not quite like the way in which Mr. Glynn was mentioned, but she could not say so, and the blush which the allusion called up passed to the account of her general embarrassment. But altogether the talk was highly satisfactory — until Kate was left alone, and began to think over how she should present it informally to her father; and then she gradually discovered that she had made little headway. A very honest regard and admiration for his mother Mr. Laballe had expressed, but the impertinent little fact remained that she was living on what might be called a brother's charity while the son was taking life easily elsewhere. That he was too poor to support his mother as he wished did not at all mitigate the fact that he was amusing himself, without any very strenuous devotion to business, and doing it on the ground that the country needed a class of elegant, learned, and leisurely men, to encourage art, science, and literature! So, on the whole, Katy — did not exactly conclude not to mention the subject to her father again, but she — pondered it in her heart so long, that the time slipped away till it seemed to her that to bring it up would look like lugging it in, and as if it were a more serious matter than it really was. For Katy herself was not in doubt. Walter was all right. It was only that she could not make the thing look to her father as it looked to her. But she pleased herself with portraying the sly revenge she would one day take upon him, when Walter's name began to be known; when he should be sought, both in his avowed and in his silent profession; when the lawyer should link his name with great causes, and the critic should adjudge righteous judgment. She heard the vague voices saying, " At last a good time has come for our country. We have a man who has sought greatness, and whom also greatness has sought. We have a mind keen and commanding in its own pursuits, but so liberally cultured that it is an authority in the pursuits of others : a many-sided man ; one who, of his own will and wisdom, against all the trend of his time and his country, has attained the calm, ripe, judicial comprehension which has hitherto been the result of generations of liberal leisure." O, Katy grew eloquent in uttering her Walter's praises, and smiled through all her soul at the thought of her father's pleased discomfiture. She inwardly vowed that she would show him no mercy. She would make him confess to within an inch of his life. He should repeat his recantation aloud, word for word, at her dictation: "I was wrong; *mea culpa.* Walter Laballe's idleness was more fruitful of the best results than other men's labor." And then she would forgive him rapturously and they would pass the rest of their lives in a state of mutual exultation over their happiness and harmonious adoration of Walter.

This was all the easier a picture to paint, as Walter presently went to town. It would be a little severe, perhaps, to say that Katherine felt relieved by his going; and yet it was something like relief she felt. Indeed, Walter found it so hard to tear himself away, and Katherine helped him to the sacrifice so cheerfully, without giving him the least excuse by encouragement to delay his departure a day beyond the specified time, that he quite scolded her for her hard-heartedness. "It seems to me, Miss Haviland," he remarked, in his grandest manner, "that you are altogether too resigned to a separation."

"Too resigned to your quickly finding your true place in the world and making all men see you as I see you," said Katy, with a smiling composure, a proud confidence, that could but flatter.

"To think how a woman will sacrifice love to ambition," said Walter, essaying a futile frown.

"How a woman will sacrifice a momentary enjoyment to the life-long ennobling of love, that is what you mean."

"But I must remember, Katy, that you can only love in your own measure. Of course, a woman can't love like a man. Here are you holding the balance as prudently and accurately as a grocer's apprentice, and coolly setting me adrift for the mere sake of getting on in the world; while I — madman that I am — am ready to cut loose from everything just to stay in your sight. That is love, Miss Katy."

"Yes," said Katy, smiling over a rose into the sunset sky, "a weak love, a feeble love, that may one day grow to stand alone, but cannot yet. Now I see the difference between a man's love and a woman's love. I have read of it but never before perceived it. A woman's love is all strong, full-statured in an hour. It does not need to be nourished and strengthened by constant presence and association. It can go into the wilderness, and live alone, and grow and flourish, biding its time. But a man must feed his love every day at the shrine of sight and sound, or it slips away from him. Poor dear, poor dear! You are honest, and love as well as you can in your feeble-forcible way;" and she gently stroked his coat-sleeve with the dainty rose before she fastened it in his button-hole.

I am not sure that Katherine was not happier after Walter went away. If there had been — mind, I do not say there was, but if there had been — the least little strain of dissatisfaction or even *un*satisfaction with him, suggested by her father's doubts, that disappeared wholly and Kate had only the lover of her fancies to worship. Him she could endow with every virtue as well as every grace under heaven. And to him she wrote letters of such length as must try any but a lover's patience — letters full of the glory of youth and love and unchecked life, plucking from earth, and sea, and sky wherewithal to minister to its joy. And Walter's letters in return were charming. All this beautiful romantic world was not lost upon him that was certain. Kate felt that if one half the fire, and poetry, and eloquence of his letters could appear at the bar or in the magazines they would set the world aglow. And that is where they will one day appear, said Katy to herself, confidently.

More and more she felt that day drawing on apace as Walter spoke from time to time of the busy occupation in which he was engaged, the many calls upon his time, and the impossibility of answering her dear letters as they should be answered. To all of which Katy listened delighted, and begged him not to think she cared more for his letters than she did for himself. She was not set up for a stumbling-block and a rock of offence to him. No, indeed. He need not answer her letters at all. She should write and write, because the reading would cost him no mental effort — alas! interjected Katy archly — but he need not even read them till it was quite convenient. Perhaps when he came home late and tired — too tired to sleep, it would soothe him, would lull him asleep to have a long, prosing letter of hers to read — in which, dear Walter, there is nothing at all of the least consequence, nothing new or exacting or that cannot wait — only one thing that is old and new, and that the letter is full of, full, full, full, and always will be, only you cannot guess what it is, poor little dullard that you are and know nothing about it. So every morning when Kate got a letter from the post-office she was unspeakably glad, and read it at all odd hours, and even ones too — and went home across the fields that she might read it unobserved without waiting to be at home; went into her own room as soon as she was at home that she might *really* read it at her leisure; remembered all through lunch that something delicious was coming after lunch, viz., reading Walter's letter; and " reading Walter's letter," meant reading it about six times every time. And when Katy got no letter from the post-office she was glad too, and walked blithely home, dreaming of Walter's eager, active life and quick-coming success, and pleasing herself with reflecting that no one *but* herself knew what efforts he was bringing to the fight because no one but herself knew how much rather he would be writing to her than poring over ponderous law-books or attending in dingy court-rooms. "I do have some influence over him," smiled Katy to herself. "I make him work, poor dear. But I will reward him." So Katy was glad and happy well-nigh all the time.

Only when Mr. Glynn obtruded into her thoughts. He was not, indeed, the ideal of a despairing lover any more than he had been the ideal of a successful one. In fact, the casual observer might think he was a little stolid in both characters. He never was very finical in dress, but he dressed neither more nor less carelessly than before. He went to town every day, and he drove his horses and his ponies — though never drove Katy behind them again. He came to Mr. Haviland's oftener after Walter had left them than before, and he was always sufficiently cheerful, and always kind and friendly. But Katy, whose eyes experience had sharpened, noted often a wistfulness that none other saw, and felt — it really seemed to her that she felt in herself the loneliness which must have been his, not hers — she was so utterly happy that she experienced a profound pity for him. She never thought of such a thing as that time should have the least effect in softening his disappointment. She was too loyal a lover herself to think that even failure could conquer love. She tried to imagine how she should feel if Walter did not care for her; but that was such an evil case as she shuddered to contemplate, and such an impossible case, that even her imagination could not take it in. So she fell back on the rather cold comfort, that things did happen, and you could not help it. And in the next world she thought Mr. Glynn would recognize his mistake, and see clearly that it was not she who was appointed to him but some other angel. But it seemed to her a very cheerless and forlorn way along which he must go through the world to meet that angel, and she was heavenly-kind to the poor man ; and he saw through it, and smiled upon her pleasantly, and bantered her about the looking-glass, which she fully believed the moon-men had set up as a signal to us earth-folk, and ground the gravel of his garden-walks under foot half the night, wild with despair at what he was losing and another man was gaining.

V.

KIND Heaven, that does sometimes find it moral to give people just what they want, permitted Katherine's only aunt, about this time, to remove from the rural city of her long residence to the great city where Mr. Laballe was making his furious fight for fame and Kate. And the letter announcing the change, announced also to Kate that her annual visit this winter would be an altogether more brilliant and stirring affair than the tame little tea-drinkings and juvenile junketings which had hitherto characterized Kate's visit, — a change proper both to the enlarged sphere of operations and to the dignity of the visitor, who had now become a full-fledged young lady.

Katherine, ever devout, felt that now she was placed under perpetual bonds to be good, since Providence had specially interposed to give her this opportunity to be near Walter. For that was what it all meant to Katy. Her aunt was highly respectable, in easy circumstances, and sufficiently well known to give Kate immediate access to good company and agreeable entertainment. And is not the city always a great, mysterious, fairy palace to the young country-girl, full of beauty and activity and promise of unimagined pleasure? But though Katherine loved all this with the love natural to her youth, the one absorbing interest which the city had for her now was that it was the theatre of Walter's life, the field of his knightly contest. Here he was laying broad and deep the foundations of greatness. And, to do Katy justice, it was not the plaudits of the multitude that pleased her most, but the underlying fact which those plaudits should certify, and chiefly, good girl, to her father's heart. She would have been more disdainful of a false renown, of a catchpenny reputation, than of utter obscurity. If, she said to herself, if Walter worked for fame simply for fame's sake, he would not be Walter at all. Underneath was the strong, solid substance, only partially manifest as yet, known in its real possibility only to her. Acknowledgment she wanted, for without that could not come the power to help and heal the world's hurts. And now she was going up to see Walter no longer first and foremost in holiday amusement, no longer at her beck and call, but steadfastly treading the vague, mysterious road along which men pass to achievement and victory. I shall not know him, mused Katy. I must make up my mind not to see him much. He will be there to meet me. He will come sometimes in the evenings, but I shall know he is near me. I shall be in the same town with him and I shall always be thinking he may come in any moment, if it is only for a moment. And I wonder if he will be very far away. I shall, perhaps I shall, just possibly, hear people speak of him, but I suppose not yet. I suppose it is too soon for him to be known. But if I should chance to overhear his name, perhaps as a rising young lawyer, or as a clever young author, how shall I ever keep my face? And even in vestal solitude, Katy began a series of furious anticipatory blushes, and laughed at herself silently for a silly, silly, good-for-nothing girl.

Time lagged and lagged, and ran with lightning swiftness, and the winter days came, and the one day of days that never would come, but came, and bore her to the city and to Walter. And Walter was there at the station, in the coach, at her aunt's, and Kate had no difficulty in knowing him — the same Walter, dark and devoted, handsome and gay, strong and smiling. "Indeed," said Katy, "winter and summer are alike to you. You will not need go into the country to recover health next summer!"

"No, Kitty, it is something else than health I shall go into the country for — something that has come into the city for me!"

"Sauciness! I came to see my aunt!"

"O! yes. That is what I called for to-night. My aunt, solely. To-morrow, perhaps, I may come to see you, and take you to see the city; or will you be too tired? Perhaps you would better stay quietly at home to-morrow, and I will look in upon you. I think I ought to be show enough for one day."

"O! but, Walter, you must not mind me. You must not think I have come to take up your time. Aunt Fanny will look after me, and anything and everything will be interesting to me. Don't think of me ever in the day-time, then in the evenings I shall enjoy you with a clear conscience."

"And pray, Miss, what is there so reprehensible about me that I am to be so summarily dismissed in the day-time, and allowed only to stalk forth from my lair at night?"

"O, Walter," laughed Kitty, "I was only thinking of you."

"So I suppose. What I wish to know is, what crime you have been so good as to fasten on me that shall keep me hid by day."

"Absurd! You know just as well as I what I mean: that I don't wish to be, and will not be, a drag on you; and that you are not to think for a moment that I am exacting your leisure or your time. Now understand me, Walter dear. Don't even in jest pretend you don't."

" But you don't mean, Kitty, that I am to dig and delve all the time you are here and leave you by yourself."

" I thought," said Katherine, faltering a little, " you would be busy all the days, just as if I were not here, but that in the evenings, if you were not too tired, and — Sundays — and perhaps some other times, I should see you, when you are not too tired."

" Tired! Nonsense! I am never tired — of seeing you, at any rate. And as for business, Missy, you let that alone. You are my business now and I mean to transact you thoroughly. I suppose you know that you have already three invitations. I hope you have come in fighting cut."

" Fighting cut! what is that? "

" O, plenty of flimsy gowns to look like a cloud in the evening, and shiny gowns to look a sun in the morning, with all the wampum thereunto appertaining."

" I have not a great many gowns flimsy or shiny ; but I dare say I shall do very well. I shall depend upon Aunt Fanny to see that I am strictly orthodox in the matter of dress."

" I don't know whether that is quite safe, Kitty. Aunt Fanny is nice, but she is, begging your pardon and hers, rather verging on the heavy composite order. You must look light, and airy, and youthful. Now don't let her make

you up stiff and poky. I hope you have brought
fluffy-up dresses, haven't you ; such as they would
call you crazy to wear at home — and in mid-
winter ?"

"I have a blue flannel wrapper, very soft, and
light, and warm," said Kate, mischievously; "but
I shall not wear that on week-days. That I shall
keep for Sundays."

"O, the vixen ! But what will you wear to-
morrow night ? "

" A gown, I think, dear ; I am resolved I will
not wear my water-proof."

" Now, Katy, if you are going to develop into
a quiz it is all up with me. Be civil to a fellow, there's a dear ! You think this is all nonsense, but I tell you honestly that I am very
proud of you and I want to be sure you don't
make any mistake. It is folly to say that dress
is insignificant. Dress makes all the difference
in the world. You are twice as pretty and four
times as sensible as anybody else here. If you
lived in town you would lead society before it
could say Jack Robinson ; and your taste would
be perfect. But you have had no chance down
in the country. That is why I wrote to you not
to make any preparations but buy your outfit
here. Then you would be sure of the style and
look like other people."

" Don't I now ? " said Kate, quietly.

" My darling, yes ; only no one else looks so

fresh and nice as you. But these day-time frocks can be seen of men and women everywhere. A rustic dressmaker could copy those and we should be sure of her. But how could she have a notion of an evening costume when she never saw one in her life?"

" O, I could give it to her."

" Why, you —"

" Are not much better! you were going to say."

" O, if *you* have been giving your mind to it no doubt it will be all right. Still, I think you had better have acted on my suggestion, and put yourself into the hands of a regular modiste."

" O," said Kate, carelessly, " Miss Brimmer and I are very clever, and you will find that I shall pass without special rebuke. But since you asked, I will tell you that my dress is not very cloudy, but quite appropriate to the weather and — me, warm, woolly, and comfortable."

Walter shrugged his shoulders, and gave a faint laugh. He was not pleased, but Kate was impracticable, and he had to make the best of it. To help him out, came a little uncertainty as to whether she was teasing him or really unversed in gala-dress. " One thing I will do *nolens vo-lens*," he muttered, playfully resolute, fingering her little *vinaigrette*, " douse you with German cologne. You shall not smell this vile American stuff."

" How do you know it is American ?" asked Kate.

" What else did I grow a nose for ? "

" Why is not American as good as German ? "

" Why is not a pinchbeck dollar as good as a gold one ? "

" What is the chief end of man ? "

" Man's chief end is to make a fool of himself for a woman, and be snubbed for his pains ; " and so Walter laughed her into good humor again.

Nevertheless Kate was uncomfortable, not to say angry, though it was so strange and unexpected a thing to be angry, and with Walter, that she hardly knew what to make of it herself. She resented his lack of confidence in her taste. I don't say that this was reasonable in her. In point of logic I think it was rather unreasonable. Walter was right. Katy *was* a country girl, and naturally would not know what was appropriate to a society with which she was unfamiliar, and she ought to have considered it very kind and helpful in Walter to take thought for her raiment, about which, also, it would have been more amiable that she herself should have some misgivings. Perhaps she had; but she was not for that to permit Walter to have any. In fact, she was not pleased that the matter should have occurred to him at all. She thought of Walter, not of his clothes, and she was vexed to find that he was not equally absorbed in her. She had prepared herself to encounter a rival in his law-books and briefs. She had reconciled her heart beforehand to being put off by business and study. But she did expect his moments of leisure, his evening hours, to be preoccupied with herself; and she was doubly disappointed that not only did he seem to have as much control of his time and as much familiarity with all sorts of amusement here as in the country, but also that he was not so absorbed in the pleasure of being with her that he could not take thought for what she should put on, and feel that it was necessary to take thought, or she would not put on the right thing! And she did not like a man to think about such things. It was a man's business to wonder, love and praise her dress, but not to know anything about it. She had really spared no pains with her wardrobe. She had studied the fashion-plates and such shop-windows as she could command, and had held sweet counsel with a dressmaker imported from the neighboring town, and had no one but Walter in mind all the time. Would he like this? Would that suit him? She had not once dreamed of what society would think or say of her, or that it would say anything; but she had a very earnest, honest wish to be lovely and pleasing in his eyes. While a gown was under her hands, her cheeks grew warm and her heart beat fast with thinking that when she put it on Walter would be awaiting her; she should go down stairs half ashamed, yet half expectant to receive his glad greeting, and enjoy his wondering, surprised glance over her unwonted finery, and the somewhat stupid compliments which she should pardon to the love that pointed them. But she meant to make him look at the bows that her own hands made, and the folds she draped, and the flowers she grouped, and he would not half see them, but would say he did — and — and — now he was asking her beforehand what she was going to wear, and his eyes would be critical, and somehow suddenly all pleasure in her dress was gone, and what made him care about such things? The idea of a *man* knowing one kind of cologne from another! What business had a man to know there was such a thing as cologne? It was not knightly. She wanted a grand scorn, rather a sublime ignorance, of such *propria quæ feminis!* And poor Katy cried herself to sleep that night and did not know exactly why.

But things looked brighter next day. Walter came and never mentioned dress, but was light-hearted and glad to be with her, and yet had to go away early to meet his partner, and could not see her again till he came to join her and her aunt for the evening. And Katy put on her evening gown with greater tranquillity than she had supposed would be possible. It was a very pretty gown too. Walter might have spared himself the trouble of being anxious. White, soft, clinging stuff, lightened up with silk, and poetized with lace, and brightened with such floriculture as girls love and adorn — not at all dazzling the ball-room vision, but very restful and pleasing to eyes that chanced to fall upon it, and chiefly to those that love it; and Walter was pleased, too. He was forced to admit that it was very soft and graceful and becoming — "though I still maintain I was right," he added, after admitting he was wrong. " I would have chosen differently — something that would have fluffed out like waves of surf all around — looked all filmy and glittering and splendid."

" But it can't be filmy and glittering at the same time," said Kate, not so much discomposed by his qualified praise, nor so much heartened by his cordial admiration, as she would have imagined.

If Kate had gone to this her first state party with her heart disengaged, she would probably have been a little more excited or agitated than she was; yet, perhaps, not much. For Kate had an intimate acquaintance with, and a great reverence for, certain persons in the best society, which somehow fortified her against feeling any uncomfortable bashfulness towards persons of inferior claims. Lord Macaulay, and Lord Byron,

and Mr. Dan Chaucer, and Mr. Whittier, and Sir
Walter Scott, and Mrs. Oliphant, and Mrs. Stowe,
and Charlotte Brontë were *habitués* of Kate's society, and she would have gone to meet them
with eagerness and delight not unmingled with
trepidation. But she had all the arrogance, ex-
actingness, and severity of youth. Except where
she was swayed by personal likings, except that
she was loyal to love, and blood, and·to the
duties and sympathies actually near her, she had
small respect for abstract goodness unallied with
distinction. The dull, honest ways of dull, honest men, the homely virtues of self-sacrifice and
self-denial in ordinary mothers and wives, the
shallow sentiment and affection of good, shallow
girls, commanded little respect and no reverence
in Kate. No amount of wealth awed her. On
the contrary, she did not give it its due, either
in respect of what it implied or what it could
accomplish. She did not credit to the rich the
sagacity and prudence which most often amass
wealth, nor that catholic culture which wealth so
largely insures. She had a very unusual, almost
an unnatural indifference to style and fashion.
Brought up in a community where fashion was
a staid and slow-paced thing, moving according
to fixed laws and not eager for change, she had
little knowledge, and therefore little awe of a
community where fashion is strenuous, versatile,
and imperious. So Katy always wondered at

flurries over an incursion into an assembly. Why, what of it? was Katy's mode of reasoning. There is no one in particular who has done anything. Some are rich and some are not, but nobody's opinion of me is worth more than mine of him. (The audacious little minx!) Most of us might as well have been some one else as ourselves. If Mr. Brown had never been born, Mr. Smith would have answered every purpose. Other people would have sold sugar, and made shoes, and preached sermons, and worn silk gowns if these people had not. Why should I be afraid of them? But Mrs. Stowe, now! There is but one woman in all the world who ever wrote Uncle Tom's Cabin, and if it had not been for her, America would never have had a woman who could write a book that should be translated into all languages and set the whole world astir. If I were going to meet Mrs. Stowe, — well, I don't suppose I should be able to help trembling, I should be so full of excitement. But five hundred people in a city are only four hundred and fifty more than fifty people in the country, — and silks and laces are the same kind of things as cashmere and cambric. Thus reasoned Katy more or less as occasion required. If she had been differently brought up and a great deal wiser, she would probably have had more respect for the elaborations of society, technically so called; but as it was, she was utterly sincere, and so escaped being disagreeable about it as she could not have done had her opinion been what such opinion often is — the mere echo, simulation, and cant of simplicity.

Wherefore Kate went to her first city party, and was not bewildered. Also she was stimulated by a lingering resentment which made her resolute to show Walter that she *could* sustain herself — that she could be trusted in dress and demeanor, as well as in life and death. And she succeeded very respectably. It is true she did not occasion a general buzz of inquiry, nor the general stare of admiration which the entrance of the novelist's heroine and beauty into a ball-room causes; and, in fact, I never saw any one who did! A woman may be never so beautiful, but the evening light and the evening dress cast an illusion over the most ugly; and moreover the guests are standing in all corners, and looking in all directions, and talking in all keys, and walking in all corridors, and there is not unity enough in the crowd to produce a common sensation, or even to see the beauty when she comes sweeping in. No, Katy did nothing of the sort, and probably would have made no world-wide impression, even had the wide world been gazing at her. But she was straight and lithe, healthy and self-possessed, less self-conscious than if she had been thinking less about herself. She danced two or three times, and could have danced more had she chosen, but she preferred not. She saw some friends of her aunt, but she was not required to say much to them, and she did not say much. When Walter brought up his friends she was more on the alert. Some girls were dressed more handsomely, more richly, more showily than herself, but many were dressed as plainly, and some less becomingly. Some were lively and chatty, and some had scarcely a word to say for themselves. Walter's male friends were mostly young men, and those who were not she did not particularly affect. In fact Katy was so young herself that she did not care much for young men. For one young man she had great regard, but for the rest she loved to smite her strong stubborn young convictions against the experience of old men ; she loved to sun herself in the mellow wisdom of ripened years. She, all whose eager life lay in the future, would fain add to her pleasure the joy of retrospect, and that she could only do by sympathy and contact with those whose lives lay serenely behind them.

And when Fate brought her that evening a college president, who was a little gray and a little bald, and the least little in the world professional, she rose with a bound to the situation and tasted solid happiness. It was such a moment of triumph as she had never expected — least of all in this visit, least of all at an evening party. Fortunately for Katy, her eye did not disappoint her hope. He was a very jewel of a college president, at least for her purpose. He had not only at his tongue's end all the learning of the schools, but he had travelled far and wide, and quite off the usual tracks of travel, so that he had stores of information not to be found in books; and he was withal, though somewhat grave, or otherwise Kate would have been grievously disappointed, also with a keen sense of humor, and with a mind still not only active, but alert and impressible. And while Kate instantly fell down and worshipped him with intellectual adoration, he too was won by her bright, rapt, sympathetic listening; he questioned her with a half amused, half tender, but altogether pleasing and stimulating curiosity; he talked to her with a flattering accuracy and minuteness; he talked to her, in short, as if he considered her worth while, and as if he were himself interested; and when it was time to go home, Kate was found by Walter, brilliant, animated, in a seventh heaven of delight. Nay, so mysterious are the ways of Providence that I doubt not the learned president enjoyed the little rencontre with almost equal zest, though he was mature, and wise, and learned, while Katherine was altogether ignorant, crude, and positive. But a bright, fresh, happy young woman has got to be very objectionable indeed in order to make herself disagreeable to an intelligent elderly gentleman who is the object of her admiration and reverence.

"Did you see anything to discourage you in the way of dress?" said Mrs. Ford to Katy, as they were performing that imperative and final duty of "talking it over."

"Discourage me? No, unless I had to make it, and then I should be discouraged at the out-set."

"Nor did I. Bella Stacy was all train, with her waist crowded down into sixteen inches!"

"So," said Walter, emphatically, "I had to put my arm round her twice to get any kind of leverage for waltzing."

"I suppose she *has* organs," said Mrs. Ford, natural-philosophically, "but I don't know what she does with them when she is dressed."

"That was a nice-looking girl with you, Walter, with hair."

"An exhaustive description," laughed Walter.

"Jane Courcy," said Mrs. Ford, whose vigilance nothing escaped; "ridiculous to see a young girl with such a wig piled atop — puffed up, and fluffed out, and rolled over, and flatted down, and twisted round. It is strange people can't see that hair is hair, and not a mere marketable commodity."

"She had a beautiful complexion, too, Aunt Fanny."

"It won't wash."

" O, no ! "

" O, yes ! "

" It was too beautiful and natural."

" Katherine Haviland, do you think I don't know paint when I see it ? "

" *I* don't, then," said Katy. " Was that tall Miss May painted ? "

" Not she. She has too much sense, and I never can tell where she got it, nor her coffee-colored face, for her mother was the handsomest fool of my early acquaintance."

" Mrs. Ford," said Walter, laughing, " you are a chaperon in a thousand, warding off every one's charms from Kate, who does not need it, by the way."

" I trust I am not afraid to use my eyes for fear it should be called backbiting," said Mrs. Ford scornful alike of men and metaphors. " Mary May is a sensible girl, and I am very fond of her, but she is coffee-colored, and does not know how to wear clothes."

" Who does?" asked Katy, "for an ensample."

" Harriet Clapham. She looked just as if she had stepped out of a picture; and Bessie Averill, who was a picture herself in that lovely muslin, all ferns and lilies. Kate, she painted that gown herself."

" Yes," said Kate, " that is the kind of paint even *I* know."

" Mr. Laballe, is that young Fraser engaged to her, or is he only flirting ? "

" Engaged, I am afraid, Mrs. Ford. It ought to be a statutory offence."

" What is his crime ? " asked Kate.

" Looking like the idiot he is, for one thing," answered Mrs. Ford. " He was standing near you half an hour, Kate, with eye-glass in one eye, and chin in the air. Did you not see him ? "

" I don't remember any suspended chin, Aunt Fanny."

" Don't ask Kate any questions this side of the Silurian epoch, Mrs. Ford. She had no eyes for anybody but that fossil in spectacles. I had to wrench her off from the old red sand-stone to bring her home."

" It was the only real enjoyment I had for the evening," said Kate, naively.

" Why, Kate ! "

" O, of course I had nice little common times. But this was something really splendid, and to be remembered."

" It was a veritable conquest on both sides, Mrs. Ford, I assure you," said Walter to her aunt. " Kate, I shall be desperately jealous if you go on in this way. A demure little country-girl, and to develop into an arrant flirt the very first night ! "

" O, don't talk so, Walter," said Katherine, a

little impatiently. "I don't like to have you talk so, even in jest. It seems to demean Mr. Franklin to use his name in such a way."

"O, of course he is altogether too superior and remote for such familiar and frivolous words; but upon my honor, Mrs. Ford, if you had kept an eye on the corner behind you, you would have seen something uncommonly like the thing under your very wing."

"If Kate enjoyed herself, I am content," said Mrs. Ford. "She certainly did not interfere with my enjoyment."

"If flirting is to have the most delightful talk with people who know things and like to tell them, then I shall always have a good word to say for flirting," added Kate.

"That is the way they all think, only they don't all speak out quite so frankly."

"Who is it that you mean by 'they,' Walter?"

"Innocent little heart-breakers like you — the most vicious kind of all."

"Aunt Fanny, don't you think you ought to come to my defence, seeing I am under your protection?"

"If I needed to come to your defence, you would not be under my protection," said Mrs. Ford, in her best Johnsonese.

"Certainly not," cried Mr. Laballe, gayly capping Johnson with Webster. "There she is. Behold her, and judge for yourselves. Going at the rate of sixty revolutions the minute. The venerable Prex had so much ado to keep up with her that his spectacles flashed like a hundred-faceted lens, cutting around sharp corners after her."

"What did you talk about?" asked Mrs. Ford.

"O, many things. The Brahmins, and all about Unitarians, and how there is always, and always will be, a right and left in all religions—"

"That is the French Assembly," interjaculated Walter. "You have got your religion mixed up with other things this time."

"It would not be worth much as a religion if it weren't," retorted Kate. "President Franklin has been in India and he was very interesting, telling me about the old astronomy, and the oneness in everything, and the Aztecs, and why you can hope for immortality outside of the Bible,—though, of course," added Kate, argumentatively and reflectively, "life and immortality are brought to *light* only through the gospel,—and about the Catacombs."

"A lively old party," muttered Walter, stroking his whiskers.

"Well," parried Kate, laughing, "it sounds differently when you just name it over. But it was not a bit funereal to talk."

"So it was for the Aztecs, and the skeletons, and such trash, that you threw me over?"

" Threw you over ? "

" Did you not do me the honor to say that all you enjoyed was the president ? "

" O, but I scarcely saw you for the evening, only to walk with you a little at first, and to dance with you once. I did not expect it, of course," added Kate, quickly. " Of course people don't go to parties to see — you ! " blushing a little at her unspoken thought.

" No ; I think we can devise something better than that," said Walter, " when it comes to personal enjoyment. All the same, don't you devote yourself too exclusively to college presidents, and that sort of truck. I am not jealous, Kitty, so I can speak my mind. There's a wife or two, not to mention a dozen or so children scattered along that presidential path, so he won't be likely to cut across mine. But you let the Sanscrit folks alone."

" In *my* humble sphere," said Kate, tartly, " *we* think learned people very respectable."

" So do we," said Walter, imitating her tone. " We take off our hats to them. We plume ourselves on being able to take off our hats to them. But we never make much headway in point of social prestige by flirting with them."

" O, there you are saying that again."

" Well, then, we don't come up from the country and put on our purple and fine linen for the sake of declining dances with half a dozen of the first men in society, and standing in a corner to talk mammoths and mastodons all the evening with a blear-eyed antique in gold-bowed glasses, who does not know whether we are dressed in gold tissue or swathed in a mummy cloth."

" O, Walter, you don't really care that I did not dance more! Indeed, I did not feel in the mood at all."

" No, Kitty, not really. If you enjoyed yourself, that is all. But I am ambitious for you, I own. I want you to shine out with the brilliancy that belongs to you. But you need not hurry. Take your own time. I only want really—under all the badinage—that you shall not waste yourself. Talk as much as you like to respectable old coves, like the president. It is an advantage to be known to be on good terms with the like of him. But don't let yourself be monopolized by them. Your star will rise far more rapidly if you circulate well among people shallower, perhaps, but far more brilliant and fashionable. It is they who will stamp you as current coin. He may certify the bullion. I want you to be reckoned sensible, dear, but I also want you to be counted — gay — not to say — now, Miss Puss, don't be shocked if I say fashionable. I am not sure that I want you to be — intellectual. That is, *be* as intellectual as you like, but don't have the name of it. Am I an exacting old wretch, Katy, wholly given over to the god of this world ? "

" But, Walter, why do you care so much how one is considered ? What difference does it make ? Why not *be* something, and never mind what you are thought to be ? "

" Because, my dear, that is not possible. It sounds very well. I admire it as a sentiment, but nobody is ever indifferent to what is thought of him."

" Not wholly indifferent. I do not mean that. But, for instance, now, if I do like President Franklin, why not let it be ? What possible reason is there why I should be known to like him, or not known ? "

" You would not like to have the reputation of being in request only among the Antiques and Horribles. You don't want to be courted by people who court a Greek root or a new kind of fish in the same way they do you ! "

" I don't know," said Kate, laughing and blushing. "I certainly don't want to be courted any other way."

" The trouble with you, Kate, is that you have made your market, and the marketing is here under your own eye, as snug and safe as Betsy Trotwood's bandbox, and you are altogether too independent in consequence. If you weren't so deuced sure of me ! "

" O, Walter ! "

" Pardon me, dear Kate, and don't avenge yourself by flirting with all the young fellows who will flock around you as soon as you hold out the golden sceptre."

" But I don't want to flirt at all, Walter. I don't know what you mean by it, and I don't care anything about it."

" O, but you will take it the natural way, when the time comes. Such austerity of virtue is too heavenly for home consumption. A girl must have a spice of coquetry to be perfect, and you are perfect, Katy. Have I not turned that well ? The rose that all are praising, O, that's the rose for me."

" I can only be what I am, Walter. I can't make myself into anything else."

" And if you *should* dare go and make yourself into anything that you are not now, into anything other than you are, it would be all over between us. It is you that I want, not somebody else." And then they drifted into pleasant little foolish talk, that says so little and means so much, and the party and the talk ended amicably.

7

VI.

BUT all the same the winter went on disastrously. Katherine fought unheeding, but all-valiantly against the misgiving that Walter was not the hero she had imagined him. He was fond and faithful, he was cheerful and gay; but she could have better borne that he was grave and absorbed, less ready to attend her, less satisfied with the present. He was always kind; but he was always more or less anxious, even as regarded her, about matters which seemed to her insignificant and frivolous. She was always, at least generally, gentle, suggestive, and acquiescent; yet she was always more or less indirectly, though not impalpably, urging him to seriousness, to duty, to application, to something which should satisfy her ideal of manhood. And sometimes he parried her, and sometimes he jested, and sometimes he overcame her with tenderness; but sometimes, too, he grew a little restive. His very absorption in amusement made Kate draw off from it. Her natural liking for fun and frolic was lost in anxiety for Walter, — in resentment against what seemed to her the insidious foe of his ability and his manhood. Had he been too much devoted to business, too much instigated by ambition, too desirous of securing place and power, Katy was just the one to have lured him into saner ways. It would have been her delight to win him to repose and relaxation, to give her own bright spirit play for his diversion and delight. But somehow she felt now as if all the weight of sobriety and responsibility were on her, as if to join and sympathize in his merry-making were to add to the velocity, the strength, the momentum of the current that was trying to drag him down — not down to ruin — she did not fear that, but to a lower level than was his birthright; to a position, to a standing, which, however satisfactory to others, would enlist her regret, her pity, rather than her pride. Her pity! She was startled at the word, at the thought, and then she was startled again at perceiving for the first time how much her fear for Walter preponderated over her hope — how much more apprehension she felt for him than she had rest in him. "I wonder — can it be " — thought Katy, "that this is the common way! It cannot be. It is not the way I thought of, certainly."

So they drew more and more apart. Not formally, not consciously, perhaps. It is marvellous how much of our mental life goes on without our perceiving it. It is as if the mind were absorbed in working out its problems, and only when the solution is complete is the mind at leisure to review its work and know what it has done. Long after these thoughts, these convictions, of which we were unaware, have crystallized into actions, we go back and interpret ourselves to ourselves. So Walter and Kate went on as they had done, long after they were really all out of harmony with each other; went on faltering, stumbling, falling out of line, but bravely keeping the same path, and not really aware that they were not keeping step. But Walter, of course, could not fail to be influenced by Katherine's misgivings. A man may be never so little inclined to change his course in life, but he knows whether his mistress adores him or criticises him. And he basks in the adoration, and is made uncomfortable by the criticism, — especially if he feels within himself that the criticism is just, and has not the smallest intention of seeking to deserve it less. Katherine, too, felt the jar of Walter's dissatisfaction, — or if that is too strong, his lack of utter, absolute satisfaction with her, — and she had the additional advantage or disadvantage, whichever it might be, of being annoyed with the cause of dissatisfaction. She was, unhappily, less disturbed at not being his ideal, than at his ideal itself. She had no ambition to become what it seemed to be his ambition she should become. And at length, slowly, sadly, almost unawares, but surely, the question arose in Kate's mind: were they suited to each other? Day and night, alone and in society, Kate revolved that question, tried many a test, decided now this way and now that, and as constantly revoked her decision; felt sometimes that she was wronging Walter, and then lavished tenderness on him by way of atonement; felt then discouraged and distrait, and as if she were beating against wind and tide. Then she resolved upon strong measures, and taking counsel of no one, wrote one day:

"MY DEAR WALTER." (Then, frightened, she waited till she was on the eve of returning home, and in desperation and weakness finished her letter, and left it for him.) "It is not quite fair, perhaps, to write to you as I am about to do; but I admit frankly that I am a coward, and have not the courage to say it. Besides, it is very serious, and I do not wish to be turned away by anything which you or I might feel. It is for all our life, dear Walter, so please to look at it exactly as it is. I think you love me. I have not a doubt of you, and not a reproach for you; but I do think we are not suited to each other. At least, I am not suited to you. I am too sober and old — not old in years, I mean, but old in my feelings. The things that you like much, I do not

care for.   I do not know how to say that you do
not suit me, for that would not be true.   I think
if you would be what Heaven meant you to be,
you would be everything that I should desire;
but it seems to me, dear, that you never will be
that, because you are so waylaid by little things,
and you do not put them down, and give yourself to large things; and that would make me
always discontented.   This sounds as if I were
setting myself up above you.   You know that is
not true, dear Walter.   It is only for yourself,
and of yourself, that I want great things, and
that because I am sure they are in you.   Don't
think I am leaving you disgusted; but you know
it would be no good my staying with you, and
just teasing you.   I cannot believe it is at all the
thing for married people to have to adjust themselves to each other.   You have to adjust yourself to everybody else; but people ought to marry
only because they are already adapted to each
other by nature.   Dear Walter, the least little
jar coming between us would be suspicious; and
if you look back, you will perceive that there
has been a continuity of jar all along.   Not in-
tentionally, dear; not your fault, nor mine; but
just that we do not harmonize.

"Dear Walter, if you only would be your
best, everything would be as I thought it.   But
as it is, let us be good friends, and never anything more.   I must always be your true friend;

but I cannot consent to be an obstacle in your path because you will not consent to take mine.

" As I read this letter over it seems to be cold and fault-finding. Let all the fault-finding be turned towards myself, if you choose, for it may be that I alone am wrong. But it makes no difference who is right and who is wrong ; if one is one way and the other the other, we are not together, whichever you call wrong. I am not cold, and I do not pretend I am happy. But it seems to me I am doing what is best. It is very little to say that I shall always be your friend."

And Katy put this letter into the post-office herself, and said good-by to her aunt and to Walter, feeling altogether a coward and a traitor ; and went home to her father, and in the new gladness of welcome tried to forget that she had written any letter. But she had written it; and when the well-known handsome handwriting that she loved appeared again, she tore open the letter with an eagerness and a hopefulness which she would have been at a loss to explain, and read :

" My dear Kate : Your letter distressed, but did not surprise me. I do not know that I can say aught to change your decision.. I never supposed I was good enough for you, for I think you are a good girl, Kate, if there ever was one, and I know that I am a good-for-nothing fellow. Sometimes when I have been talking with you, in your most fiery-souled moods, I have felt a stir, and if there had been any 'push' in me, you would have pushed me ahead. But there isn't. I can't lie to you, Katy, and it would be no use if I did. I am a humbug, and I know it, and despise myself for it; but I am not any the less a humbug for that, and the worst of it is that you have all along been finding it out. I was not a humbug in loving you, for I do love you honestly and dearly, and if I had anything to live on I should not let you go so easily; but should hold you fast, and let you try your hand at making me over. But as it is, I only jog along from hand to mouth, half the time, as you know, at the mercy of my crabbed old uncle, who doles out his dollars with innuendos and lectures that swallow up more than the money is worth, and be hanged to it all. I hate my profession, and I don't love any other. I was born to spend money, not to earn it, and it is a confounded shame and misplacement that I was not endowed according to my talents. I hate to give you up. The best thing in my life will leave me when you go from me. I would be a good husband to you, Katy, if I could be your husband at all. But, miscreant as I am, I have too much manhood to keep you watching and waiting for an improvement that will never come; or to waste the bright years of your youth in bothering over a man who will never do you the least credit. I am no great shakes, but I am too great a shake for that.

"So here ends the first lesson. You certainly are not wrong. I think sometimes you have been a little hard on me, just because you were built on so energetic a scale that you could not appreciate the difficulties that beset a fellow whose walls and dome looked strong enough, but whose underpinning was somehow left out. But I don't know that it is any use to quarrel with Destiny. I suppose I can breast fate that dooms me from within as well as another who is ruined from without. I have at least pluck enough not to whine. The burning tears are in my eyes, but I can dash them all away. God bless you, Kate, and give you to some man more worthy of you than I. I have felt all along that I did not suit you, and I knew the tears you shed at parting were more of disappointment in me than sorrow at leaving me.

"Good-by."

Katherine sat stunned after reading this letter. She had received a blow as violent as unexpected. She did not ask herself what reply she had looked for to her letter. She knew perfectly well that she had not contemplated any such issue as this. She was not a hypocrite; but in writing to Walter, in thinking to give him up, she had not really looked such relinquishment in the face. She had all along an underlying hope that her heroic treatment would cure the patient, not kill the physician. What she had really counted on was that Walter would see the seriousness of the emergency, that he would be once for all shocked out of his versatile life, out of his unworthy aims, which hardly seemed more than aimlessness, that he would concentrate his power, grasp the opportunity that awaited him, and bring forth fruit meet for repentance. Kate looked for a letter full of love and pleading, self-reproach, and resolution, and remonstrance, and she was in a melting mood before it came, and prepared to forgive, and encourage, and console, — poor girl. And now Walter had taken her at her word! and she was as amazed and appalled as if the blow had originated with him. She read and re-read the letter, comprehending more and more clearly with each perusal that it was final. She was so wretched, so forlorn, so despairing, that she felt one moment as if she must go to him, — must throw herself at his feet, and beg him to forgive her and take her back, let come what might. Then she re-read the letter, and her self-respect, beaten down by her love, rose again, miserable but inflexible, and told her that he had relinquished her without a struggle. He had accepted the first overture of release.

He made no resistance. He begged no delay. He resigned himself to the situation without remonstrance, and it was not for her to rebel against it. Besides, was it not even too evident that, though she had taken the initiative, he had been sensible of relief? There was love; Kate felt that he had been sincere. He had not simulated a feeling which he had not. But O! what kind of love was it? She who had so worshipped heroism; she who had been so exacting; she who would admit nothing less than the greatest, who demanded that love should be unperverted and all-conquering, — she had been able to inspire only this feeble and powerless passion, something subordinate to commonest circumstances, something that had no influence and no impulse, something that gave way under the first stress, — why, how was Walter weighted in the race more than other men? And then she stabbed herself for having stabbed him, and saw it was only because she was not strong enough to inspire him. Katy was so perturbed and miserable over the main point that she had no eye for side issues. She was not amused by the weak, whimsical frankness with which Walter admitted his shortcomings. She did not observe the comical ease with which, towards the close, he lapsed into self-pity, quite warming into enthusiasm at the thought of his own wrongs and sufferings. She did not clearly see the fatal selfishness out of which neither duty nor shame could rouse him; the manhood, the bravery which would nerve itself to relinquish her calmly, but not to become worthy of retaining her. She only saw that between herself and Walter all was over; that she had suggested it, that he would have it so, and that it was better it should be so. Her pride, her dignity, her love, her perception were alike aggrieved. She was wounded and suffering at every point.

Nothing of all this showed itself in her demeanor. She received and returned all glad greetings. She interested herself in all home ways and in all the happenings of her absence. When she was alone, it is true, she often found herself arrested midway in any errand whatever, and gazing fixedly at nothing, while her sad mind travelled its weary round of reflection and forecasting. But one day at eventide, when she had become so familiar with her loneliness and misery that she thought she could mention it lightly, she said, gently, "Papa, I have a thing to tell you that you will not grieve to hear. It is all over between Mr. Laballe and me."

"No, Katy; but is it, really?"

"Really, papa."

"How came that?"

"There was nothing else, dear. It was best," she replied, thoughtfully.

"Did it seem best to yourself, Kate?"

" Yes, papa, to me. You were right from the beginning. I am sorry, but you were right."

" Did it come about because you found I was right, or from some other reason ? "

" Only that. Walter was not to blame at all, and I do not think I was, or that he thinks I was. It is simply that I feared we were not suited to each other. I was not quite content with him, nor, indeed, was he with me ; and I suppose we never should have been content. But the suggestion came wholly from me, without any provocation from him, and he accepted it as the best thing. He is utterly blameless, papa. You need have no feeling against him, even in your thoughts."

" My dear Kate, I am too glad it is over to blame him. Even if it had come from him I should still have been glad. But that your good sense should have discerned him, that you should have done this of your own free will, is too good news for me to higgle over the manner of it. I would never spoil your happiness, and I certainly would never force your will, (as if the dear man ever would have tried! Katy did a much larger business in forcing his ;) but I never thought him a fit mate for you, and I shall breathe the easier that you have found it out."

" But don't be severe on him, papa. I have given him up wholly. We shall never be anything more to each other than we are now. But

I feel very warmly and kindly towards him, and I think he was — true to me — in his way. You must think very kindly of him."

"Trust me for that, Kitty. I shall not think of him at all, so make yourself easy. He is not a man I should ever think of twice, except for you."

Kate was too absorbed to feel the slight put upon her choice. She was silent, and her father said presently, as a new thought struck him, —

"How is it, Kate, you are not unhappy? You have done this of your own choice?"

"Entirely of my own choice, papa. But you know I was very much in earnest, and — and — I cannot say — it would not be worth while to be perfectly light-hearted after having made so serious a mistake. I feel sure I am right now; but of course I don't feel yet quite as I did before."

"Yes, deary, I understand. You would not be yourself if you did. I cannot, to be sure," said Mr. Haviland, reflectively, "understand how you ever could have set a value upon him. You are so clever and discerning, and he is such light weight. But never mind. I cannot tell you, Kate, how relieved I am that it is over." And so Mr. Haviland dismissed the subject. It is really wonderful how an elderly gentleman can be exceedingly fond of his daughter and yet fail to put himself in her place. Mr. Haviland simply transferred to Katy his own opinion of her lover, and had no idea of the blank dismay which lay over her mind, brooding and shadowing it.

Otherwise, matters went on much as before. It was not a village where engagements are considered as public matters as marriage. Girls did not treat their lovers as wives treat their husbands, and had not forgotten to blush at the mention of one name, or the approach of a certain footstep. It is all very right and proper, no doubt, to do away with all this blushing and backwardness and shy secrecy; but somehow, in laughing away the bashfulness of love, is not something of the bloom of love also brushed away?

So had Katherine no questioning, surmise, or banter to meet. The engagement had not been known, the acquaintance had not been visibly interrupted. Only to Mr. Glynn — of all persons in the world — Katherine felt, was the revelation due. Utterly sad and straightforward, it did not occur to her that her motive might be misconstrued. She had as yet learned to look only, or chiefly, at the thing to be done, and not at the attitude she might present in doing it. Fortunately for Katherine, her lack of wisdom was not revealed to the world, but only to one man, who knew her too well to mistake simplicity for design; though even he did not at first quite comprehend the purpose which actuated her, while yet fully comprehending what was not her purpose.   Nevertheless, a great rush of joy filled his heart, every trace of which he sought sedulously to banish from his face.

"Miss Katy, I don't know how you expect me to feel about this, but I cannot regret anything in it except your trouble.   I don't know what to say," he confessed, ingenuously, — a fact which must have been clear to the most casual observer.

"I do not expect you to feel, and you need not say anything," said Katherine, with the ghost of a smile; "only I wanted to tell you because it makes me feel easier towards you — about you."

"You do not mean —" he began, eagerly, and stopped abruptly.   He knew she did not mean *that,* and throttled the suggestion on the spot.

"When I was most happy, I could not forget that you were — not, and that it was my doing. It seems strange that I should have power to make you unhappy and none to make you happy — nor myself — nor any one — " Kate threatened here to go off into a long, silent reverie; but she thought better of it, evidently, — "Everything is so strange.   But it seemed as if it was selfish and heartless to be as happy as I could be; because why should I be favored and you not?   If some one else had troubled you, it would have been bad enough; but it was all through me.   All my joy was your sorrow.   Now — I do not know that I can make you quite understand — but I feel that it is a sort of justice fate owes you, to know that we are equal in trouble."

" Kitty, you surely do not think I could be so base as to rejoice in any misfortune that could befall you. To be unhappy in one love will not, I suppose, make another more acceptable."

" I do not mean that at all, or anything against you. But it satisfies me towards you. I no longer must conceal my feelings from you lest they give you pain. I do not have to feel heartless in being happy when you are not. I want you to know that — if I ever — caused you — any bitterness, I have tasted that bitterness myself in full measure."

" Yet the separation was your own doing ? "

" In a sense it was. In any sense to be indignant about, I did it. But I am so lost, why should I conceal it ? It was — he who rejected me. On the outside I released him first. But I feel more and more, every day, that he was glad to be released. Yes, Mr. Glynn," looking straight into his eyes, " it is I who was rejected."

" Fool ! " ejaculated Mr. Glynn.

" No, he was no fool. In some points he was not wholly strong. But he had every talent, and if I had but possessed the power to influence him, he would be a king among men."

" Better be content with a republic," said — shall I say sneered ? — Mr. Glynn, divided between anger and — such is man — delight.

"At some time," continued Katherine, "there may come a woman who will be able to inspire him with a love so warm as to kindle his purpose. That is what he needs — that is what I thought to do ; and then I shall be surprised at no achievement. But I do not hide from myself, nor from you, that I failed."

"Katy," cried Mr. Glynn, with a gesture of impatience, "I can't say what I think, because it would vex you and pain you, and perhaps do me a mischief; but I want you to understand that " — that Laballe is a fool, and you are another, was what was in his mind, but the one fool occupied in his esteem so different a position from the other, the folly of the first had served him so good a turn, and the folly of the second was so harmless and even pathetic, and moreover he was a man and she was a woman, — so, altogether, he minced words and ended lamely, — "that I don't subscribe to your opinions."

"Do you not?" said Kate, listlessly.

"Not a jot. It is simple nonsense, as I could show you if you would stand it, which you will not. You are a sensible girl, but you have not the data."

"I do not know whether it is sense or nonsense," said Kate, only half heeding him, and gazing steadfastly into the fire, "but I have lost my life."

"And I have found mine," cried Mr. Glynn,

abruptly. Katherine looked up with languid inquiry. She could not have seen the color flush into his swarthy face even had not the firelight cast its glamour over him ; and she was in any case too much concerned with her own thoughts to know how deeply he was moved.

"Kate, I do not know how I should have felt to see you married to a man worthy of you. It might have been a sharper pain in some ways, but there could not have been the madness of seeing you fall into the hands of one incapable of appreciating you. I have escaped so great a danger that I count myself this day a happy man."

"You?"

"Yes, I," (half impatient at the slight surprise in her tone, it so plainly asked what had he to do with it.) "I thought you were going to be lost to me in that worst of all deeps, an unequal marriage. And here I have you, before me, in your own house, free, never to be sullied by that —not to waste your life in trying to hold up a dead weight; never to experience the long anguish of a slow undeceiving, when it is too late. Now it is not too late. Thank God, everything is saved."

"I thought not," said Katy, with a touch of her old mischief. "But never mind. I have told you what I wished you to know, and we need speak of it no more."

"But, Katy, I want you to be happy."

"Happy!" said Kate, incredulously. Happiness was a thing from which she had so long parted, a thing from which she seemed so forever remote, that the mention of it appeared incongruous.

"O, I do not mind happiness. I shall do very well. It is only that my life is over. I wonder how long one can live after one is dead. O, I wonder if in the stars one can ever, ever forget!"

Mr. Glynn left the room abruptly, and Katherine did not so much as know that he went.

The days dragged on, and Katherine nerved herself to pleasant words and cheerful looks and apparent interest, though heavy at heart. Everything seemed to her so insignificant. She found herself in a certain set of circumstances, and though it by no means seemed worth while to try to get out of them — as, indeed, what was there desirable outside? — still, there seemed nothing worth while where she was. She marvelled that Tishy should feel concerned about the whitewashing, or that her father should be particular to have the morning paper, or that Donald should be in loud-voiced grief because a brood of chickens, too impatient of life to wait the slow coming of summer-warmth, had perished in the cold spring storms. What joy was there in farming, or politics, or housekeeping?

But a heavier blow was to shake Katherine out of the apathy of her grief.

VII.

MR. HAVILAND had never aspired to be a rich man, but he would have scorned to be a poor one. He was born and bred of a stock that looked upon debt with horror, and counted independence the one necessity of life. He was by no means a money-making or a money-loving man. He had inherited the ancestral farm with the ancestral principles and the ancestral pride. He knew very little about stocks or bonds, and dealt scarcely at all in them. He made what little money he had added to his inheritance by the old-fashioned, commonplace methods — industry, prudence, thrift — a very slow and ridiculous way of making money, but still adhered to more or less in the rural districts. But in this comical way he had accumulated a modest fortune, quite ample for his own wants, and enough to assure him of Katy's wellbeing through life. In an evil hour, in one of those lapses from prudence to which the wisest are subject — no, I will not say that, for the wisdom of an act is not determined by its event; the highest wisdom may result in disaster. Rather let me say that Mr. Haviland, though himself well content with narrow ways, distrustful of experiments, and particularly adverse to meddling with what he did not understand, was nevertheless of a most kindly and obliging disposition. One of his neighbors, a farmer of ingenuity and intelligence, believed himself to have discovered a chemical process by which certain farm products could be so treated as to become of vastly more than their ordinary market value. The process was not costly, but to make the matter a business, buildings and machinery were necessary, and Mr. Haviland and one or two others were asked to form a joint-stock company, which, not having any of the immunities of ordinary corporations, left each partner responsible for the debts of the whole. Of this, however, Mr. Haviland was not aware.

He had not much faith in the project, but rather from a general lack of faith in projects than from any special mistrust of this. Indeed, if all men were like Mr. Haviland, enterprise would soon come to a dead stop. But if there were not some men like Mr. Haviland, who would foot the bills of the enterprising who fail? Mr. Haviland, then, was not confident that his neighbor had found the philosophers' stone in his cornfields and orchards; but he did not wish to be unsympathetic and churlish, and as the sum required from him was not large, not so large that its loss would cripple Katy, he pleased his friend and himself by putting down his name and paying in his money. The first year there were no dividends because the business had not been under way long enough to reach the remunerative point; the second year, Mr. Haviland jocosely promised Katy, who was then at school, a fur cloak with the proceeds; but some mischance happened to the crops, and they did not harvest a fur cloak. Then the machinery moved on undisturbed by Mr. Haviland, and the capital and dividends occupied his mind only enough to point an occasional mild jest. But Fate was moving on him from another quarter.

He and his neighbors shared the habit of investing their surplus funds in the county treasury and the neighboring savings-banks, contented with small percentage for the sake of greater security. But one day a scheme arose, smiling rich promise, and the next it swept the land with the besom of destruction. It was a scheme of public benefit, in the hands not simply of honorable but of religious men. It was advertised and advocated in the religious papers. The clergy and the church patronized it; and men who would have been deaf to the cries of " wild-cat banks," and who reckoned " speculation " as one of the seven deadly sins, left their county funds and their savings-banks, and followed this golden-mouthed Chrysostom into the wilderness.

But the religious men blundered, just as if they had been worldlings, and the counsels of the religious papers were brought to naught; and just as wide-spread disaster fell upon clergy and churchmen, farmers, and widows and orphans, as if the trap had been set by scoundrels. It was a disaster that fell not alone, nor chiefly, upon men of business, whose losses of to-day are neutralized by the gains of to-morrow; to whom loss means only checkmate; only a little change in their account-books, or at most a temporary crippling of business. It was a disaster that smote the weak with an irretrievable blow. It went into the country towns and swept away the hard earnings that could never be replaced. It made in many a home the difference between ease and uncertainty, between rest and comfort for old age and harassing uncertainty, or a chilling and hopeless certainty. It went into Mr. Haviland's house. It found him a healthy and happy man, content with himself, at peace with the world. It dealt the blow, and left him dazed, smitten, overwhelmed.

The disaster was no direct fault of his own. He had invested no money in the ruinous scheme. But the sudden collapse touched many other affairs. The neighbor, in the application of whose invention Mr. Haviland had helped, was an honest and ingenious man, but he had, like many other inventors, small business ability. His affairs had been financially mismanaged, and the sudden pressure of the times forced a stoppage and a settlement. Then the ruin began to disclose itself. There had been not only no profit, but the debts, for a rural village, were of appalling magnitude. Then the law crept into light, and showed the unsuspected fact that the corporation and contract had, perhaps unwittingly, made each stockholder responsible for the whole business. Since the firm had been formed one partner had died, and his estate had been divided and scattered; another found himself involved and destroyed in the larger disaster; the chief and inventor had nothing, and in short Mr. Haviland was left to bear almost alone the whole liability — a liability before which his small but sufficient estate would disappear.

The shock of the loss was scarcely less than the shock of the surprise. The original occasion of it was so slight as to have almost passed from his memory. Many a time had he good-naturedly lent money to a needy neighbor, and not infrequently had this bread cast upon the waters failed to return even after the lapse of many days; but he had always been scrupulous never to scatter insecurely more than he could afford to lose, and these small lapses had never dis-

turbed him. Precisely this was what he supposed himself to have done in the present case,
and he stood not only appalled but confounded.
In earlier years he might have thrown it off,
though he was never of the temperament to rise
gayly above it; but whatever his possibilities
might have been, the time for elasticity and
conquest of circumstances had gone by. Kate —
Kate — was stripped of her possessions, of her
inheritance, of her independence. Nor did the
proud man fail to feel the wound in his pride. It
was himself that had done it. His own cherished
prudence had failed to discern the fatal flaw.
His own hand had robbed his beloved of the
ease and luxury and dignity of life. In his
sudden anguish he grew weak and almost wild.
He made incoherent statements to Katy, explanations that were half confessions and half bemoan-
ings ; and Katy, who by no means comprehended
him, but who saw clearly and instantly that there
was great loss and trouble, and that he was in
mental confusion and distress, came up instantly
out of her depths, kissed him, fondled him,
scolded him, and enveloped him with comfort
and consolation. Money, money! what did she
care for money? And in her own temporary
suspension of hope and happiness, she spoke
with more real indifference than she might
otherwise have felt, though, perhaps, not more
than she would in any case have assumed.

Poor, indeed! As if she were not fully able to take care of herself and him too! Bad, avaricious man! Ungrateful, unnatural parent! To think she minded anything, if only her dear, sweet, cross old daddy would behave himself, and not think she would mind the loss of a little money, or a good deal either! Not she! And Katy hung about him, and caressed him, and read to him, and sung to him, and soothed him. But for all that was the wound not stanched, and the yellow dawn of one peaceful Sunday morning found him stretched upon his couch, stricken, speechless, unconscious.

Katherine, unacquainted with illness, and hitherto unshadowed by the mystery of death, was awed but incredulous. This familiar and beloved being had passed through the portals of a subtile and awful change. All her heart and soul and life seemed to fuse itself in his with an imperious and inextinguishable sympathy that would but could not penetrate his secret. Neighborly kindness and succor were unintermitting, as they always are in our village life. Mr. Glynn, who from the beginning of the perplexity and danger had occupied himself almost unceasingly with Mr. Haviland's affairs, — to whom, indeed, the unhappy gentleman had relinquished them with pathetic hopelessness and helplessness, — was unwearied in attendance and service. As hours and days went on, the assailed and overpowered soul struggled faintly back to life and love. Into the eyes there came wistfulness, recognition, affection ; and then, alas! pain ; and Katherine hushed her breaking heart, forced her sad face into smiles, and softly soothed the trouble into peace. But always the pain came back. Only it seemed to Kate that when Mr. Glynn was by, the eyes whose every glance she noted rested upon him with peculiar satisfaction, followed him with interest, watched for him sometimes with strange intentness ; and Katy told Mr. Glynn her fancy, and he left as little as possible the sick man's side. Once, when they had been sitting long in quiet and silence, thinking he slept, the dear eyes opened suddenly, and fastened on Mr. Glynn with start-ling eagerness; the feeble lips made such earnest effort to speak, the vanishing mind strove so forcibly to convey its wish, that both eager watchers bent over him with eye and ear alert, to grasp the smallest fragment of his meaning.

. "O, *can't* you catch one word ?" moaned Katy, wringing her hands in helpless agony.

"Hush," said Mr. Glynn, softly ; and then in clear, tranquil, assuring tones to the dying man : "Katy? yes, I will take care of Katy. Never fear. I will take every care of Katy always. Trust me." The assent, the satisfaction were so immediate and obvious, that Kate, who thought not of herself at all, cried, joyously, "O, darling, is it that? Is it only me? O, don't think of *me*, dearest, dearest!" Slowly into the pale and beautiful face stole a look of repose, of ineffable tranquillity, of immortal holiness, and from the calm and peaceful sleep that followed there was no awakening.

If sympathy could have lightened Katherine's burden, that burden would have been small to bear; for none but sorrowed with the kind, happy young girl, motherless from infancy, and now fatherless and alone in her desolate youth. And this sympathy found its way to her heart, and was sweet and consoling; yet was there nothing she so much wanted as to be alone. She was so young, she knew so little of affairs, that she contemplated her situation only on its emotional side. She did not think of the material change that menaced her. She wanted her guests to go when the sad occasion of their assembling should be past; she wanted the house to settle into its old ways, that she might face her loss in its worst aspects, and see what it was to be, with this void that should never be filled. And while her relatives, friends, and neighbors were wondering what course she would take, and hesitating what suggestions to make, and fearing to seem rough and hard by intruding business upon her sorrow, Kate was entirely unaware that there was any cause for suggestion. Her nearest relative was her aunt; and Mrs. Ford, finding Mr. Glynn already apparently in charge of affairs, knowing him somewhat in his business relations, and still more as Mr. Haviland's long-time friend and neighbor, naturally took counsel with him, and leaned upon him as the nearest strength, after the manner of women. And, having vainly tried to induce Kate to return home with herself, not as a matter of necessity, but of sympathy, Mrs. Ford was insensibly persuaded by Mr. Glynn — so insensibly that she fancied the idea originated with herself — that it was not best to obtrude any change or suggestion upon Kate, but to leave her a while to her coveted solitude, to the tranquillizing touch of time and the healing springs of youth.

" I would so much rather take you home with me, dear Kate; but if you really cannot bring yourself — "

" Yes, dear aunt — "

" We are leaving you only for a little rest and quiet. But our house you must always consider your home, and I shall run down again before long."

" You are so kind always, Aunt Fanny."

" It is no kindness, Kate; it is only the natural order of things. And you will send for me immediately if you want anything. I should be so happy to take you home with us."

"O, no, aunt."

"I know, dear. I shall not urge it any more. I have no doubt it is best; but we cannot bring ourselves to be content at leaving you here alone."

"I shall really be so much happier here than anywhere else."

"So you say, dear; and I suppose it is so. And there is no hurry."

"Hurry about what?"

"Nothing, my dear; nothing at all. There is no hurry about arranging your future."

"I think perhaps that will arrange itself."

"Perhaps so; and at any rate we shall not help matters by worrying about them."

So it came to pass that Katy had her heart's desire, and was left alone in the deserted house; and the clock ticked on the stairway so loud that it seemed to ring through space; and the easy-chair stood empty by the south window; and the cat purred in the sunshine that moved slowly along its old round over the carpet; and Tishy's voice sounded strange in the distant kitchen; and the house seemed hopelessly given over to the deafening resonances of silence and the heart-breaking order of an ever-present absence.

"I could bear it all," said Katherine to Mr. Glynn, to whom she could talk more freely than to others, because he needed no explanations;

"I could bear the separation, the being without him, because that is all my own. It is those last days of mental torture. To know that his dear, good life was clouded at the last — that I cannot bear."

"But it was only for a little. It is all over. And your love never failed him, nor even your cheerfulness. I could see how he rested on that, even at the worst."

"O, I am afraid not even that."

"My dear child, you cannot see clearly now. You are tired and grieving, and you dwell on regrets. But try to believe me. The heaviest blow was softened to your father when he found you unchanged."

"But he never could have supposed that any such thing could have changed me towards him."

"No; and he was also too unselfish to care less for your loss than for your reception of the news of loss. Nevertheless, I know well how your loving-kindness and good cheer comforted him. I assure you, Kate, that to me he spoke of it quite as much as of this trouble which you did not mind."

"Ah, but I minded the other too much."

"I think he did not know it," said Mr. Glynn, after a pause.

"I hope not — not wholly. But I thought because I was not happy, there was no other unhappiness but that. It did not seem to me anything then, that I had my father. To think of it — that I should not have thought anything about that! And I fear I was often morose, at least sad. I thought of myself more than of any one else. O, if I had known that papa was in trouble!— if I had known, if I had thought I could lose him so soon, — how I should have thought of him and no other!"

Vain regret! and old as vain.

9

VIII.

"KATY," said Mr. Glynn, one day, apropos to nothing, "do you remember a question I asked you long ago — last year?"

"A question?" said Katy, quite at a loss for his meaning.

"A request that you could not grant — on the last drive we ever took together."

"O!" sighed Kate, faintly, and blushing a deeper crimson than her cheeks had known for many a wan week.

"Pray don't remember that," she said, softly, as Mr. Glynn was silent. "Pray do not remember it; I do not."

"I do not renew that request, Katy. I make you another, wholly different. I want you to marry me."

"I do not understand," faltered Katy.

"When I asked you then, I thought I might win your love, but I could not."

"I am very grateful to you," said Katy, pitifully. "I can never tell you how grateful I am.

You have been the truest of friends. My father — " and her voice failed her.

" I know it," he exclaimed, suddenly taking her hand, and as suddenly dropping it. " I know. You have been sweet and perfect, as you always were. You would have loved me if you could. As you could not, you have been everything that was kind and gentle. I also would have kept from loving you if I could. No, not that," he checked himself, smiling, " I would rather love you, Katy, hopelessly, without return, than to love triumphantly any other woman ! " And after a pause he added : " That is an amusement not in your books, — is it, Kate ? "

Kate could only turn away her eyes in silence.

" But," he continued, " that is not what I came to say. What I wanted then was your love. Without that I could have nothing. Now I want you. Katy, if you had married me then, I should have stood in the way of your happiness. I should not stand in the way of your happiness now ? "

" No. Because — but — "

" Loving you as I did, dear, I could never have been willing to make you wretched. Had fate put you into my hands, you not consenting, I would not have consented. But now — "

" O, now I am not worth your taking. O,

Mr. Glynn, you know I have no love to give. No, you do not know how desolate I am."

"I think I do know, however."

"Then you could not want me."

"But, Katy, I love you. That you naturally forget, because you do not love me."

"I have a great respect and — a real liking for you, Mr. Glynn."

"That is right. That I hoped for, because without that we should have little to go on indeed. This other love, Katy, you do not count on?"

"O, no."

"Answer me, Katy, truly, and forgive me, but answer me for the sake of your father's friendship. You do not mean ever to marry Walter Laballe?"

"O, no; never, never!"

"And you have no thought of any other love?"

"How could I? No, no."

"As a friend and neighbor you do like me? I am not disagreeable to you? It is not unpleasant to you to see me and talk to me?"

"O, no; much more than that. I am very grateful to you. It is more. Grateful sounds cold, hard. My gratitude is very warm. I have great confidence and trust in you. But O, Mr. Glynn, you do not want that. You are too good to be put off with that."

"Little Katy, I am not too good to be put off

with anything you can give me. If it could have been love—but that we will not speak of. What I want now, what will make me happier than anything else can, is that you should come and live with me, and let me take care of you. It is all that is left me in life, Katy. It would not be robbing you, and it would be giving me infinite wealth."

" But, Mr. Glynn, I will be just as good friends and live here. I will always be your true, faithful friend. I will never marry any one else, and I will never go away. I should like always to live here. I could be just as much to you here as to — change."

" No, Katy, that is not possible. There are many reasons. Do not ask me to give them, but trust me. You say you have confidence in me — that it is not possible. You must either do this one thing for me, or you will go away out of this house, out of my life ; and that I cannot bear. I thought I had lost you once. Now that you have come back, it would be worse to lose you than if you had never gone. You are tired and lonely. You have no heart to leave all the old life, and strike out into new paths. You would be successful by-and-by, because you are young, and strong, and buoyant. But it would be a weary way."

" I have not thought of it," said Katy, shrinkingly. " I do not want to go away."

"No, you do not; and you shall not go away. Come to me, Katy. I will take the most faithful care of you. I know you better than you know yourself—I have studied you more. I will be so careful of you, dear, that you shall as little as possible miss what you have lost. You shall have just the life you like best. You shall be wholly free and independent to go your own way. Remember, you lose nothing, and if there is any happiness for you in life, I will find it for you."

"But, O Mr. Glynn, it would be wicked, and base, and mean, and vile in me to go to you — as — I — should have to go."

"No, my — Katy, not with a full and fair understanding. If you should come to me pretending to love me, and I should find afterwards that you did not, that would be fatal. But you have never deceived me. You have never been otherwise than wholly frank and true. I know what I have to expect."

"But you — you could not be happy with so little."

"Should I be happier with nothing?"

"But suppose it should not always be nothing. It might be that — that some other — fate, some other love should come to you. Then you, too, would be wretched, and it would be a horrible and hopeless sort of wretchedness."

"Let me be the judge of that;" and he added, with a quiet smile, "If you had done me the honor to become a little acquainted with me, you would know very well that no danger is to be less dreaded."

And Katy smiled too, in a sort of hopeless recognition of the love that was so patient, so frank, alike in its assertion and its abnegation.

"Katy, dear little Katy, you were the dearest little pet and plaything in the old times — infinitely dearer now. Do not be afraid of me. I will never be hard or harsh with you, or constrain you in any way. I will never be displeased with you, whatever happens. I will not ask you what is in your heart. That shall come in its own time. But will you trust me enough to tell me whether you are held by any, ever so lingering a doubt whether you might be barring the way to your own happiness. Is there still in your mind a hope that one day a way may be open to you for another marriage? Do not misunderstand me. I ask you out of the very depths of my love and my reverence. Nothing is so sacred to me as your confidence. O Katy, be kind to me!"

"Mr. Glynn, it is all one as if I were dead; *any* marriage is impossible. What you want is not natural. You are very, very good — but — I cannot think it would be right. Right for you, because — but not right for me. It would be false for me."

"Not false assuredly. No one is concerned

except you and me. You shall not be bound by any promises that you cannot fulfil. Listen, dear, would it be unnatural for you to come and live with me and let me take care of you if you were my sister?"

"O, no. If I could be born again, and be your real sister, I would do that. I would be glad to do that. That shows how much I like you, how truly I like you."

"You think your father trusted me? Did you never think, dear, that your father wished to intrust you to my care?"

"Not in this way. I never thought that. I do not think he thought it. O, I know he never thought that!"

"But if he could have thought it, if he could know it now, do you not think he would approve?"

"If — if it were all right. He would not wish me to do wrong."

"Nor do I wish you to do wrong. Trust me a little, Katy."

"I do indeed. I trust you wholly in everything but this."

"Your father's wish would have been in any case a sacred obligation. But in this case it is my dearest wish too, and my strongest hope. But how can I fulfil it unless you will come to me? How can I take care of you unless you will give yourself to me? Mind, dear, I am not threatening. If you refuse me, I shall stay by you and keep watch for you all I can ; but that is so little, and you are alone, and you will go away, and I shall lose you. O Katy, come to me and let me fulfil the promise that gave your father peace ! "

" But let me live here. I will do everything as you wish if you will only let me stay here and not be married."

" O, my dear, you must be married, of course ! That is a little ceremony quite indispensable. But that need not frighten you. Just let me come over quietly some morning and take you home with me. Do not fancy you will be en-slaved by it. I will not even weary and worry you with my love. I will not. Did I not keep my promise before ? Did I not, Katy ? Speak to me."

" I suppose so," faltered Kate, not in the least remembering any promise given or taken.

" It shall be so in the future. I give you my word. Do not vex yourself with fancies. Think of me as your best friend. You can let me be that. You shall have no duties only such as you choose. I will impose nothing on you."

" Mr. Glynn, I do not know how to answer you. I cannot do it ; I cannot accept it. My father will know. You are good and generous and kind ; I feel that. I do not know what to say ; but I cannot do it."

"But you can do it, Katy. This is just what you can do. I do not ask the impossible. Hear me, Katy. I am not used to ask favors; but see — to you I beg, I plead. Katy, Katy, my life is in this; all that I ever wanted in all my life is this."

"But I must save you. You do not know what you are asking. I should be taking all, and giving nothing. You do not know what a forlorn and spiritless ghost I am of the girl I once was, of the girl you knew. O, Mr. Glynn, please go — please let me go! You are good and true; I thank you from my heart; but you do not know what you are asking. I will save you from your own generosity."

"I know perfectly well what I am doing, and I am not at all generous. Good heavens, Katy, look at it! Here," — he grasped her hands and drew her nearer to him, — "here is everything in the world that I love. Without you, the world is empty to me. What I want is you, in my house, before my eyes. You, unhappy, that I may console you; alone, that I may take care of you. Think of that supreme happiness — when I thought you were gone from me forever. Did I dream of this? There seemed no way open to me; not a ray of light. And now my happiness will not diminish yours. Perhaps it may bring something of yours back. Darling, I am not thinking of you at all. I forget your poor

little broken heart. I only think of the great
joy coming to me, to live with you, and see you
my care, my charge — to love you, Katy, to lav-
ish all my life on you. Katy, say that this shall
be ! ''

" But I have nothing to give you in return,''
gasped Katy.

"Give me the opportunity. It is all I ask;
nothing more. Be at peace, my dearest. I love
you wholly. I ask nothing from you. You shall
settle it all with your own heart at your leisure.
Just to live for you, with you, is — is my heaven,
Katy ! ''

" But tell me ! '' cried Kate, earnestly. " O,
please be careful ! Do not let me destroy you.
You think you will be content. But are you not
deceiving yourself ? Is there not in your heart a
thought that I shall one day change ? When the
days and the years go by, and the Katy of old
never comes back again, and there is only a
colorless woman in her place, with a pallid mind
and a dull, dead heart, and all the spring and
vigor gone out of her, then will you not be dismayed and disgusted ? Then even in the grave
where I live I shall feel another pain of death.
Tell me if you really look this in the face and
accept it ? You are thinking that some day I
will change ; but I cannot change.'' And Kate's
voice was shrill and tremulous with excitement.
Ah ! it was not the voice of the dead. Out of

no grave of feeling came that eager, wailing cry!
And her innocent, searching eyes pierced deeper
than they knew. Again his swart face flushed
unseen as a gentle hand unwittingly touched the
heart's hidden secret, revealing it thus first, perhaps, to the slower mind. The flush and throb
passed swiftly by.

"Katy," he said, looking honestly into her honest eyes, "who can tell? Perhaps I do think
that my love may win to your heart in time. I do
not know. Perhaps if you do not hate me at the
beginning, it may be that I have a hidden hope
that a little love will come to me by-and-by. But
I assure you, Katy, it is not that which moves
me. I put that out of sight. I am sure of your
kindness, of your sweetness, of your friendliness.
And to breathe in always that kind, sweet friendliness from the eyes I love, and the heart I love,
when I thought I was doomed to utter dreari-
ness! O Katy, Katy, how can I show you what
love is!"

"I wish I had loved you," cried Kate, ingenuously. "I wish it had been you that I loved."

"But since it was not, let it be me that you
will bless. I would not ask this if it were not
for that other love. I should not dare—I should
not know to what fate, from what future, you
might presently find yourself bound. But now
I think I do know, and I dare. Have no misgivings, Katy. If I knew surely that you would

never look at me with other eyes than now, if you should surely never have another shade of tenderness in your heart, it would be all the same. If you lay before me helpless, wrecked, with only the breath of life on your lips, it would still be the same. It would be my dearest joy to serve you, to cherish you, even if you did not see my hand or know my voice. What will it be with your dear eyes looking upon me — clear, if sad ? Your heart is heavy; but I shall know that it answers me. Do you not see that I am wholly self-seeking ? "

" But if I cannot be true to you? If I cannot wholly cut myself off from the past, even though the past must be outwardly as if it had never been ? "

" Dearest, for name and fame I lay my honor in your sweet hands, and it shall bind me to their sweetness and sanctity. For happiness, for tranquillity even, I am content to wait — for yours. Mine is already assured.

" But," he added, hastily, " I put no check, no guard, upon you in word or thought. You shall not be true to me by rule. You shall not curb your heart. If you think of — that other, you shall not feel you are wronging me. Think of him all you must. For your own sake I shall wish it otherwise ; but you shall not bend your thoughts to my pleasure. I will not be your tyrant. Katy, how can I make you see that it is

not to imprisonment I urge you, but to the largest
liberty?—only to protection and care that I cannot give you here? Grant me this, Katy, which
you can, which you surely can, and out of the
wreck which menaced both our lives you will
have saved me something most precious."

Beaten down by her own griefs, disappointed
of her young dreams, uncertain and despairing
of herself, overborne by his unsuspected impet-
uosity, with no words or strength to withstand
him longer, yet with the instinct not to yield,
Katherine looked up into his eyes, silent, imploring she knew not what. And as he met that
upturned face, so innocent, so sorrowful, so ap-
pealing, a sudden passion seized him, a sudden
flame leaped along his veins, a sudden wrath
against the fate that had barred her from him, a
sudden frenzy of will to grasp and gain her. In
an instant he had swept aside all pleading. He
gathered her in his strong arm, he crushed the
soft hands to his breast, his flaming eyes held
her. "Katy!" he cried, "I will no longer ask
you. I will take it into my own hands. You
shall come to me. You are mine. You belong
to me. You are mine — mine — mine — from
the beginning. Kiss me, my own. I will not
ask it again ; but this once — this once for a seal,
for a pledge that I am come to my own." And
he bent to her troubled brow, he pressed close
the drooping eyes, he touched the trembling lips

with long caress, as if the repressed passion of his life should pass into her soul in that one slow, sweet moment. And as Katy, pale, panting, powerless, sank to the storm that swept over her, as she felt herself held in that iron clasp, felt the smothered fire of his burning eyes, and the firm lips' compelling tenderness, some wild, new thrill quivered through heart and soul and spirit, and she was suddenly aware that this man had forced in from the outer darkness of indifference where he was wont to dwell, across the line of complaisant liking or calm, instinctive dismissal, in to her own warm world. It was not love, but it was recognition. It was no lesson learned, it was an illumination.

IX.

SO then Mr. Glynn having snatched victory in high-handed fashion, carried it with a high hand. He knew well that if he would secure the momentary conquest he had gained, he must make sure of Katherine while she was yet in the trough of the sea. Once riding the waves again, stanch and sound, with sails set and colors flying, she would slip away from him over unknown seas. It would have been wise and prudent for him to reflect whether wooing and winning in this Sabine fashion were safe and suitable in our day, — whether a reluctant will, overborne in weakness, would not rise again with returning strength, not only to reluctance but repulsion. But Mr. Glynn, moderate and cautious in the ordinary affairs of life, in this most vital affair of all was neither cautious nor moderate. He took counsel neither of prudence nor wisdom. He was a man. He was bent on the one sole purpose, to get possession of this woman, to have her within his reach, to hold her in his power. It is true that he meant everything that was high and honorable by her. He would bear himself chivalrously towards her. But, had it not been his own love that was in question, he would have seen how little that detracted from the risk. But it was love that impelled him, and he trampled under foot all doubt, all hazard. He did not pause to consider what fatal consequences might result to himself or to Katy should heart and soul and will awake from their temporary trance to find that tranquil liking, too hard pressed into unnatural service, had changed into irrepressible distaste. He never faltered at thought of what would come should all his hope crumble, and, availing himself of her depression and despair to secure her passive acquiescence, he should fail to possess himself of his ultimate object, her inward and spiritual allegiance.

He was a man, and he resolutely refused to be hampered by any secondary consideration. He loved Katy; he wanted her, and he would have her. He sincerely believed — let it be said for his extenuation — that he could secure her happiness. She had followed her own path, and stumbled, and been sorely bruised. He believed he could have prevented that if she would have permitted; and he believed that now he could take her and heal her and hold her up. At any rate he could take her! And he looked neither to the right hand nor to the left till his purpose was accomplished.

Mrs. Ford was instantly summoned, and to that excellent lady, who could neither bring herself to burial with Katy in the country, nor coax Katy away to her own city home, and who was in sore perplexity over her much-loved and not quite comprehended niece, Richard Glynn seemed the angel of the Lord sent from Heaven for her deliverance. Although her own marriage had been very far from an ideal one, none the less did this devout believer in the existing order of things count marriage the one gateway to female dignity, the sole path in which life could move forward with decorum and coherence. Partly in thoughtlessness and partly in misliking for such speech, and partly in the rush of events, Katherine had never told her aunt of the sundering of her engagement to Walter Laballe, though a tolerably certain suspicion of the true state of things had crept into the lady's mind. Nor was she by any means sorry; for, though she liked the young man well enough, she had not been able to discover that he possessed those solid charms which could never claim her approval alone, yet without which all others would have been equally vain. She would have been very much and very justly shocked to have been called mercenary, or to have supposed herself willing to assist in a marriage of convenience for her niece. Only if she could have seen in black and white a convincing evidence that Walter Laballe had, either in possession or in fair prospect, a handsome and well-established income, she would have been inclined to pass over any little traits of instability, or even inability, as belonging to his years and desultory life, and altogether likely to yield to the exigencies of his profession and the serious responsibilities of married life. She certainly would not have descended upon Kate to find the engagement off and a marriage with a questionable income immediately impending, without making the most vigorous efforts to stem so disastrous a tide. But to find this doubtful affair closed, and Kate claimed by a man of high standing and ample wealth — the good lady folded her hands in pious resignation, devoutly thanked Providence for uncovenanted mercies, and felt that her cup was running over.

That Katherine should be quiet, undemonstrative, even uninterested, seemed to Mrs. Ford but natural. That she should be indifferent to so admirable a marriage, that she should have anything to oppose to so perfect an arrangement of all her difficulties, that — let us be just — Kate could for a moment contemplate a marriage in which her heart was not enlisted, Mrs. Ford could not suspect, would not have admitted to herself if she had suspected it. Mr. Glynn saved Katy the trouble of explanation, and Mrs. Ford the perplexity of surmises. He made known to her all of the situation that it was proper so near a relative and so warm a friend should know, and thus seen, the situation commended itself entirely to Mrs. Ford's reason and approval. The intimacy of the families was sufficiently significant of the satisfaction with which Mr. Haviland would have greeted such a marriage. Kate's loneliness and the condition of her affairs were ample reasons for the apparent precipitancy. Mr. Glynn's assurances to Mrs. Ford were calculated to satisfy and gratify the most devoted mother. And in short it came to pass that, compassionate, dutiful, bewildered, and sore beset, Katherine found herself in that most immoral of all positions, the position of an unloving wife, yet did not deem herself degraded and did not feel herself debased.

For weeks after her marriage Katy was like a flower beaten down untimely by an untimely storm. The long-continued sorrow and fatigue to which she was wholly unused culminated in a low, slow fever which seized her impalpably, but held her fast in its languid yet deadly clutch, and Katy looked for an easy path out of all her confusion through the gradual slipping away of life. Mr. Glynn was even more alarmed than Kate, who, for that matter, was not alarmed at all. Unversed in feminine ways, Katherine seemed to him so small, so fragile, so unable to cope with illness, that he felt his hold upon her loosening, and had, too late, a terrible misgiving as to whether his own inexorable insistence might not have helped to lay her low. But Doctor Blount, who was familiar with every droop and drag of ailing womanhood, who had known Kate from a very early period in her life, who saw Mr. Glynn's misery but did not see all its cause, and laid it only to the account of his over-anxious love, — Doctor Blount laughed his fears to scorn, assured him that it was but the natural reaction from her great excitement and grief; that Kate was a sensible girl, and knew what she was about, and was doing the best thing possible under the circumstances, namely, lying by; that when this enforced rest had brought about the desired equilibrium she would be all right again; that as for Kate being delicate — bah! the thing was absurd! She was as strong as her husband, and likely to live as long — and longer if he could not keep a stiff upper lip. He knew her stock, and could take out a life-insurance on Kate any day. She was as sound as a nut. There was not an infirm fibre in her. Good *Gad*, Glynn, every man has his price, and it took a wife, it seems, to show what an uncommon fool you are. And in all those anxious weeks nothing was so cheering to the poor man as the doctor's unmeasured abuse. And presently, sure enough, Katy honored the good doctor's faith, and was herself infinitely surprised to perceive that not only was vigor slowly surging back into her veins, but the elasticity of life into her heart. She began to feel that the years which could not bring her satisfaction might bring tranquillity; that though she might find little to enjoy, there might be much to do. And then she went even further, and fancied that, though she might never measure the heights and depths of happiness, she might walk in serene peace on the table-lands.

And as for this friend of her father, — this friend of her own as she could not choose but consider him, though she could not bring herself to call him husband even in her thought, — coming out of the far-off, listless atmosphere of illness into the clear light of health, she felt towards him the moving of a strong, compassionate gratitude. She could not love him. Her love had gone from her past recall. Her power to love was exhausted. Power to love him had never existed. This was fate, and no wish could change it. There was no room for duty here. But this man who claimed nothing from her, who with all his importunity had sought only the opportunity to bestow, seemed to her worthy of exertion to a cheerful and helpful life. All the love she had lavished had

brought her no return. If his must be alike
wasted, it should at least not be wasted on selfishness and self-indulgence. Through her illness
she had only vague recollections of a kindly
face, of words inexpressibly gentle and reas-
suring, of loth and lingering withdrawals. But
as she climbed slowly back to health, and as
with health came observation, reflection, and
renewal of interest in all outward objects, Kate
saw not only how constant and watchful he was,
but how solitary and self-contained. Her own
home had been full of sunshine and companionship. Everywhere was friendliness, equality,
confidence. Her father had not been a man to
be formally feared or obeyed or respected, but
to be loved and fondled and made much of, to
be teased and confided in and first considered,
not from duty but instinct. Tishy was no servant, but sovereign in her own right, worship-
ping Katy, and tyrannizing over her, and rejoicing beyond measure in every good thing that
befell her. From that house to this the transition was but gloomy. Even Tishy, who came
up often to tend her, looked strange, sat about
forlorn, and was evidently ill at ease. Mrs. Palker, the housekeeper, Kate fancied, looked at
her as if she were a curiosity, and poured out
volumes of confidence, which tired Kate inexpressibly. In the house was too much stateli-

ness and too little sunshine, and Kate, home-sick and heart-sick, shed some bitter tears, unseen, for herself; and then went back over the lonely life that Mr. Glynn must have led, and cried again for him; and then suddenly thought with a pang of something like horror that she was his wife, that she was married, that all her hopes and imaginings had ended in this — his wife, his wife, *his wife,* — forever and forever; there was no way out; all the dreadful, eternal future shut her in against this blank wall. And if there were a way out, if she were herself outside, what then? Would the grave give back its dead? Would she find life other than she had left it? If she had not been borne hither, would she have found herself still in her home of sunshine, full-fed with hope and love, buoyant, unstricken? Katy uttered an inarticulate cry to Heaven, and if in it were mingled some unspoken invocation to the saints, some instinctive, dumb appeal to the father so lately lost, to the mother never known, why, Heaven I think is not jealous of such prayer, and not for that should Katy forswear her firm Protestant faith; and then — for Katy's moods and tenses followed close upon each other's heels — a swift thought came to her, and she looked at the clock, and dried her eyes, and put up her hair, and put on a gown, and adorned herself, and went down stairs with heart throbbing and ears ringing, not daring to hesitate, knowing she should not have the courage to conquer hesitation. And even with her hand on the door-knob of the dining-room, her courage gave way, and she shrank back trembling.

X.

BUT somehow, whether through the diabolical acuteness of love, Heaven knows — if Heaven will pardon the collocation — that irresolute feeble fumbling at the door reached the ears of Mr. Glynn, who was about taking his seat at his solitary dinner-table. He came quickly to the door, opened it with an eager, expectant look, which, on seeing Kate, changed swiftly into such gladness of surprise and gratification as smote her like a reproach. He drew her into the room, and stood for a moment holding her two hands, intent, battling valiantly with the impulse to shiver all his promises, and had grace given him to conquer and be wise — let us not say honest — and speak lightly to Kate, who had too much ado to keep herself well in hand to be very observant of him.

"It is not possible that you have really come to dine with me, Kate?"

"Then, perhaps, to give you your dinner, if you like."

"If I like! If I adore! But, dear, how you tremble! You are cold."

"No indeed, I am not cold, not at all. It is only the — the coming down stairs. I have not been down before."

"And you are weak. You should not have attempted it alone. That was very imprudent. I was so glad to see you that I forgot to scold. Will you consider yourself scolded? Will you send for me and let me bring you down the next time?"

"O, there is no need. I am quite strong. It was not that alone, but — coming here and — all."

"And feeling that I should certainly eat you up. Confess, Katy. I confess that I should like to."

"I should certainly disagree with you," said Kate, grasping out feebly after Sydney Smith's baked missionary, by way of support.

"Don't mind manners, Katy. Especially don't mind or mend mine. I must stare at you. I was hungering and thirsting for you, and it was angelic in you to come down of your own accord."

"I suppose angels always come down of their own accord when they come at all," said Kate, demurely.

"I know one angel who did not come down to this house of her own accord, and for a while I surely thought she would spread her wings and glide away after I had got her here. But you won't now, will you, Kate? Promise me you will not be so cruel and inconsiderate as to fall ill again."

"Not if you are good to me," said Kate, smiling.

"Good? Just wait and see. But get well while you are waiting."

" But I am well now, quite well."

"Yes, to be sure. You are so well that you are almost dangerous. But come, this is giving you the cold shoulder for your first dinner, which is not hospitable. Now, what shall we eat and what shall we drink? Katy, why did you not tell me you were coming, that I might kill the fatted calf?"

"I was not coming till the moment I thought of it. But it does not signify. I am not a very prodigal son."

"Was not that an unlucky figure? You must lay it to the account of a general mental perturbation. See here, Katy, I fear I don't know how to keep house for a lady."

"And I am sure I don't know how to keep house for a gentleman; so we are even there."

"But you," said Mr. Glynn, "you don't have to do it while I — here I am — and very much afraid of you, Katy. I am indeed. If I only had the knack of trembling, you would hear the very spoons rattle. Tell me, Kate, is this a nice table to ask you to sit down to or not?"

"Indeed," said Kate, laughing, "it is a nice enough table, but — if I can't tell a lie — I think I could do better."

"Bless your heart, so you shall — turn and overturn, as the good parson asks the good God to do at five minutes before eleven every Sunday morning. And I remember that you are a worshipper of idols — graven images, and table-tackling in particular. You will have a wide field for operations in this house. But first you must eat. Shall it be here?" he added gently, indicating the seat of honor at the head of the table.

"Just as you please," said Kate, growing tremulous again.

"Then you shall be an invalid still, and sit by me and be dictated to. And a well-ordered dinner-party we shall be; for you being a convalescent ought to be hungry, and will naturally eat when you have nothing to say, and I who have been hard at work all day am ditto, and so willing to listen between whiles. Whereas if we were both determined to talk all the time, how sad it would be!"

Poor Kate felt that she would be more than willing to give up her share of the conversation, but she did not say so. She had come down determined to put her own self aside and to pleasure him, not at all virtuously, but for self-preservation, and she was not the girl to give in lightly.

"Mr. Glynn," she said, somewhat abruptly, trying heroically to work the stiffness out of the situation, moved also by real sympathy, "have you always lived alone?" She had thought so much of this in her solitary musings.

"For years, Katy. Ever since the death of my grandmother. You remember her?"

"Just a little. And of course I ought to know that you were alone. But somehow I seem never to have really thought about you till — lately. How could you bear it?"

"Very ill indeed. But I hope you will make it up to me now by thinking of me frequently."

Katy stared at him a moment, half deceived by his sober look. "I shall begin to think you deserve to be alone," she said at length, "if you take pains to misunderstand."

"I think perhaps if I have a genius for anything, it is for living alone. Why I want you, Katy, is because it is you, not for dread of solitude."

"I wish it were for dread of solitude."

"Why?"

"Because then I should be sure you would not be disappointed."

"O! but I have you; so I am just as well secured against disappointment. You see, Katy, if it were any one supposed trait, or person, or influence that I sought, I might be mistaken; but you can't fail to be Katy."

" And I suppose you are so used to solitude that you do not mind it?" said Kate instinctively, bearing away from the point upon which he was as instinctively verging.

"So, so. My father died before I was born, and my mother I do not remember. Fancy what a savage I must be. But you will civilize me gradually, only be patient at the slowness of the process. Of course my life would have been different if they had lived, but I cannot miss what I never knew. It was natural to me to be alone."

" You had only your grandmother, and her not long."

" And though but a boy at the time of her death, I had long felt more care of her than from her. Her loss was a great sorrow to me, but it did not leave me orphaned, or deprived of any protection. It did leave me alone. I think I was as happy as most boys, but in a different way. I was very grave and sober. I had a frolicsome little neighbor then for a companion."

" Yes," said Kate, " I have heard of her."

" She was the most wild, whimsical, wilful little witch in the world, and she kept me in spirits constantly."

"She has grown grave and sober herself, now."

"I wish I might be able to give back to her a little of the heart and courage she gave me."

Kate thanked him with a look. "I am glad you were rich," she said, "so you could have everything else."

"Yes, little lady; but I remember you have not a great respect for money!" Mr. Glynn glanced mischievously at her and she blushed scarlet, for she too had vivid recollections.

"However," he added, "you will do well to think twice before condemning it outright. Don't you know the Bible meanders into a gold mine at the very outset. The gold of Havilah is good. Moses was a sound financier, and hardly got the thing started before he slapped in gold as the running-gear of the whole machine!"

"And how long do you suppose it was before the Pentateuch people got tired of specie payment, and set up their First National Bank?"

"But banks presuppose bankers, and that you know is taboo in a mixed audience like you and me."

"O, I did not know you had so inconvenient a memory," said Katy, frowning away another blush.

"Ah, Katy, my memory is a merely local and partial one. I think I remember all the things that you ever said or did. Otherwise my memory is not remarkable. It certainly does not go back to the Pentateuchs. I don't believe a mother's son of them ever had an honest five-dollar bill in his life."

"Then they were spared the vexation of having their porte-monnaies bursting out at the ends, because they were always made a little too short."

"No, that is because they are too full! We have changed all that now. Am I not a man and a tyrant?"

"But a rich one, as you have confessed in many a thoughtless hour. How came you to be rich?"

"Inheritance, partly, and partly indifference. I never cared much for money, and so it came in from all quarters. My poverty in relatives is the rather grim cause of some accumulation of property."

"And I suppose you have been doing it yourself, too?"

"Certainly; I like business. I like activity and adventure, combination and calculation. I like to see means converging to ends. I like the game, that is, I care not overmuch for the prize. I dare say if I had had a more attractive home life, I should have been a poorer man. But now, Katy, I am very glad I am not a poor man. You have instantly put value on all my possessions."

Kate's quick and vivid blush was not only

11

a shy retreat from praise, but a sad, regretful consciousness of the meagre part her heart acted in the drama. She resolutely, though silently, pledged herself never to fail his faith. If self-abnegation and self-consecration could avail, he should have all the happiness she could give him, if not all that he deserved.

Mr. Glynn noted the suffusing color, and quickly changed the subject.

"This is a great improvement on yesterday."

"What was yesterday?" asked Kate, brilliantly.

"A club-supper in town."

"O! did you stay in town yesterday?"

"You mean to say you did not miss me?" And then, as Kate looked up guiltily, "Don't look so horrified, dear. I always thought that a selfish, whining, not to say snivelling song, 'Do they miss me at home? Do they miss me?' Yes, I came down in the theatre train."

"I did know that you did not come up to see me, but I thought you were busy. I did not know that you had not come home. What is a club-supper?"

"Tobacco-smoke, whiskey, cards, and men — which things I hate."

"Why do you eat club-suppers, then?"

"Heaven only knows— or the other place."

"If it were not for the cards and the whiskey

and the tobacco, I should think the men would be nice."

" The men, to be sure, I do barely tolerate."

" I should think men would like to be by themselves best. Clever men, I mean. If there are women you have to be polite to them."

" As if that would come hard."

" But men know so much more than women."

" Is Saul also among the prophets? I never thought *you* would turn traitor, Katherine."

" *You* must not say it, but *I* may. One would not permit it in public, but in secret, I fear it is true."

" I see. Officially you let the feminine light shine, but personally you think it ought to be hidden under a bushel."

" But women have no chance to know things, and men have. So many things happen to them that are interesting."

" But don't you remember the Chinese proverb, ' All knowledge is by nature implanted in the heart of a woman ' ? "

" I shall quarrel with you about that some time. I shall not quietly let you consign women to ignorance, even in polite phrase."

" But you will wait until I have forgotten that you began the quarrel by yourself concluding all women in ignorance."

" Of course that was only in a general way. Some women are very learned. There was a

Mrs. Winstone, whom I met at Aunt Fanny's last winter. It is just like reading a book to hear her."

"I don't like people to talk like books."

"You could not fail to like her. It was not a stiff, dull book, but a lively and entertaining one. What I mean is — that — now you know for instance, when I talk, I talk all disorderly, in a heap. I can't get things to come right, and I go back and begin again. But she talks in sentences that are just perfect."

"O, you cannot convince me. I shall never, I trust, have to take her out to dinner. I suspect perfection here below. Give me Miss Ready-to-Halt, who has to dance with one crutch in her hand, but who foots it well, I promise you."

"If you could only once see her you would agree with me instantly. And there was another, Mrs. Leveridge."

"You don't mean to say you saw Mrs. Leveridge!"

"Yes; do you know her?"

"Know her? She was the best, almost the only female friend I ever had. And you met her? She is a brilliant woman indeed. I shall agree with anything you say about her."

"If I had known — " said Kate, and blushed into silence.

"Yes," said Mr. Glynn, laughing, "if you had known and known, how you would have talked me over, would you not ?   But I suspect it was lucky for me, for she knows five times as many of my sins as I ever committed.   She has a wonderful faculty of setting things out — what we may elegantly call the gift of language.   I have no doubt that if you had been at all interested in the subject, she would have readily given you sixteen graphic descriptions of my character, which she would call analyzing it, each one clearly and cleverly drawn, and standing out in bold, strong relief, and no two alike ; but where *I* should scramble into daylight under such a superimposed weight of portraiture, you would be puzzled to ascertain.''

" That is true," said Kate, with interest.   " I have seen that myself.   She had been to see some pictures one day with me.   She was very good and took me.   And afterwards people came in, and she talked about them, and it was wonderful.   And I had not liked the pictures much.   Of course it was because I did not know enough to see in them what she did.   It was as if she had seen a dozen pictures, one under the other, like a palimpsest.   I liked her talk a great deal better than the pictures.''

" Of course you did.   There was a good deal more in it.   I used to be under the same spell when I was in college, and she was a brilliant young lady in town, ruling with absolute sway, no sister near the throne.''

"O!" breathed Katherine, looking up with smiling inquiry.

"O! are you there? Not quite. I believe it is generally understood that all the men on the Merrimac River have at one time or another passed under her yoke. But I never aspired so high. She patronized me, and younger-brothered me to the endangering of my soul through pride and vainglory; but she was too good and simple and dignified to trifle with me. We were very good friends then; but, dear me, she has since taken a husband and children, and I honestly think she now cares more for her smallest child than she does for me! Eh?" to Kate's little laugh of surprise.

"I am glad you think she is good," said Katherine. "I think she is magnificently good."

"She has need to be. If she were not the best woman in the world, she would be the worst."

"O, no!"

"O, yes. Don't you see? She is so diabolically clever and creative. Give her the knee-pan of a man's character, and she builds up the whole beast on it. It may be a quite different being from the original animal, but it is sure to be so strong and spirited, whether for good or evil, that it instantly supplants the original in the gaze of all beholders. Now, if she were ill-disposed, don't you see how mischievous she would be?"

" But she is not ill-disposed."

" Just what I say.   On the contrary, she overflows with benevolence towards all created beings.   Like all great members of the universe, she is ruled by two forces.   Her preternatural clearness shows her all salient points, and her wit instantly seizes them, while her inexhaustible kindness claims all her sympathy for the side of humanity.   So between the two she takes the curve of piquant popularity."

" Yes," said Kate, " every one brings her tribute."

" O ! but does she not come down hard on a poor fellow if he takes the wrong tack ! " said Mr. Glynn, evidently with vivid recollections of such descents upon himself.

" He should not take the wrong tack."

" To be sure.   But only few of us are perfect."

" But it is only certain kinds of bad things that Mrs. Leveridge will not tolerate.   A great many things she is far more patient with than I could be."

" Ah, Katy ! the mischief with all you good women is, that none of you have charitableness. I suppose it is the necessary result of being good. Spots must show blacker against white than against the party-color of weather-beaten humanity."

" Your pill is round and sweet, and looks like

a sugar-plum; but as I roll it around in my mind, it seems to me that it *is* a pill."

"O, you have great store of Christian charity, broad enough for the human race, unlimited forgiveness for sin in the abstract, the wildest schemes of redemption for sinners in general; but let one of your friends do a definite wrong thing, and there is no atonement."

"Well," said Kate, stoutly, "the Bible only says forgive your enemies. I don't know that we are anywhere commanded to forgive our friends."

"Well done, Kate. It is you for the application of Christian precepts to daily life! But is it worth while to keep a small flaw of a friend — or even a large flaw — so near the eye as to shut out the whole character?"

"My friends do not have flaws," said Kate, sententiously.

"Stick to that, Katy," said Mr. Glynn, laughing. "I think I like your law better than your gospel; a fellow feels safer under it; only don't turn it around. But you are certainly getting better. You hit back."

"Are you afraid?"

"Of course I am. I have been afraid of you, you little witch, ever since you were two years old, and used to go into the divinest little rages. What fun it was to see you sputter, and scold, and stamp your little feet, and strike out with your little fists like chain-lightning, a great deal faster than you could talk — ”

“ Amiable creature ! If I may be allowed to interrupt.”

“ O, a comment is not an interruption. The worst thing about ladies’ symposiums, Katy, is not that they don’t know things, but they are always passing the salt or something in the middle of the sentence. Of course I cannot be stimulated by an intimation that a potato is of more value than my remarks. Now you, Katy, have not really interrupted me once.”

“ No,” said Katherine, “ I was not hungry.”

“ The saints defend us ! They are certainly attacking us. And in truth, Katy, you have eaten nothing, and you are tired, dear.”

“ Just a little. I think I will — ”

“ O, don’t go. Don’t run away. Come into the library. I will settle you as comfortably as you can be in your own room. I won’t even talk to you. Only stay a little while with me.” And Katherine suffered herself to be drawn into the library.

It was a large, low-browed, and not altogether cheerful room. Books were everywhere — not only ranged against the walls, but under the tables, piled in zigzag rows and tottering columns along the floor, and overstrewn with pamphlets and papers, which also obtruded from behind every shelf or frame that would hold them up; so that it required no little care in Kate to pick her way safely among the débris. Old engravings in old frames, quaint and odd, coarse and fine, were hanging, and standing, and falling everywhere, very curious and valuable as illustrating the progress of the art, but less successful as ornamentation. Most of the chairs had their arms full, and most of the drawers were open, and all that were open staid open, because they were too full to shut. Wherever the over-burdened carpet could dim twinkle through the storm, it did not serve to mend matters. One or two fine bronzes were — shall I say chucked — out of harm's way under the bay-window, but not in a position to bring out their beauties to advantage. A plaster Socrates with a very dirty face, as is perhaps biographically proper, viewed the world sidewise from the top of a book-shelf, the heads of several Roman emperors kept him in distinguished company, and an unhappy Cleopatra glared with broken-nosed disgust upon the situation. Evidently Mr. Glynn was no disciple of Eastlake, no devotee of the Renaissance, but a heathen man and a publican whom the Gospel of Furniture had never reached, dead in trespasses and sins against Morris and Household Art and the Expression of Rooms. But he, good man, had no misgivings. He brought Kate into this den in perfect good faith. He gave the dying embers on the hearth a vigorous poke,

and thrust and piled on the wood till the dancing flames sent a glow through the gloom. He
cleared a large reclining-chair by the simple process of suddenly tipping it aslant enough for
every book and paper to slide out, and with
great muscular force ploughed it through the
rough field, scattering books right and left, to
a small clearing in front of the hearth. Therein
he bestowed Katherine, and with such careful
and gentle arrangement of cushions and foot-rest
and fire-screen, that she could but admit she was
very comfortable. And even as she smiled her
thanks, the treacherous tears rushed into her
eyes, and her wilful breath came in a quick,
gasping sob.

"O Katy!" was all her unhappy husband
could moan, standing over her in helpless blank
dismay.

"I am not ungrateful, believe me," cried Katherine. "I am not unhappy."

"You must not speak or think of gratitude,
dear," he said, softly.

"But I must. You are so good. Do not
think I do not feel how kind you are. You
have been ever since — ever since — "

"It is you who are good to me, Katy. You
gave up the solitude you craved and came to
me. All my life I can never thank you enough
for this — this, which I know was a sacrifice."

"But it shall not be a sacrifice," cried Kate.

"I did not mean it for that. I do mean to make you happy and be pleasant to you." If he smiled inwardly at the under-meaning which Kate did not intend to convey, his face gave no sign.

"My dear little girl, you are pleasanter to me than words can tell. You have made me happy already. You do not need to intend anything. The mere fact that you are here, never to go away again from me, is enough. It is like perpetual sunshine. When I am in town all day, I am never without a secret consciousness of something pleasant awaiting me. When I come in sight of the house, I look up first at your windows, and think what is behind them for me, not to-day merely, but for all the days of my life. You see, Katy, how I am past remedy. Be at peace, dear little heart, for my happiness."

"You will not think I am troublesome."

"Never;" smiling in spite of himself.

"Nor unhappy."

"Not if you tell me you are not."

"Indeed I am not. Truly I am not. Only be patient with me. Give me time. It is all — so — strange."

"I know, Katy. You have had a great loss and a great change. It will take time to adjust yourself to your new life. You have been ill too. You must remember that, and not be impatient with yourself. You are a brave, good girl, and all will surely come right if you will be patient. It is not *I* that am waiting, dear. I am happy because I have you. I cannot be happier — only in seeing you grow strong and cheerful. Unless — O my darling, *have* I done you a harm? Do you feel I have wronged you in bringing you here?"

"O, no, no," said Kate, eagerly and sincerely.

"Does it trouble you to be here?"

"I do not think it does;" trying to be at once honest and kind. "Nothing could make me anywhere — light-hearted."

"No, dear, you never could have taken up the old life. It is only that you begin the new with me instead of alone — to my infinite content. So you must try and think friendly thoughts of me."

And then he sat by her side in the soft idealizing fire-light, silent, caressing the passive hand, firm and strong no longer, but dearer grown by weakness.

"You don't care for this," he said, playfully. "Kissing hands is only a sovereign courtesy. That is not breaking my pact."

"You need not do that," said Katherine, in the fullness of her remorseful gratitude. "You may kiss *me* if you wish."

"Ah, Kitty, it is very sweet in you to say so; but the kiss I am waiting for is not the kiss you will offer me."

Nevertheless he did not decline the offer, though fearful as soon as he had spoken lest Kate should take alarm and feel herself called upon for a love which had no value and no existence except by spontaneity — an alarm which he knew would only delay if not defeat his eager hope of one day possessing her heart. But Katherine was not yet sufficiently released from herself to take much heed of him, and she detected no plot against her peaceful, if monotonous, future. Mr. Glynn rang for lights, and busied himself with books and papers and — watching Kate; and Kate lay flushing in the fire-light's rosy glow, wide-eyed and thoughtful, trying to realize rather than to remember, but remembering only and not realizing, till it was in good earnest time to go; and when she left him, his last words lingering softly in her ears and falling softly on her heart, rewarded her for the effort she had made to come.

" You have given me the happiest evening of my life." And she was comforted.

XI.

AFTER this nothing seemed so hard. The ice was broken; and she could meet Mr. Glynn, and take her place at his table, and feel herself not wholly a stranger. He helped her much by his cheery and genial, but unchanged, scarcely more than accented friendliness. He never frightened her by even seeming to wish for more than she was glad to give. He betrayed no discontent if she was pensive. Whenever she came to him, she was received with such warm welcome as could not fail to put her in heart with herself. If she held to solitude, she was not chidden or questioned by so much as a look. In all things she felt herself wholly free to consult her own pleasure; nor could she ever fail to see that he sought the same end. There seemed to be no effort, no duty, about it. It was only that his life lay in hers. He found his happiness in the paths where her feet wandered. Of course Kate would have been a monster to disregard this generous seeking. And Kate was no monster, but a good girl, somewhat cast down by adverse fate, but trying earnestly to do the right thing, albeit with a heavy heart; and in so doing and so trying, her heart came gradually to be lightened of its load. In the steadfast love of this strong friend she felt no triumph. It was to her no opportunity for self-indulgence, for pride, or caprice, or petty tyranny; but a great trust, which had been committed to her unsought — from which, indeed, she had shrunk; but which, accepted, she must discharge with sacred fidelity. If she had loved him, — not as she did regard him, with a true respect and friendship, — but if she had loved him as she *could* love, she would have known what to do. But — well — and if she loved him, what would she do? Why, of course, make his life as happy as possible; and first of all, make herself and the house pleasant to him. And after all, why was not that the very best thing to do as it was? Besides, said Kate to herself, resolute to be at least for him victorious, how many girls have married the right man, and have found him bad! I have not gone my own way; but how good he is! Nobody could be better. And if he had been bad and tyrannical and selfish, and yet had made me marry him all the same! Such thoughts were running through Kate's mind in an under-current while she was listening to her loving aunt, who had come down on a visit of mingled inquiry, condolence, and congratulation to her niece. Many praiseworthy sentiments regarding her good fortune in having attracted so unexceptionable a man, and secured so desirable a husband; the unbounded duty she owed him; and it must be added, too, the unbounded use she must make of her position and possibilities, were passing tranquilly over the unrippled surface of Kate's mind without at all disturbing her real thoughts. But presently a little too pronounced emphasis on her good luck jarred upon her. Kate was ready and forward herself to ascribe all goodness and unselfishness to Mr. Glynn; but it was a matter altogether between herself and him. She had no mind to be congratulated as a lucky girl who had made a good match.

"Aunty dear," she said, a little mischievously, "what a very poor opinion you must have of me."

"A poor opinion of you! What can you be thinking of, Kate?"

"Certainly you must have supposed my deserts of the feeblest, or you would not make so much of my having married a respectable man. Now, for my part, I don't think I was a bad match for any one. Your niece, aunty! It is not very manly in you to put me down."

"Put you down, Katherine?"

"Certainly, aunty. You have been edging me down into the Valley of Humiliation ever since you have been here.   Why don't you say what a lucky man is Mr. Glynn to have coaxed such a nice girl as I into marrying him?— handsome, stylish — now, aunty, you look severe.   Don't say I am not handsome, if you can help it; but, above all things, don't say I am not stylish, for I cannot bear it — not in my present weak state. You know I have not recovered my full strength yet, and if I am not humored I shall have a relapse."

" You little trollop ! to be talking to me this way !" said Mrs. Ford, with good-humored indignation.

" I.never saw such austere virtue, aunt.   You won't even be dragooned into a compliment. And you have been praising Mr. Glynn for the last half hour, without once stopping."

" Well, my dear, I never heard that praise of a husband was dispraise of a wife."

" Nor I, aunty, until this sad hour."

" I don't mean to say, Katherine, that you are not good enough for any man in the country ; but, at the same time, there was no reason why you should expect anything remarkable.   You were a match for anybody, but not a catch."

" An epigram !" said Kate, solemnly.   " A match, but not a catch ! "

" And Mr. Glynn has behaved so extraordinarily well about the property."

" What property, aunt ? "

" Yours, my child ; or what should have been yours."

" You mean about poor papa's trouble ? "

" Yes ; the whole arrangement."

" I do not know what you mean by his behaving well.   He had no chance to behave ill, if he had been ever so ill-disposed.   My father lost all the money before Mr. Glynn had anything to do with it.   I don't know that he could have done any-thing except turn around and make faces at me. But then, you know, I should not have married him."

" My dear Kate, you are a little fool, especial-ly for thinking I am such a great one.   I suppose Mr. Glynn has not told you the whole state of the case.   He asked me to say nothing about it at first, as you had trouble enough, and we were very glad to save you any more.   But I supposed you did know now."

" I did not know there was anything to know," said Kate, faintly.   " I have been ill, you must remember.   And perhaps," she added, with some-thing of shame-faced loyalty to the relation in which she stood to Mr. Glynn, " perhaps you ought not to say anything now, if Mr. Glynn chooses not."

" Nonsense, Katy.   It is my affair as much as Mr. Glynn's.   And besides, you ought to know, that you may understand what I have been say-ing ; besides, there is nothing to tell.   I think your poor dear father died without realizing the extent of his losses."

" I am glad of that," gasped Kate.

" So am I. It was the most extraordinary thing that a man so careful, so prudent, and I think I may say so wise, — but there," and she dried her good old eyes, " did you know, Kate, that he lost everything ? "

" I did not know particularly. I knew he had great losses that troubled him much."

" He gave everything over into Richard Glynn's hands, and he was still at work on it when your dear father was taken ill. It was as bad as it could be, Kate. The farm would have been sold under your feet and the house over your head ; and what does Mr. Glynn do but pay the whole valuation himself, declaring to me that you should not be disturbed in your trouble, and simply making it a matter of business with the other side ! And not a word was to be said to you about it. But now that you are married, and moved, why should you not know it ? "

" Why, indeed ? " said Kate.

" Now you know very little, Kate, about anything ; but I can tell you that there are very few men who would have done that, especially when they were just going to marry you, and would naturally have said, ' Why, let it all go. You are to have another home. What could you do with two ? ' A good many people would call it mere sentimentalism, and I don't say they would call names!"

"Mr. Glynn," said Kate that evening, looking up from the book she had been vainly trying to read, "I know about the farm."

"About the farm?" he queried, guilty but parrying.

"Aunt Fanny told me."

"Is it possible you two had come to the end of your tether and were reduced to real estate for conversation?"

"O, Mr. Glynn, I know why you did it; but you must see it comes a little hard on me."

"If I must, I must; but as a mere matter of fact, I don't."

"I did not know that, added to everything else, I came to you a beggar."

"No more did I. As I remember the course of human events, it seems to me that I was the one who did the begging. You only granted grace — and not even that. I took grace by main force and carried it off."

"But, Mr. Glynn — it was kindly done, I know, most generously done — "

"Not a bit of it. It was bare-faced pillage. You could prosecute me for abduction in any court in Christendom and stand a round chance for damages. But mind, Kate, I will fight you to the very last, and I will carry you off at the end. So you won't make much by that move."

"But *do* you think," said Kate, not to be diverted from her purpose, "that it was quite fair to let me go on so, knowing nothing. I was a woman grown. Ought not I to have known where I stood?"

"Not in the least. Because, if you had, you would not have stood there!"

"How could I know, then, what I was doing?"

"You could not, dear. That is the very thing I did not want you to know, because then you would not have done it. Don't you see? It is as plain as a pike-staff to me."

"But I was in a false position all the time."

"I should have been in a falser one if you had not been."

"I do not see why."

"Why? Because, as it was, all I had to do was lie low. If you had known, I should have had to lie high and low, right and left. And I have a conscience which never permits me to deceive more than is absolutely necessary to the end in view. Don't corrupt me, Katy."

"And you feel perfectly justified, even now, looking back upon it?"

"Justified? Glorified! Why, look at her! I had hard work enough to get you, as it was. If the question had been complicated with pennilessness, independence, working for a living, and such high and mighty abstractions, when would

I have seen the end of it? Justified indeed! See here, Kate. I would have burned the old mill and machinery with my own hands, rather than not have the chance at you!" Thus this unblushing machinator.

"And I was thinking all the while I could stay on the farm," said Kate, musingly.

"Well, so you could. It was your own. Only I ordered you off. But don't you know of a certainty that if you had been told the farm was forfeit you would have flown instantly into a factory, or a school-house, or some demnition grind or other, (it is a quotation, Katy; it is not original sin. There is a vast difference between literature and profaneness,) and then where should I have been? Instead of that, I kept you under my own eye where I could work to advantage."

"But in your honest, inner mind, don't you think you ought to have given me a chance?"

"Chance to what?"

"To manage my own affairs?"

"Not a bit of it. I wanted to manage them myself! In my own interests! I could do it a great deal better than you."

"But I ought to have done — I ought to have had a chance to do what was dignified and self-respectful."

"Ah, that is precisely the tangent you would have gone off on — dignity! Did I not know,

Kate, what a close shave it was ? Now you may dignify as much as you like, I have got the law on you ! A pretty piece of business it would have been before you were in my hands. That is the beauty of the existing order of things. Once get a woman in the clutch of marriage and she can't help herself. So, Katy !"

"But I am a Woman's-rights woman," said Katherine, dubiously.

"So am I," said Mr. Glynn, cheerfully, soaring above sex.

"Then I think I ought to have my rights."

"You shall, Kate, if I can get them for you. What, to begin with ? "

"The right to be poor, and know I am poor and earn my own bread and butter."

"But you are not, Kitty. You are really quite a rich woman. You own a good house — two, for that matter — and considerable land, and some live-stock, and bank stock, and state and city bonds, — upon my word, Kate, it is a pretty joke calling yourself poor."

"But I did not come fairly by it. How would you feel to find that you had just nothing and took all from me ? "

"I will make it all over to you and see."

"I don't believe you would dare try that," said Kate, smiling.

"Dare ! It would not make a day's difference. I would have it all out of your hands again so quick that you would not know it had ever been in."

"You would not speak so contemptuously of my business abilities if I were a man."

"Of course not. I should not think so."

"But you have never tried me to know whether I had any financial sagacity or not."

"I never mean to."

"Mr. Glynn, you are perfectly lost in the gall of bitterness and the bonds of iniquity."

"I am afraid I am."

"Why can a man not treat a woman on the basis of equality with himself — at least till he finds out to the contrary? I don't mean," continued Kate, hastily, "that I knew about things as you did, but if I had been a boy as old as I was, even though I had known no more than I did, you would have acted so differently."

"Certainly I should. What did I want of a great lubberly boy?"

"But you would have consulted him. If a man found 'a great lubberly boy' sitting idle in a house not his own, he would never pay his debts and say nothing to him about it."

"By no means. He would take him by the scruff of the neck and pitch him into the street."

"And don't you think it would be better for girls — I won't say to be pitched into the street by the scruff of their necks — I don't know what that is. It does not sound very elegant."

"It is not, Katy. It applies only to boys. Girls have a ruff instead, which is very elegant."

"Well, then, don't you think it would be better if these girls were taught to depend upon their own resources and make their lives strong and self-supporting, and so command respect instead of extorting pity?"

"No, I do not. I think the best thing for a girl, if she is in trouble or if she is not, is to have the man who loves her go to her and take her, peaceably if he can, forcibly if he must, and bring her to his own home to love her and serve her, and keep her out of harm's way all the days of his life, for the good of his soul."

"That does not seem to have the ring of reform. What are the girls to do who don't have a Thracian and a soldier to carry them off?"

"Katy, you need not try to convince me of sin. I will agree to everything you say, up and down. You can't bring forward a theory that I won't subscribe to. All the same, I am glad I hoodwinked you, and blindfolded you, and bejuggled you into this house. I have been glad ever since. I would do it again, twice as bad, if necessary. I wish I could look back upon any virtue I ever practised with half as much complacency as I do on this flat burglary. Come, now."

"Why, this is being dead in trespasses and sin," sighed Kate, her breath fairly taken away by his audacity.

"Katrina, come and sit here by me. You are not really vexed?"

"O, no, not vexed. Not that at all."

"If you are, there is one way you can have revenge."

"What is that?"

"By thanking me."

The blood rushed into Kate's cheeks, the tears into her eyes.

"My dearest, sweetest, best," he cried, serious enough now, "it is such a little thing you are beating against! If I had loved you less, if I had been only a common friend, a decent neighbor, I could hardly have done otherwise. As it was, what was it? I would not have had you leave me then — not for a thousand fortunes. I made a pen-scratch and kept you. That was all. What were a few thousand dollars, more or less, to me? I wanted you. It was a pure piece of selfishness, Katy, and it has prospered greatly, as most selfishness does."

"I do not believe a word you are saying," said Kate, smiling through her tears.

"Never mind, dear; I have got you, and you have got the farm, and possession is nine points of the law, thank Heaven! Now, what shall we do with it?"

"O, I should like to keep it," said Kate, earnestly; "that is — now —"

"Of course you will keep it. You would be

a very mercenary girl to go and sell it after I have run the risk of my life to prevent its being sold. Besides, I shall not let you. I am a Woman's-rights man!"

"That you are!" said Kate, energetically. "One of a thousand!"

"So the farm shall not be sold; that is decided."

"Then what else can — we do?"

"Ah, that is a sweet word, Katy. That little 'we' pays for the farm twice over."

"I thought it was men who kept to the point," said Kate, shyly.

"Not when women drop little golden apples for them to nibble at."

"Please to nibble at *my* farm, then."

"What shall *we* do with *our* farm, then? Well, dear, anything that will give us pleasure to think of. We must remember that this is the home where our Katy was born, and where she lived all her happy years, and grew to be — "

"O now, Mr. Glynn," interrupted Kate, "I am not anything remarkable. Please not think I am, because you will surely be disappointed."

"Remarkable! Did I ever accuse you of it?"

"No;" blushing a little; "but I know you were going to say something — not very wise."

"I was going to say that you are the light of my eyes; and that you are, and you can't swear off. If this be folly, make the most of it.

Kate, do you think I am a fool to be loving you so?"

"It begins to look like it."

"Well,—

> 'Among all the follies that I know,
> The sweetest folly in the world is love.'

Now I have quoted poetry at you; so you may be sure the evidence is all in. Katy, I don't know whether you are remarkable. I don't even know whether you are pretty. I only know that you are Katy—my one woman in all the world —my little old Katy-girl."

"I will tell you what I should like to do with the house."

"What house?"

"The one you bought away from me with malice aforethought."

"Whose house now?"

"O, I believe it is a sort of joint-stock property —a Glynn-Haviland affair."

"Very handsomely spoken. Go on."

"I am afraid you will think it foolish and impracticable, but I don't see why it should be."

"Nor I either."

"Why, you don't know what it is."

"I assume that is the very reason."

"O, please don't laugh at me. I am really in earnest. I want to do something very much. I used to think about it a great deal before —long ago. I never could quite see how to bring it about, but I used to picture it all out to myself many and many a time. And now I think perhaps it may be possible; but please don't laugh even if it is not."

"I promise you I won't, dear, as soon as I know what it is. I only laugh because I am in the dark and have nothing else to do, and because I am so happy."

"Well, you know the charity-places for children in Homes and Convents and such places ? "

" I have seen a little of them; yes."

"Of course they are all very good, and there is no help for them, but they seem to me dreadful. Do you not think they are dreadful ? "

" To be wholly truthful, Katy, I cannot say that I ever thought much about them. I know there are such places, and I thought it was a fine thing to have the little oafs made comfortable. But I can't claim any credit beyond putting my name down for any Institution that was presented, and Heaven knows that is very meagre credit."

"I suppose, naturally, you would not mind it particularly, but to me it always seemed dreadful to have little children in an institution. They need some one in particular so much; and to have them sleeping all in rows, and living all in rooms together, and only one place to play in, — it looks as if they were cheated of their birthright."

"My dear Kate, if you knew the wretchedness from which they come."

"And the impossibility of doing otherwise. Yes. But what if I could do a little otherwise?"

"What could you do, dear?"

"Why could I not turn my house —"

"What house?"

"The house of commons," smiled Kate. "Why could I not — you see, Mr. Glynn, I cannot bear to think of — of its going the way of all houses. There is no real reason why it should not. It is not that it is better than other houses, only — I love it so."

"Perhaps that is the way of all love," said Mr. Glynn, softly. And Kate gave him a grateful glance.

"And so I do not like to think of some one else — of anybody there. O, I think I could not bear to see —" and poor Kate's voice was choked by tender memories.

"You shall not," said Mr. Glynn, hastily. "Everything shall be just as you want it — just as you will like it best."

"At the same time," continued Kate, bravely recovering herself, "I do not want it to be wasted. That would not be better. It would not be pleasant and it would not be right."

"*You* are right, dear Katy."

"Now, then, why would it be impracticable

for me to find three or four, or five poor little
children — little wee children — even little bits
of babies, the smaller the better — enough to
make a nice little family ; not a hospital, not a
regiment of them, but a lovely little home family, and make for them a home there? I think
I should like to see the poor little innocents toddling and rolling about in my old places ; and
there they could be real children, and natural
and wild and bad, you know, and grow up
healthy and happy. I think that would be perpetual sunshine and blessing falling on the
dear old house. O, I should like it so much!"
and Katherine clasped her hands eagerly, and
looked into her husband's face intently for his
opinion.

"You shall certainly have your liking, Kate.
Bless your sweet heart for thinking of it!"

"You think it is nice yourself; do you not?"

"I think it is very charming indeed."

"O, thank you a thousand, thousand times!
Not in the way you don't like," she added,
quickly, "but because I can't help it. It is so
nice of you not to laugh at me or ask me down
with unanswerable questions."

"Not I. I am too much relieved. I was horribly afraid you were going to adopt the brats
yourself."

"The what?" queried indignant Kate.

"The — the — cherubs;" putting up his hands

as if to ward off a blow. Kate laughed, but discreetly concluded to accept the amendment.

"It will cost a great deal of money. Have you thought of that?"

"But I have married a woman who has some money in her own right, and a good deal more by marriage. Don't grow avaricious, Kate. I *shall* be disappointed if you turn out to be a miserly woman."

"And it won't be all expense, because there is the farm."

"Don't try to get out of it that way. Do you expect the infants to carry on the farm?"

"No; but the farm ought to carry them on, and a good deal more. You will see. You may be able to bank better than I; but I know all about a farm — witch-grass, and timothy, and ploughing in clover, and seeding down. But then I don't suppose they will eat much but milk for a good while."

"Undoubtedly the consumption of witch-grass will be small the first year or two; you are right there. See what it is to have a knowledge of farming — especially baby-farming. Who is to be farm superintendent?"

"There is not going to be any superintendent. That is the very thing I don't want. Don't you see I am going to set up an opposition to this forlorn superintendence, which is what makes the orphan-houses so dreary.   What babies need is a mother, and I have one all picked out."

"You have!   And does she take kindly to being picked?"

"She will as soon as she knows it.   It is Tishy's daughter, who used to live with us.   The best creature!   Only she would be married."

"That *was* a downfall."

"It was indeed, for he was a wretch.   She never would have looked at him, for she had a good deal of sense — at least about most things. But it was his three children.   She could not stand the temptation of those children.   And she thought she was going to have a home, poor thing!   O, shall I not make Martha a happy woman?   And Tishy will stay and keep everything just as it was.   This I could not have done at all.   This is your doing;" and Kate fairly beamed upon him.

"But, my dear, are you sure this ne'er-do-weel of hers will be the right kind of man to have about our infantry?"

"O, he is gone.   Nobody knows where he is. He went away and left his three children for her to take care of; and then her own little baby was born, and she had four on her hands.   But it was just as well.   He never was any good — only to throw the spare-rib at her when it did not suit him."

"A greasy scamp! And what is become of the three children she married?"

"I believe Tishy engineered them upon their mother's relatives. Tishy was enraged with Martha for marrying, but after he went away she came forward and said she would take care of Martha and the baby; but his — what you call cherubs — she would none of. So as Martha had a baby of her own, she consented to let the others go. She is fond of them, too. I suppose she would like to have them here with her, but I will not. It is bad blood; and besides, they are too big, and they are already taken care of. I will have only little, helpless, friendless midgets that don't know any better. And Martha has no home, and she is a beautiful housekeeper, and the silliest soft heart you ever saw, and will just turn slave for children. She shall have — how many do you suppose she can take care of? No; I will hunt up only just as many as she can be a real mother to. O, how shall I begin? I must see Tishy instantly. You will help me, won't you? Not about Tishy, but about finding the children, and getting started. I won't trouble you in the least afterwards, if you will only help me a little at the beginning."

"No. I certainly shall not enter into any such limited partnership. You want me to throw the whole weight of my intellect into the business, and then retire. Thanks, madam. I enlist for the war or I enlist not at all."

"But you are a man," said Kate, frankly. "You won't be any use. Besides that I did not wish to trouble you, you can't do anything."

"I might milk the cows and bring the wood."

"O, you may do anything you like outside the house. I was only thinking of the inside. Yes, certainly, you can be very serviceable in supporting the family."

"A trifling duty, and a humble, — but still — something."

XII.

THIS old project of Katherine's, fanned into new life, gave new life to herself. She had Tishy up for frequent and animated consultations, and found in her an enthusiastic partner.

"It is too good news to be true, Kath*erine*," said Tishy. "I never was so put to't in my life to know what to do."

"What to do when, Tishy?"

"Ever since you was married, dear. Mr. Glynn he just told me to hold on, but I knew there must be a change some time."

"But, you dear Tishy, you did not think I should let you be turned out-doors?"

"Well, of course, Kath*erine*, I wa'n't going to be beholden to nobody. Nor I don't mean that I was afraid of comin' on the town. I have got money in bank, and my two hands into the bargain. But it is dretful hard to change, dear, at my time of life."

"You won't call this a change?"

"Not to speak of. Nothin' to what I was afraid of. I have been dretful uneasy. I was afraid you might want me to come up here."

"Afraid, Letitia Midkins! And I here!"

"I know, dear child, but you are young. 'Twould be dretful new and strange-like for me to come up here with them foreigners-like. I have had my swing too long to play second fiddle."

"And now, Tishy, you will play first fiddle in your own house. You will get along comfortably with Martha,— won't you? You and I always got along well together."

"You and I? Lud-a-mercy!" and Tishy rivalled Lord Ronald with her laugh of merry scorn. "You, child? Well, you're Mis' Glynn now, but I can't realize to myself you're anything but Katy."

And Tishy laughed again at the idea of her getting along well with Kate — Kate whom she had served with a devotion so unswerving and so affectionate that it never called itself service.

"And you must remember, Tishy, that Martha is married too, and has a son of her own, and must be treated like a mother as well as like a daughter."

"If I can't manage Martha Midkins without your help, Kather-ine Havil*and*, I can't with—" said Tishy, with good-natured but very Tishy-an asperity.

"Yes," said Kate, laughing; "but you lorded it over us both so long when we were under you, that I am afraid you will forget to treat us with proper respect."

"I will look out for respect, Mis' Glynn — I suppose that is respect. But if you think I am going to call Martha Midkins Mis' Bostwick, you will lose your guess, I can tell you. Ketch me calling a child of mine after one of the Old Boy's unaccountables, if she married him seven times over!"

"Tishy, that is the only misgiving I have — for fear he will come back and trouble us."

"I ain't in the least worried about that," said Tishy, rocking back and forth in her chair, teeth hard set, and looking altogether vicious.

"But if he *should* come?"

"I'll pay him my compliments with the skillet. It's what I ought to a' done in the first place. Instead of which I tried to reason with Martha. But, Lord! I didn't rightly know what carron he was then."

"Very well, Tishy, I will come down as soon as I possibly can and look over the rooms, and we will see what needs to be done; and I think Martha better come as soon as she can. Now you remember, won't you, that Martha is to be the mother and you the matron. And you won't encroach upon her — will you?"

"Lord love you, child! Martha is Martha, and

I am Tishy, and I ain't likely to forget it, nor she nuther. Don't you worry. But I wanted to tell you, and come nigh forgettin', that there's a poor creetur up there near where Martha lives. She was a weak, washy little thing — never had no hold onto her. I used to tell 'em she'd ketch cold going to bed barefoot. Well, her husband he was a carpenter — a clever sort of man enough, but no faculty — never forehanded, and he fell from a roof now goin' on three months ago, and only lived about a week, and his wife she went into a gallopin' consumption, and last week she died, and there's the baby just four months old — a poor little pindlin' thing that must go to the poor-house, and that means the grave. Martha she has nussed it the last week, but, Lor! thinks I, there's a windfall for Kather*ine*."

"I don't know about taking *such* a baby," reflected Kate.

" Why, it is the Lord's poorest," said Tishy, piously.

" True ; but I am afraid it will die, and then we shall be discouraged. Don't you think we ought to begin with babies that will live ? "

" Why, law, Katy, no babies don't have a sure lease of life, and sometimes the ones you least expect it of clings the longest and strongest."

" But you say this poor baby's mother died of consumption ? "

"So she did; but consumption ain't ketching."

"Only, Tishy, it seems as if it is as much as ever a baby can live, any way, little weak thing! and if it is born to consumption, there isn't much hope."

"O, law now, Katy, you're all out there. You've no idea what a sight of hold-on there is in babies. Why, they live through what would kill a grown man. You see they haven't no nerves and no worries, and they only have to take what comes, nor never fret about to-morrow. Very like the child took all the health the poor mother had, and left her to die; but the child will grow up into an old woman."

"Very well; if you think the chances are that she will live, we will take her."

"There's no chance at all she will live if we don't take her. She's dying daily where she is now, and the poor-house 'll fetch her up. But then, if she dies, it will do no harm to ease her off."

"Certainly; but what I think is, the babies that die go quickly into the hands of the good God, and are sure to be happy there. But those that live must take what comes, and so they ought to be well furnished with health and good principles and good habits. If we could take them all, we would; but as we can only have a very few, I don't think we can afford to waste ourselves on those who are going to be happy in Heaven so soon. We must help those who must stay here. That is not hard-hearted, Tishy, don't you see, though it sounds sort of business-like."

" O, well, Katy, you can't tell who is going to live and who isn't. We must just trust the Lord for that. And, besides, wouldn't it be sunthin' to take a poor peaked baby and build him up till he's as strong and frisky and antic as a kitten ? "

" Yes, if he is suffering only from want of care, and can be cured into firm health. But if he is inwardly sick and weak, and can only be kept in a feeble half-and-half life, I think I would not do that. I think I would let him die."

" Why, Kitty, you frighten me ! "

" O, I will not kill any of your babies, Tishy, don't fear. But, don't you see, where is the fun of being miserable ? Why should any one live in disease and discomfort ? "

" But, don't you know the Lord works some of his mightiest wonders in poor, feeble folks that never did a day's work in their lives, nor knew a minute free of pain ? "

" O, I know he does not actually throw us overboard when we have made wrecks of ourselves. But, all the same, Tishy, I want to take care of the children that have got to live whether or no, or that have bodies at least worth saving. So you better look out and keep your charges in good condition, or I shall gobble them up some fine morning."

Kate had not expected to open her nursery quite so soon, but Mr. Glynn agreed with her that the prompt appearance and the unquestionable forlornness of this very young person were signs not to be disregarded. Tishy indeed declared that she would rather begin with the two, and get the hang of it, than have all come together. So then it became necessary for Kate to visit the old house at once. She had not entered it since she passed out from its shelter on the morning of her marriage.

" I am going with you," said Mr. Glynn, when she asked him for the keys of some of the rooms which had been closed at Tishy's request.

She could not help it that a blank disappointment fell for a moment on her face at this announcement, and he could not help it that his eyes darkened with a sudden pain at that unintentional avowal. Yet he had been as well aware of her preference as if she had spoken it. But she put down her disappointment instantly, and he thrust back the useless regret.

" I knew you would rather go alone," he said, simply, " but indeed I cannot let you."

" I only thought of going alone," said Kate, as simply, " but it does not hurt me to have you go ; " and then they walked down the silent road together.

Afterwards Kate felt that it was well she had been companioned. The little restraint helped her to self-possession. Mr. Glynn had ordered all the rooms to be opened; cheerful fires were burning, and the familiar sunshine flooded the familiar rooms. It would have been a luxury to Kate to sit alone in the silence and solitude, and dream herself back into the irrecoverable past; but it would not have been strengthening, and what Kate wanted now was strength. So it was well that she could not abandon herself to tender and sorrowful recollections, while yet she felt herself held back only by the most heartfelt sympathy and consideration to which she was in honor bound to respond with deference at least. And while every word and look of her husband's was softened with the memory of the past, he gradually, almost imperceptibly, won her to think and speak of the future, so that somehow the tearful and tender forms of a vanished home melted into the bright and beckoning fancies of joyful promise, and Kate's vision peopled the rooms with dimpled figures, round, rosy faces laughed up at her from the cosy corners, and hope and cheer nestled in the nooks that she had feared to find so desolate. It was only the old story of the chilled traveller warmed and saved by the loving effort lavished on his frozen comrade.

XIII.

HEARTENED and energized by her successful activity in this direction, Kate next
turned her energetic attention to the house,
which was now her own home. It was old and
square, and spacious and stately, with broad pi-
azzas for summer shade, and broad balconies for
winter sunshine ; low-roofed and heavily raftered,
with ample corridors and a hospitable hall, and
wide, welcoming rooms ; and wise beyond its
generation in great, windowed closets with over-
grown drawers and sweet-smelling chests. The
débris of a seafaring and foreign-trading ancestry
had drifted down the years, and lay scattered
about in jars of priceless value, huge and hideous,
convolute with dragons and serpents and scaly
monsters in heat of fiercest action ; chairs and
tables curiously twisted of bamboo work, or end-
lessly carved in a gloom of massive blackness ;
wondrously wrought cabinets ; inlaid boxes, iri-
descent with mother-of-pearl ; lustrous trays be-
skimmed by impossible birds, berayed with the

golden glint of impossible suns; many-folded screens, brilliant with peacocks and butterflies and slender-legged storks in radiant embroidery of vivid silk and shining gold; caskets polished and quaint, opening one within another, like a fairy story, or hiding each its treasure of fragrant fan, or hieroglyphic silk, or mystic necklace, or ivory ball and bauble cunningly carven, sphere within sphere. Wider travel, cosmopolitan taste, and the Great Exposition, have brought these things home to men's business and bosoms — especially to women's; but to Kate they were utterly novel and fascinating — like a peep into the Orient itself. Her earliest convalescence had dallied languidly with such curiosities as lay around her, and with each fresh accession of health she penetrated further into the fastnesses of the house, freshly enchanted with each new discovery, till the faint, sweet, pungent, musty old sandal-wood smells seemed the very breath of Araby the Blest, wooing her over purple seas to the grotesque Barbaric Lands. The wide waste of garret, uncrossed by partition-walls, was itself a museum. It was not simply that the taste for bric-a-brac had not then become a fashion, but the absence of any mistress of the house had rather ruled out taste and banished to the garret's safe shelter much that was rare and perishable. The burden of broken crockery and yellowing silk and moth-eaten tissue weighed heavily on the righteous American soul of the good housekeeper, and many a bit of exquisite porcelain had mounted from mantel and cabinet and the flirt of the chambermaid's duster to the strong, solid cupboards of this unvisited wilderness. Persian rugs, heavy and dense and dim, with blended beauty of hue, had been folded away in camphor, against summer depredations, and been deliberately forgotten upon return of winter, wasting their dusk splendor in cedar chests. India shawls, faded and soft; creamy crape, overswept with dense floriage and foliage of silken handiwork; golden-fretted velvet and finest silken sheen, that had draped the fair forms of dead women, were folded into forgetfulness beneath the cobwebbed eaves. The sweet dead women had passed away, and of their memory remained to Kate not so much as a name; but she left all reverently, as it lay, undisturbed. She was too new a comer, she was too much of the outer world to touch the inbreathed life of these personal belongings. But what else was there she inspected with fearless minuteness. Many an unheeded hour she spent over vases and bowls, and nondescript bits of translucent fabric and spirited drawing and marvellous changing color. A tiny tea-set, the very soul of fragile loveliness, made her fall a-moaning with delight. And one day Mr. Glynn coming home unexpectedly early from town, vainly hunting for Katherine, followed the clue of the open garret-door, and came upon her shawled and muffled, and crouching before a motley group of Chinese mandarins, beggars, mugs, and vases.

"At your devotions, Kitty. Saying your prayers to your little gods. So I have been harboring a pagan."

"I did not know you had got home," said Kate. "I am trying to draw this high-shouldered jar for Aunt Fanny; the shape is so lovely. I am making sad work of it I know;" as Mr. Glynn looked over her shoulder; "but it will give her some idea."

"You have blocked the shape out very accurately. Are you going to try to capture those fellows cavorting across the bulge?"

"I have been studying those. Is that a man in the boat, and are those two women in the water, and is he trying to get away from them frightened? Or are they frightened, and he mocking them, and they begging him?"

"Life-like, to give such scope for argument — but *I* am frightened," feeling her purple-cold hands. "Katy, you are thoroughly chilled! You must not do this. You must come down instantly."

"No indeed. Don't be disagreeable. I come up every day, and it does not hurt me in the least. No; I won't go down till I have finished;" clutching her paper, laughingly, as Mr.

Glynn would have taken it from her. Whereat, without further protest, he quietly picked up sketch, artist, and all, and carried them down stairs together. It might be considered a frivolous attempt at wit to say that Katherine was very much taken aback; but she had the presence of mind not further to sacrifice her dignity by resisting.

"There," said Mr. Glynn, debarking her before the library fire, "that is the way we Bluebeards treat our wives when they don't obey us."

"And you call yourself a Woman's-rights man?"

"What do *you* call it?"

"A rose by any other name would be more correct."

"But could not be sweeter. Why don't you have that truck brought down stairs into a Christian climate if you want to see it?"

"O! there is so much of it."

"Room enough here."

"And I have not thought of it. I have not been cold, really. Only my hands were cold because I could not wear my gloves. You need not be afraid. I do not wish to be sick again any more than you wish to have me."

"But you must not continue these garret explorations; not till warm weather."

"I will tell you what I should like to do," she

exclaimed suddenly. " It has been coming into
my mind a long time, and it is all in now."

" Out with it, then."

" I have a strong impulse to commit sacrilege.
I suppose it is that."

" Upon my word, Katy," said he, surveying
her critically, — her hair was somewhat rough-
ened, her dress somewhat tumbled, her face aglow
with fervent heat after the long cold, and she had
a mingled air of adventure, resolution, and *sparkle,* — " upon my word, you look at this moment
capable of achieving anything you undertake.
You surely won't need any assistance from me in
rifling a church."

" It is only the church in thy house that I want
to rifle."

" Whose house ? "

" Philemon's ! "

" Checkmate."

" I suppose you want everything in this house
to stay just as it is."

" Only you, Katy. I want you to stay just as
you are. Everything else may slide."

" And I am the very thing that will change.
I shall grow wrinkled, and my teeth will come
out, and my hair will get gray, and I shall have
an ear-trumpet and 'roomatiz'; and that is the
time when I shall depend upon your liking me
vastly. It is not much matter now; but then I
expect you to come out strong."

"I must begin now, then, so as to get my hand in."

"I want to tell you what I should like to do."

"That is just what I am pining to hear."

"But I am really afraid that you will not like it."

"I promise faithfully not to murder you, in any case. I will not even imprison you in your chamber with one grim warden for the remainder of your life."

"Will you promise not to be in the least degree vexed, or even inwardly annoyed, or think I am finding fault or want to break things?"

"So completely that even if you do break them I am ready to swear you did it as a military necessity."

"I think this is a beautiful house, a most interesting house. I don't want to alter it in the least particle — not to harm it; but I should like to — develop it; you understand?"

"I shall, as soon as you have enlightened me a little more."

"I used to think about it when I was getting well; just lie and think idly of this and that as my eyes happened to fall. You did not suspect you were nursing such a viper back into life, did you? But I had no plan, really; only idle, sick fancies. But now I am all alive and awake and well."

"You look like it."

"And as a — a — housekeeper," said Kate, blushing and hesitating a little, "of course I must know everything and do everything."

"So that is the limited scale on which the oppressed sex acts," sighed Mr. Glynn.

"And if I say there are some — incongruities — in the house, you will not mind it."

"I will fling them out of window. I never ordered an incongruity into my house in my life."

"No ; it was Mrs. Palker. She told me herself, dear soul, as innocently as possible. She was only too conscientious and careful. But I would rather have things where I could see them and enjoy them, even if they do get broken and worn ; would not you ? "

"Certainly."

"When I first came here it looked — I am afraid you will not quite understand."

"I will make a violent effort."

"Cold and cheerless — a little. I was so sick and faint-hearted, I had no courage. I am not complaining ; don't think that. Every one was as kind as could be. But the very sun seemed gone."

"I know you had a hard old time of it."

"And on the top of it all I was sentimental. That was silly, but I could not help it then. And this kept going through and through my mind:

    ' They've made her a grave too cold and damp
      For a soul so warm and true.'"

"You poor little Kitty!"

"O, *that* was only sentimental," said Kate, surveying her past self loftily from towering heights of superiority. "You don't mind my telling you this now?"

"I want you to tell me everything."

"Now," said Kate, "I can see, not by melancholy, but as a matter of fact, that the house is a little dark and gloomy; but it need not be. And it is a little — not to say — dingy — O!"

"Dingy — eh?" said Mr. Glynn, with the utmost good-humor. Dingy was not half so dreadful a word to him as it was to Kate.

"Not an antique, Oriental dingy, but — "

"Dirty-dingy!"

"Well, a worn dingy at least."

"And American dirt is so much less picturesque a thing than Persian or Turkish grime. Item: to order scrubbing-brushes."

"No, indeed. That would not do at all. Mrs. Palker is very neat. She would surely slay us. That is not the kind I mean. It does not look fresh and cheerful. And where it is fresh, it is — horrid," said Kate, candidly.

"That is right, Kitty," laughed Mr. Glynn; "free your mind."

"Now in my room there are many things that are exquisite — well, poetic, finer than I ever saw in my life before. But it is spoiled by such an ever-present carpet. I would far rather have

Tishy's rag-carpet that she wove herself. All the time I was sick I could not help staring at it. I think I might have got well sooner if that had not given me a congestion of the brain. I don't mind it now I am well. And Mrs. Palker told me twenty times the tale of her search for it."

"Item : a new carpet for Katy's room, and to fend off Mrs. Palker."

"And not hurt her feelings. But I don't want to buy things. I never thought of that. If you would let me bring the wasting sweetness down from the attic. That garret is a perfect treasure-house. It is only that the rooms are big, and that makes them look bare, and that makes them look dreary. And some of them are so hermetically sealed, and they haunt me. I do believe the house has been emptied into the garret. Everything down-stairs is fine, and rich, and pretty — "

"Except what is cheap and nasty."

"Exactly. Now if you would be willing to let me open the house ; make it look open, and bring those heathen gods and their trappings down into the inhabited country, they would become household gods. I believe myself that they all belong here."

"They certainly do if you order them down."

"A man does not know how to take care of himself, does he ?"

"Not the least in life. I don't quite know whither you are tending, but I strive to double and turn fast enough to keep you in sight."

"You say that because you do not choose to fight. But it is a solemn truth. I have discovered it since — since I knew you better. I have discovered many things since I came here. Now listen. I am about to utter an immortal saying: A man can take care of a woman a great deal better than a woman can take care of herself; but also a woman can take care of a man a great deal better than a man can take care of himself!" and Kate nodded defiantly.

"That is a saying worthy of immortality," returned Mr. Glynn, with a solemn and responsive nod. "Show your faith by your works."

"That is what I wish to do," said Katherine. "You are the application of my text. Here are you, saying, no doubt, in your mind this very minute, how absurd it is for me to set up that I can dispose of this house better than you who have lived in it for generations. But I can turn this house upside down in a fortnight so you won't know it. I can do it, Mr. Glynn. You don't know what you are talking about — but I can do it!"

"Talking about! I don't even know I am talking. It seems to me I am in the grasp of a young goddess who threatens to tumble my roof about my ears, and looks as if she could make her word good."

"How strange it is to be a man! Of course you were the master of all, yet it was Mrs. Palker who ruled and reigned."

"Still it was an autocracy tempered with indulgence. Let me beg you to remember that and be merciful."

" O, I am not blaming Mrs. Palker. She is as nice as possible — that is, nice enough for — for Mrs. Palker. But why did you not care about things? Did she just go her own way without consulting you ? "

" O, no; she often comes to consult me; but she seldom has time to hear my opinion — barely time to express her own."

"I suppose she would not like very well to have the hands on her dial reversed ? "

" I believe she is to resume a husband soon, so she will not be a constitutional objection."

" Yes; she told me she expected to change her situation soon, and then she should work no more."

" If she would stop talking, too, it would make quite a difference. I think she talks more according to what she says than most of my acquaintance put together. But she is perfectly harmless, Katy. What next? "

" Why, next — next — " said Kate, looking

around. "Seems to me this room ought to be humanized."

"This?   O, my dear, now I think this room is perfect;" and Mr. Glynn surveyed it with serene satisfaction. "Reform, take any shape but that."

"It is a room capable of perfection," said Kate judicially; "but its light is hidden at present under a bushel, under a great many bushels.   It is dark, and light, and romantic—"

"And ever so convenient.   It is a rendezvous for all my wants.   There's a place for every-thing—"

"And everything in it."

"Well, at least, then, one is sure to come across it in time.   Ah, Katy, I think you must leave me to taste the sweets of liberty here."

"I don't know.   If the mania for improve-ment fairly gets possession of me, I won't promise I can keep my hands off you."

"Don't try," he said, stretching out both arms towards her.

"You would not like," said Kate smiling, but not choosing to see his gesture, "to be Gid-eon's fleece, untouched when all the rest of the world is dewy.   And I was struck by a mighty leathery odor when I was in your dressing-room a little while ago."

"You were?" said Mr. Glynn, innocently. "I can't think where it came from."

"Nor I, for there were only eleven pairs of shoes on the closet-floor."

"I know. I always keep my stated supply under the lounge."

"Yes. I saw them peeping out. Peeping out? Creeping out, tumbling out, fighting out. Eight pairs more. What makes you wear so many shoes?"

"I don't wear them all at once, ma'am."

"But why do you wear them all at nineteen times?"

"Upon my word, Katy, I don't know. I give it up. But I suppose one must have some amusement living alone, and I take it out in shoes. Your coming puts a different face on the matter. Item: to build a new wing on the north end to accommodate shoes. What are you going to root me out of next? This is getting exhilarating."

"This is only beginning. Things will do themselves when they are fairly started. And I understand that you give me leave to rage through the house?"

"How can I give you leave, Katy? The house is yours — the pottery and trumpery are yours. All is yours. Shall you not do what you will with your own?"

"It does not seem so," said Katherine, suddenly overcast.

He was leaning back in the large library-chair

looking up at her as she stood before him, rosy, intent, alert, a little disordered in dress and hair, but the very picture of fresh, eager life, with the turbulent sensitiveness of girlhood flooding her cheeks and veiling her eyes that shyly avoided his serious and tender gaze. He took her hand and drew her to him. He laid her soft, cool palm on his forehead and pressed close the "tired eyelids upon tired eyes." Kate's cheeks were suffused with a deeper crimson, but she stood by her guns manfully.

"Have you the headache?" she presently asked, softly, for want of something better to say.

He shook his head, then gently removed her hand and put her away from him, and Kate left the room quite awed and confounded.

"O, what have I done?" she bethought herself, in the swiftly sought solitude of her own chamber. "I did not think that he would care. I did not mean anything that would be unpleasant to him, or that he would not like. But I suppose he has lived here so long, and is attached to everything just as it is, and the thought of change pains him; and he thinks that I am dissatisfied. O, I wish he would know that I do not really care! Of course it is all very dear to him here. I suppose I should not have been pleased to have any one come in and overhaul things at home. Mine! As if that made any difference! As if I could take any pleasure in it if it should give him annoyance. How sorry I am I ever mentioned it or thought of it!"

The upshot of Katherine's perturbations and meditations was that she went boldly back into the library.

"Mr. Glynn, do let me take it all back and think no more about it."

"Take what back, pray?"

"All that I was chattering about. It was only talk. I do not really care. I would not tease you for the world."

"Tease me! Who has been teasing me?" resounded his cheery voice.

"Why, I thought I had;" quite discomfited by his breezy manner.

"Not you! You tantalize me horribly, sometimes, but tease me, never!"

"I was afraid that — I thought perhaps — I did not know but that you might fear I was discontented and wanted to meddle with what is dear to you."

"Not a bit of it, little sweet-heart. *I* want mightily to meddle with what is dear to me, but I don't dare to! You are mistress here. Everything that belongs to me, or everything that did belong to me when I was an independent gentleman, is in your hands. My subjugation is complete. I only and humbly beg leave to make a mental reservation of this room."

"An Indian Reservation is what you want to

make of it," rejoined Katherine, greatly relieved. "Of course I would like to do — what I said. It is nice to do, and it would make everything nicer. But — I want to please you too."

"The way to please me, Kate, is to do whatever you like."

"But I mean that I want to give you pleasure. You must not make me wholly selfish. I want to make it pleasant to you. That is stupid, for of course it was always pleasant ; but I should like to make it more home-like and happy to you. That is selfish too, for that would make me happiest. I wish I could ever say what I mean. *Do* you understand ? "

"With all my heart. It is like you. And nothing can make the house seem so happy and homelike as to find you in it, and over it, and about it, doing what you will with your own."

" You know once you said I was not pretty," said Kate, rather at right angles with the tide of talk, as her manner was.

"Never ! " said Mr. Glynn, firmly.

" Or words to that effect."

" Never."

" At least you said you did not know if I was pretty ; and of course, after all these years, not to know it is to know that it is not."

" *Non constat !* "

" Now, I am going to return good for evil. Not that you are handsome, exactly — "

" But interesting ! "

" Perhaps I should not quite characterize you as an interesting man, but as a man with interesting points in you — "

" What an abominably discriminating creature to have about ! And as to looks, then, what *were* you going to say ? "

" Why, that you have a sort of rich face, after all ; as if there had been plenty material to make it of. Don't you know some people have a tightly drawn, pinched look, as if it was a close fit with them ? "

" Good heavens ! Katy, just wait till I can — Where are all the looking-glasses ? "

" You need not look in the glass, for you won't find what is best there. Are you doing me the honor to listen ? "

" To be sure — and will keep at it as long as the listener hears such good of himself."

" He will hear better. He will hear that you always ring not only true, which I should expect, but — understanding — which is not so indispensable. It is a pity sometimes to get at the northeast side of people and find it so different from the southerly and sunny exposure. But you, Mr. Richard Glynn, on whichever side one approaches you, you are always southerly and sunny. That is where you get your face ! "

" I declare, Katy, if you were not talking at a face which has forgotten to blush for these dozen years, you would fancy all the world was turning red. My soul is blushing furiously."

" O, you need not try to laugh me down. All the time I have been here you have been nice to me. You have not been cross once, nor snubbed me — "

" A remarkable case of self-denial."

" O, I know. I have been sick and stupid and dull, but I have not been so dull as not to know that I have not been a nice person to have about. Yet, all dead as I have been, I have lived just as keenly, and seen just as clearly as if I had been alive. If you had trespassed I should have been just as severe as if I had been perfection myself. But you have never once angered me, or displeased me, or disappointed me — only that you have been so much better than I could have dreamed."

" Why, Katy, I did not know you had so low an opinion of me."

" I did not have — I only never thought much about it. Yet somehow I find that whenever I accost you, you never fail me. And that is quite remarkable, I think. It is so different from — O ! " and Kate brought herself up short with a dismayed moan.

Mr. Glynn mentally finished out her remark to his liking, but gave no sign.

" Is it not just possible, Katy, that you bring

a little of the atmosphere you find? You are not exactly a souring ingredient yourself."

"I will not have you taking up my line of remark," said Kate, loftily. "Be original."

"But being stigmatized in this categorico-biographical way, I must turn the tables on you, or perish in the attempt. What do women do under a course of flattery?"

"Flourish like a green bay-tree. It is our native air — with variations." 'He began to compliment, and she began to grin.' "But I want you to understand that I have given you a piece of my mind!"

"And I want *you* to understand that I shall put in a claim for a great deal more — for all the remaining pieces, in fact;" but Kate skipped away far more light-hearted than she entered.

XIV.

AND yet it had been a shock to her to find
herself actually instituting a comparison between Mr. Glynn and Walter Laballe, and to
the latter's disadvantage. And then it almost
gave her another shock to apprehend vaguely
that the thought of Walter had somehow grown
indistinct of late. Good heavens! was he fading
out of her mind? Good heavens! then, was her
mind fading out? To be sure, she was married to
another man, but this other man had, in a way,
given her leave to think of him. She had certainly not the smallest intention of being false
to her husband, but she had as certainly in-
tended to be true to herself, to Walter, to her
idea of love. She had meant to be a living mon-
ument to constancy. She would prove that love
was immortal; that it could live with no delight
to feed on. All her life long she meant to be
unfalteringly faithful at this sacred shrine. Poor
Walter! One constant corner in her heart was
little to give to him to whom she had once given

so much, to whom she had looked to give all. And yet it was true that poor Walter had disappointed her — kept disappointing her; that she had always, in some sense, care of him, responsibility for him, anxiety about him — never rest in him; plenty of pleasure and pride, but never peace. Mr. Glynn was a quiet and sober-going man, — though, after all, more lively than she would have supposed. She had fancied him not caring much about anything that she cared for, yet he did have likings and dislikings, opinions and ways of his own, which she had come to respect, and to be interested in finding out. She had only thought of him as a member of the human race, and he had turned out to be a distinct personality. He was not so brilliant as Walter. He was not anything like a society man. The stage on which Walter shone he shunned. Kate smiled to herself to think of the incongruity of Mr. Glynn figuring in any of the youthful caprices of play and picnic, but she could not hide from herself that she was gaining a confidence in him, a respect for him that Walter had never been able to inspire. She was acquiring a habit of mentally referring all things to him. He was coming gradually to be her judge, her standard, her oracle.

Not arrogantly. No man could assume less; but he was helpful. His opinion, his judgment, was given with a warmth of interest that gladdened and encouraged her in whatever quest she engaged it. And as she gradually entered more deeply into the circle of his life, she saw and was impressed and influenced by the sight that he was held in high esteem of men. The sagacity, the gravity, the even balance of faculties and steady poise of mind to which she had recourse at will, and for any lightly occurring incident and slight emergency, were sought also as she saw in matters when fate and fortune were at stake. And sometimes Kate resolved that she was too trivial, and that she should forfeit his good opinion if she did not cease to bring upon him the details that at any time perplexed or perhaps only interested her. Yet all such resolutions melted away before his friendly face, and however sagacious and self-contained she had meant to be, she invariably found herself talking out everything that was in her mind and in her life, lured on by she knew not what of playful and sympathetic interest that was in no respect prying or imperious, but a sort of caressing and constraining solicitude—something that asked while it gave.

And while Kate worked and waited, and wondered whereunto her life should grow, and marvelled to find so tranquil what she had feared to find so troubled, and was grateful to her deepest heart that the white stole of peace should be folded about her who would have snatched the glittering garments of happiness — lo ! the summer had come round again, and all the windows of her house and of her heart she flung open to sunshine and the birds. Her own home had prospered. Her deft swift hands had dispelled what of gloom the years had gathered in it, and her quick wit, her simple and delicate taste, her bright and loving spirit, had disposed its wasting resources in the interests of good cheer, and over its costly and cumbersome magnificence had diffused the airiness, the grace, the charm of a sweet feminine personality. Kate enjoyed it herself as she enjoyed all pretty and pleasing things. In a quiet way, too, she enjoyed presiding over its hospitalities. She welcomed her neighbors out of her own loving heart, but she liked also to have Mr. Glynn bring his friends from the city, and to see their pleasant and plain-spoken surprise at the changes wrought. She liked to see them come in all stately, on their best behavior, feeling that a house with a wife in it was not theirs as the bachelor house had been ; and she particularly liked to thaw them out with gracious friendliness and gentle freedom till they "owned up" merrily, and loudly proclaimed themselves unfairly but completely conquered, and declared that a house with a wife in it was a thousand times better than a bachelor's den. She enjoyed also ordering Mr. Glynn to enjoy it, which he did with

prompt and profound obedience, and needed no
order from Kate to admire the ways of Providence in bestowing upon a woman the mysterious, the incomprehensible gift of creating the
domestic world, all blossoming and beautiful,
out of those same materials which in masculine
hands had but stretched into a wide waste of
cold existence. And in all this rose-blooming
wilderness of his was nothing so sweet and en-
trancing to him as she, under whose breath it
sprang to blossoming. Deeper and dearer grew
she daily into his life, half maddening him sometimes with the mockery of a possession who did
not possess. For what was his opportunity
worth if it availed him nothing? In some
sense it availed against him, for he saw clearly
that what might have been manly wooing would
be most unmanly, since Kate had no resort from
himself. What pleasure to command her duty
if he could not command her love? He knew
well that he could break her heart, but he could
not compel it. So, never for an instant repent-
ing a single step, feeling that these disturbed and
tumultuous months were sweeter than all the
tranquil years that had preceded them, he grew
ever more discomposed and uncertain, distraught
with the storm and stress of a love that was baf-
fled of its natural outflow, whose tide was ever
turning on itself. And sometimes the very
depth and intensity of his love made him cow-

ardly, and he despaired of ever wearing this flower that he had won — drooping and forlorn enough indeed when he won it, but lifting itself into fairest freshness and fragrance under his constant and loving tendance.

And so he could only wait.

Kate's orphan nursery flourished greatly. Four little waifs, gathered in from the wild wide sea of sorrow and poverty and despair, were already mothered there, and promised fairly not to die under Martha's fond and sagacious watch. And Kate grew learned in baby ways, and found great pleasure in the snapping eyes and outstretched arms and leaping little figures that greeted her approach, and had many grave consultations with Tishy about accounts; for Tishy deigned to consult her regarding expenses, though displaying only sovereignest contempt for all suggestions as to the treatment of the younglings. Thus the world prospered greatly with Katherine.

But when the first picnic of the season loomed above the horizon, Kate said instantly and incisively No, and then feared she had spoken too positively.

"Do you want to go?" she turned to Mr. Glynn.

"Want to go? My dear Kate, it was *peine forte et dure* when you were decoy-duck. What use now, when the game is decoyed and done for ? ”

“ It will be tiresome — won’t it ? ”

“ I can tell you exactly what it will be — a ponderous attempt at pleasure. There will be some very pretty boys and girls in the highest spirits, which will be likely to reveal that they have not the highest breeding — joking generally shows the threadbare places of the mind ; there will be several people who would like to enjoy the woods and water, but who cannot because they must talk to people who don’t ; and when they are all reduced to the deepest melancholy, the eating will effect a momentary diversion, overshadowed, however, by the speaking which will speedily supplant it, wherein one forlorn automaton will try to pump all the others, who will say, each in his turn, that he did not expect to be called on, but will just say, &c., &c. ; and when human endurance can no more, we shall come home with that elastic cheerfulness which only release from merry-making can produce.”

“ That may be your picnic,” laughed Kate, “ but it is not mine. I think we must go.”

“ Young boy, we must.”

For Kate had suddenly and rapidly recognized a reluctance to resume her old associations, and to that she was resolved not to submit. Her future should in no respect be slave to her past. She would cherish her love, but it should not rule her. If Mr. Glynn read her purpose, he only rejoiced in it. But neither he nor she was prepared to see Walter Laballe walk upon the scene, jaunty and festive as of old. They had not known he was in town. It was his wraith, not himself, that Kate had feared, and resolved to subdue.

She saw him before she had alighted from the wagon, while chatting for a moment as to the best place to leave the horse, and Mr. Glynn saw him almost at the same moment. Some sudden impulse laid his hand on Kate's — not with a clasp, but a grasp — less a grasp than a grip. It was not endearment or succor, but a certain instinctive and imperious assertion of ownership, a swift and forceful dominance that would brook no intermeddling. It was but for an instant, and Kate looked into his eyes with clear, level gaze, pale and proud.

"Do you wish to stay?" he asked.

"I *will* stay."

"Shall I stay by you?"

"I do not need you."

There was undaunted strength in the brave, bright face, in the prompt confident voice, and the chilled flood of life rushed back and warmed his heart again. This careless cavalier had once imperilled more than life for him, and he felt that the smiling face boded him no good. It was no vulgar outbreak that he feared, but a check and set-back to the current that he hoped was—but with such invincible slowness—bringing Kate to himself. For Walter Laballe as a man he had a mere, perhaps an unwarranted, contempt—the contempt of a direct, determined, and successful man for one of vague purposes and puerile accomplishment. It was Kate's unfortunate entanglement that lent to Walter Laballe not only importance but existence in Mr. Glynn's eyes, and it added a sort of fury to his disappointment that he should be thwarted by one who seemed to him so insignificant. His aspiration to Kate and his success with Kate had invested Mr. Laballe with a dignity which Mr. Glynn would never have conferred upon his own claims alone ; but, now that aspiration and success had been alike swept away by Kate's marriage — now that the unsuccessful suitor had nothing to gain, while the successful suitor felt that he had yet everything to gain, what was he here for ? Why should he come to meddle and mar where he certainly could do nothing else ? It was an unreasonable griev- ance, for of course a poor man cannot be banished from his old haunts because he has failed of his wife. He could not know that his rival's victory was so hollow a victory — was as yet no victory at all in regard to the prize which he had set himself to win. But, reasonable or unreason- able, there he was, curled and comely, tall and impressive, talking to one and another with the same grace as of old, with just a shade more of melancholy perhaps in the large, languid eyes that took so kindly to melancholy, even in his gayest moods.

Mr. Glynn and Kate walked leisurely over the grounds, accosting various friends, and greeted Mr. Laballe as they entered his group.

"I am glad to see you," said Kate, cordially. "I did not know you were in town."

Mr. Glynn strolled away, and as they talked Mr. Laballe gradually led Kate from the group where they could talk, not unobserved, but unheard.

"I only came Monday evening. My stay is to be very short, but I shall give myself the pleasure of calling, with your permission. I suppose I may present my congratulations now?"

"Good and evil have befallen me since we met last," said Kate, seriously. "I have lost my father."

"I know it. I should have written you at the time, but I was in great trouble myself. I was not sure that I had the right."

"I was as sure of your sympathy as if you had written; but in such an hour nothing makes any difference. You said you should be here but a little while. Where do you mean to spend your summer?"

"Nowhere," he said, smiling.

"That is not easily accessible," rejoined Kate.

"The fact is, I found myself rather suddenly pulled up by the roots, and I don't take kindly to transplantation. You know all growths do not thrive equally in all soils."

"Have you left town?" asked Kate, surprised.

"No, not permanently; but I seem to have no hold on anything."

"I hoped you would have a strong hold on the law by this time. You know I always had the belief that there was nothing you could not accomplish if you tried."

"I have lost one great incentive to trial."

"Do you mean me?" queried Kate, out and out.

"What else should I mean?" he said, a little startled out of his melancholy by her directness.

"It strikes me," said Kate, with slight amusement, "that I never was very successful in the character of incentive."

"No," he said, stung evidently by something disappointing in her manner; "but you succeeded extremely well when you went into business on your own account."

It was very coarse; but he was very angry.

Still, if the coarseness had not been there, anger would not have brought it out. And if he were not aware that his little affectation had laid him justly open to ridicule, he would not have been so angry. Kate was slow to comprehend. She had a vague notion of what he meant, but could not really believe her own understanding, and stared at him in sincere surprise. At length she said slowly, —

"There is much in my relations with you that I regret. But I should regret most of all to despise you."

"O, Kate, don't say that!" he exclaimed, the real man in him coming uppermost.

"No, I won't," said Kate, kindly; "but you must not make me."

"But you ought to be fair to me, Kate. I must remember, I suppose, that you are Mrs. Glynn."

"I am Mrs. Glynn, certainly; but how am I unfair to you?"

"Why, certainly, Kate, — Mrs. Glynn, — you will not deny that I thought your heart was all mine, and suddenly you left me in the lurch for a poor devil, — which I admit I am, — and married Glynn hand over fist."

Kate was breathless with astonishment. The case as he had boldly stated it certainly bore the outlines of truth, though false in its whole scope and spirit. That it could ever have presented itself thus to him she had not dreamed. She was too loyal to love ever to have fashioned, even in her thought, such an infidelity. After the first rush of surprise she believed that it never *had* presented itself thus to Mr. Laballe.

"Walter," she said, gravely, "answer me truly, out of your best, your honorable consciousness. Do you think it was because you were poor and Mr. Glynn rich that I left you and married him?"

"N—no, I do not," he replied, after a moment's hesitation.

"Do you think that before I left you, or at the time I left you, I had any thought of marrying him?"

"I cannot think so, indeed."

"Do you think there was the faintest germ of a grain of insincerity in my regard for you and my interest in you?"

"I'll be hanged if I do, Kate; and I was a beast to say what I did. But I have lost you, and Glynn has got you, and all his money into the bargain; and I am not very happy besides. Forgive me, can't you, Kate?"

"Entirely. And now we understand each other, and will be good friends, and never speak of this any more. There can be no more thought or talk of loss or gain, you know, when one is married."

"But I really meant no harm. Only I am so wretched, and you looked so blooming, and I felt very tender towards you, and you laughed at me; and then it really was not such a very long time, you know."

"There is a great deal that you cannot understand. But then it is now not at all necessary that you should understand, — only that I wish to be your friend, — if you have faith enough in me to make my friendship seem worth while. Why are you wretched? I want you to be happy."

"Happiness is not for me," he said, in his most pathetic tones. "Love and life have gone against me."

"I wish that I could help you, and I know that Mr. Glynn will gladly do anything possible."

"You had better not bespeak him;" with a sudden dropping into conversational inflections. "He does not look at me as if he loved me."

"He does not love you," said Kate, simply; "but he will befriend you for my sake."

"Well he might. He has had all the luck in life, while I have gone to the dogs by lightning express every time."

Kate sighed inwardly. It was the old song; always luck, — never patience, purpose, will.

"Is it anything in particular that has gone against you, or only that you do not get on as fast as you wish?"

"It is that I don't get on at all. The law is a hideous bore. The very smell of the court-room is intolerable to me. And then I am having a deuce of a time at home."

Some one came up to bear Kate off, and she

had no more private conversation with Mr. Laballe. Nor indeed did she seek any. She went
hither and thither. She was often with him,
and there was a good deal of lively talk; but
through it all she seemed to be living a sort of
double life. She was friendly and facile with
old and young. She helped amuse the children,
and she helped to lay the tables, and she talked
with the old ladies, for whom she had a special
liking, and was never wanting to the young men
and maidens; but all the while her own musings
seemed to go on uninterruptedly. What was
this change that had come upon her? Or what
had come to Walter Laballe? She strangely
felt a return of her old disappointment, but in
different respects, though she would have been
at a loss to say how or in what. She looked at
him from time to time, and somehow character,
strength, promise seemed to have faded out of
his face. It had grown too smooth and round.
The dark eyes seemed to be looking not to see,
but to divine what others thought. There was
in them no repose, no self-confidence. His very
paleness seemed to be a pallor of the flesh, not a
signal of the spirit. Her glance fell involunta-
rily on Mr. Glynn, who was sitting near a group
of children, listening to the music. What a
sombre face it was! Yes, sombre was not too
strong a word for its expression at that moment.
But the thought sprang into Kate's mind that it

was a face into which she had never looked in vain. And while her eyes yet rested on it with wistful intentness, he turned his glance suddenly upon her. And after one fraction of a second Kate came to her senses, and half blushed at the consciousness of being caught in the very act of spying upon him, and smiled a little defiant nod at him, as who should say she did not care if she was. But there was something of good-fellowship and light-heartedness in the slight pantomime that communicated itself to him, and it seemed as if a cloud lifted from his brow and the sudden sunshine brightened his whole being. He tapped with his fingers the seat beside him, and answering his look, Kate arose and joined him.

" Kate, why don't you tell me I am a brute ? " he said, lounging rather indifferently perhaps, but thereby disabusing the interview of any look of confidential conversation.

" That would not be good manners," said Kate, gayly.

" Did you think I distrusted you ? "

" Distrusted me !   When ? "

" In the wagon when I clawed at you."

"O, no.   I think too well of you for that."

" Kate, you are an angel. Do you suppose it would surprise the people if I should pounce upon you with a tremendous **hug** ? I could find in my heart to do it."

" I think old Mrs. Beardslee over there would stare."

" Why should she? You are my wife, you know."

" The very reason why it might strike her as strange."

" Katy, I think I felt for an instant like a wild beast when she sees the hunter coming for her cubs. She does not distrust them, you know, but her first impulse is to take tooth and claw to them, and run."

" How much better is a man than a beast! It would have been foolish to run."

" Seeing I had not a fool to run with. Katy, if you were a fool, I suppose I should love you just the same. But you could break my heart."

" In that case it would be such a foolish heart it might just as well be broken as whole," said Kate the heartless.

" What a little weak thing a woman is," he presently began to soliloquize in an undertone, looking down askance at her from his brown, brawny heights. " A little bit of soft prettiness lying in her lap there she calls her hand. I could crush it with the mere foreboding of a grasp. And to think that all a man's strength and soul and life and death lie in that little soft hand! Katy, I think I could not live if it were not a sweet hand, a tender hand, a divinely sweet hand. I wish that boy would tumble out of the swing, to make old Mrs. Beardslee look the other way a minute."

"See here now," said good Doctor Blount's rough, gruff voice coming up from behind; "it is too countrified by half, a man sitting down at a picnic and spooning his own wife. I never thought that of you, Dick Glynn. Clear out! I want to spoon her myself."

"If you had only come a minute sooner," said Kate, "you would have seen what you never would have believed without seeing, — me, obeying a look, and coming away from the big chestnut over there to sit meekly beside a domestic autocrat. Can you believe I am that high-spirited creature you once knew and loved?"

"I could believe anything, seeing you such a wreck," he declared, glowering at her from beneath his shaggy eyebrows.

"Does me credit, doctor?" asked Mr. Glynn. "Looks well, does she not?"

"Too well, by half. That is sensible, Glynn. Take yourself off. Nobody wants you here. *You* don't want a molly-coddle for a husband, Kate?"

"Yes, I do. Not that I know what a molly-coddle is; but I am confident it is just what I want."

"I warrant it! There never was a woman yet that had a grain of horse-sense. Give her a fuddiduddle that will dance around her on tip-toe, and fetch and carry, and she thinks he is a man, and calls it devotion, and for such a pop-injay will send to the right-about any time an honest, manly fellow who will lay his life in the dust for her silently, but does not know how to mouth sentiment or make eyes at her."

"The dear doctor! He is painting his own portrait. But he has painted out the mole. You never went down into the dust to me; never! You were fond, honest, and manly, and all that, — fond, but you always scolded me."

"If Glynn weren't scowling straight at me, I would give you a kiss for your impudence, you jade. Look at that flopdawdle over yonder bowling the silly girls down with his big, black eyes."

"That? Why, that is Mr. Laballe!"

"Mr. La Fiddlestick — without the fiddle. There is nothing of him but his looks. And yet without a thimbleful of sense in his skull, he has it all his own way with a lot of tittering women."

"Doctor Blount, you shall not speak so of Mr. Laballe," said Katherine, with rising wrath.

"High-diddle-diddle! Who's to prevent?"

"*I* prevent. I order you to be civil."

"Ho!" in a sort of subdued howl, and turning full upon her; "I did think the wind was setting in that corner once."

"Well, you see it was not," said Kate, crossly.

"No; but if it had, I should have been sorry I did not strangle you once upon a time when I had the chance."

"Here you are," said Kate, "with money and fame and troops of friends, yet devoured with envy of a poor young man because he happens to have a little beauty to recommend him."

"It is a mighty saucy and snappish little beauty that is recommending him at this moment."

"Now, then, Doctor Blount, as you have got off a pun and a compliment in the same breath, — and you know, though punning is easy, compliments come hard to you, — suppose you rest on your oars, and be good-natured, and call it even with Mr. Laballe."

"Me — even with that Jack-i'-the-box!" laughed Doctor Blount.

"What do you *mean* by your Jack-i'-the-box?" fired up Kate again.

"Come, come, you need not go off in a huff again, Mistress Glynn. You did not marry him."

"I dare say I should if he had wanted me to," said Kate, careering recklessly along the single-rail track of truth.

"No," said Doctor Blount, blandly, "if worst came to worst, I should have forbidden the banns."

"I suppose my father would not have been considered authority on the subject."

"My old friend Haviland was a fool, a soft-hearted fool, with sensible streaks in him, as I have often had occasion to remind him. And one of the pleasantest things I look forward to is sitting with him on some heavenly hillside and hearing him confess I was right."

Katherine smiled. She knew too well the old, close friendship between her father and Doctor Blount to dream for a moment that his sharpest nip was for anything but "true heart and not for harm."

"But don't you see you are abusing me in abusing Mr. Laballe? You slight my judgment because you saw for yourself we were friends, and we are friends still."

"Not at all, my dear," said Doctor Blount, seriously. "A girl may amuse herself with many a young man whom she would demean herself by marrying."

"But you reviled the poor girls yonder for amusing themselves."

"O, well," said the doctor, acknowledging with a shrug that he was caught, "I suppose an old fellow may be allowed to growl with an old friend."

Kate looked at him with a smile that would have made it difficult to growl at her.

"You see, Kate, I have been fool enough to

care so much for a silly chit like you that I was desirous you should not throw yourself away. I always had a weakness for your father, and you were a catching sort of girl yourself; and I think, my dear, it was uncommon sensible of you to give the go-by to the like of that mooning young Laballe, and your hand to my old friend Dick Glynn, as sound-hearted and level-headed a man as the round world harbors."

"Thanks," said Kate, smiling. "I certainly have nothing against your friend. But why are you so bitter against Mr. Laballe? The world is wide enough for both."

"Laballe has no substance in him. He is all show and no go. He has never done anything in life but spend his mother's money. Look at it, Kate. He must be hard on to thirty, and has never boned down to anything, but helped his mother through twenty thousand dollars, and leaves her to be handed around from pillar to post in the family, while he goes gallivanting with the girls. That's a pretty kind of man to tie to! And yet some girl — and a fine girl too, no doubt — will tie herself to him any time, and minister to his selfishness with her money, or drag down after him into a shameful poverty. Do you think I would have let you do that, Mrs. Glynn? No, ma'am; I would have shut you up in my drug-shop first, and brayed you in a mortar with a pestle."

" Till I came to my senses."

" Such as they are."

" Thank you."

" Or would have been before you could have contemplated such a lapse from common sense."

" I have a suspicion, dear doctor, that I am hungry."

" And I suppose I may find and bring you a piece of frosted fruit-cake or lemon-pie. I don't know but that I might find something more senseless and sickish, but I don't think I could. I'll try, if you say so."

" No, I don't dare trust myself to you. You will be making experiments on me, — out of pure love to science, doubtless; but I am indifferent to science and devoted to frosted cake. But out of sheer cowardice I will compound on cold chicken. Let us make an onset together."

It was the same old song of Walter Laballe that had been sung to her once before for warning, but somehow it seemed colder and crueler from the lips of the living than it had from those of the dead — more cruel, but, alas! more convincing.

XV.

THE next day Mr. Laballe called. Katherine received him in the little breakfast parlor, where she happened to be sitting. It was cool and shaded, opening through one great window upon a piazza overclimbed with honeysuckle and roses, overlooking a sloping lawn dark now with luxuriant leafage. In Kate's old home everything had been dainty and refined. In this new home all was costly and elegant as well. No eyes could be quicker to take in the costliness and elegance than Mr. Laballe's, no mind could be more deeply impressed by it, and no heart could set a higher value on it than his. And here was Kate, part and parcel, owner and dispenser of all this state. She, who had never in the least cared for wealth, had come into possession, while he, to whom it would have been the path to fame and fortune, almost the very staff of life, was hopelessly enslaved by narrow and narrowing fates. Such bitter thoughts he revolved as he sat in Kate's morning room. To Kate herself, all modest and unpretending as she was, the mild state and splendor were far from unbecoming. She had acquired, perhaps, just a little more dignity and self-possession, the latter of which at least she sorely needed; but she had lost nothing of girlish grace. Too simple and sterling to be awed by or indifferent to position, she wore her matronly honors with gracious and winning meekness. Now, as she sat there, all white and fair and pure and strong, embowered in the warm summer gloom, "green-dense and dim-delicious," breathed upon by the morning's fragrance, sung to by birds and lulled by soft summer sounds droning through the wide-flung lattice, she was the same Katy that so little while ago had flushed at his footfall, had listened to his fluent words with all her soul in her eyes, had flattered him with her highest hopes, her wildest expectations. She had loved him then. Whether or not she loved him now, who could tell? She certainly was the girl in all the world who would not have married for money; but severed from him, what might she not have done to gratify and satisfy a dying father? He himself, Walter Laballe, had loved her. He considered that he had loved her profoundly and truly, "as a man is able." True, he had lightly let her go; but then it was because he loved her too honorably and unselfishly to bring her down to poverty. If he could have shrined her in such a home as this, would he have let her go ? What ideal, what idyl, could be more perfect than the life they would have led had but fate put him in Glynn's place — Glynn, who was simply heavy and respectable, who had alertness neither of love nor taste! To be sure, Glynn had not wronged him. Glynn was not on till he was off. Nor would the house or fortune have come into his hands if they had not been in Glynn's. Still he felt — what indeed it was always easy for him to feel — a vague sense of outrage. He grudged Glynn the possession of what had been fairly won, and not from himself. He forgot, indeed, that fortune and love had once been in his own hand and he had lost both through light esteem. He could not cherish a grudge against Kate. He had indulged in one outburst of anger against her, and she had instantly reduced him to dust and ashes. And as she sat before him, composed, observant, forever removed from him, she had never looked to him so attractive as now. Never, he felt in his inmost heart, never in her free girlhood, when he had wooed her in free fashion, and won her as a young man may, though he had loved and valued her, never had she seemed to him so altogether lovely, so immeasurably desirable as now, when she was wholly beyond his reach. The very luxury by which she was surrounded heightened her charm to him, who had been content to relinquish her because he could not command luxury. If sudden fortune had come to him, no memory of Kate would have hindered him from amusing himself. If with his own fortunes unchanged he had met her in poverty, he would have been full of compunction and friendliness, but would have congratulated himself that he was free from entangling alliances. Seeing her in sanctuary, he abandoned himself on the instant to the remembrance of his love, and rage against his hard fate.

A subtile change in her manner towards him did not escape his notice ; but he attributed it to anything but the true cause.

"Mrs. Glynn," he said, abruptly breaking in upon the ordinary topics which they were pleasantly enough discussing, "I can never forgive myself for my rudeness, my brutality towards you yesterday. But you know that I am not given to brutality."

"I know," said Kate. "Let it all pass. Do not bring it up again. Let us forget all that."

"I cannot forget. I only want you to do me the small justice of measuring the bitterness of my disappointment by the recklessness of my words. If the *bouleversement* had been less, my speech would have been more careful."

"I was sure you meant no harm. I am sure you can never cherish any harshness towards me."

"Thanks, Kate. You only do me justice there.

I have blamed you for nothing; but indeed I have suffered."

"It would not have been creditable to either of us that such a change should have come without suffering. But it is for all the rest of your life to be better and stronger by it."

"No, that is not my way. I am like a dial, good for nothing except when the sun shines. Affliction never had the least tendency to sanctify me. I can but admire the delicate discernment of Nemesis in hunting about to find the particular kind of things I hate, and then furnishing them to me in inexhaustible profusion."

"But, Mr. Laballe," asked Kate, ever ready to enter upon missionary work, "is not that partly because you are too eager in seeking the things you like rather than the things you ought to do? Does not the trouble come because you are so unwilling to learn the lesson Nemesis wants to teach?"

"I dare say. You cannot accuse me of any weakness that I shall not freely admit."

"O, I am not accusing you — am I? I certainly did not mean it."

"I accuse myself, then. I have failed in every relation of life. And I have failed worst of all at the crisis when success was possible." The great eyes grew humid, and this touched Kate. She forgot, or at any rate overlooked for the moment, the selfishness which lay at the root of the failure. She relinquished conversion, and gave herself only to consolation.

"You have surely not failed," she said eagerly. "You are too young yet to speak of failure or success. Everything is still before you."

"Everything is before me — true ; but I cannot touch it ; " and his eyes pointed the meaning of his words.

"Everything that makes success, and most that makes happiness, you can not only touch, but grasp," said Kate, gravely.

"Once it was possible to me."

"It is possible still."

"No, Kate ; you laughed at me yesterday, and justly enough ; but you do not know, I did not know, what strength went from me when you left me. The one defect of my life is — redundance. I can do too many things tolerably. I needed a power to clamp me to one. O Kate ! if you could have borne with me a little longer!"

"If you could have held me a little stronger !" was the response that leaped to Kate's lips ; but she wisely forbore, and only said, smiling, "We will look at the may-be now, and not at the might-have-been."

"But the might-have-been is the only thing that has any attraction for me. Kate, you sit here peaceful and prosperous, and you forget the love that once made your life. You do not know what it is to be beating about the world, barred

from the career you long for, bound to the career
you hate, and the one pure spirit you worshipped
wrested from you forever. Kate, I feel like a
fugitive and a vagabond upon the earth. I cling
to you with the grasp of the dying. I cannot
loose my hold."

"I wish you would talk with Mr. Glynn. I
am sure he would help you."

"The devil he would !"

There was some excuse for the man's rough
speech. What vague evil intent was in his heart,
heaven knows, or the other place ; probably the
man himself did not. He certainly had not come
with any definite design of winning Kate's heart
back again, nor even of destroying her peace of
mind, or her husband's happiness. He was not
so bad as that. But finding himself there, and
finding Kate still winsome, and feeling under no
obligation to consider Mr. Glynn's happiness as
in his keeping, it seemed easy and natural to fall
into a semi-love talk with Kate. She was very
pleasant to him, and regret and melancholy were
very pleasant to him, and her sympathy had always been exceeding pleasant to him. He had
always been interested in talking about himself,
and Kate had never been tired of listening. Now
he had a real grievance, a palpable and touching
sorrow, and he never inquired whether its indulgence might involve or in any way disturb Kate,
or lead to or reveal any dissatisfaction in her life.

Whither his talk was tending he had not duly considered, perhaps; but what he really wanted to make out was, that Kate was not in love with her husband, and was in love with himself, or was not so much in love with her husband as not to be still susceptible. He did not for a moment think of tempting her from duty, from respectability rather; but it would have been exhilarating to find that her husband had not been able to oust her lover from her heart. And then — he was just the kind of man for it — he would have established himself in a semi-questionable position with her, — a sentimental friend with all the immunities of friendship and all the luxury of love, — an enjoyment all the more piquant for the flavor of doubt and danger. It could not be a tranquil or a secure, or a happy position for Kate, but it could be a very stimulating and very delightful one for Walter; far better suited to his poetic temperament and æsthetic culture than a humdrum marriage with its every-day duties and prosy responsibilities. In short, Walter Laballe, without being a very bad man, without formally resolving to be bad in the least degree, was through sheer self-indulgence starting out to be, what many another has been before him, just as bad a man as the woman would let him be. His salvation lay in the simple fact that the woman would not let him be bad at all. She had no thought of rebuffing him, or of reminding him of her position. It had never occurred to her as possible that he should put himself in a situation to be rebuffed. Kate was married, and that fact made it as impossible for her to have a sentimental talk with Walter Laballe as if she had been dead — at least the kind of sentimental talk which he was constantly trying to push into. If his eyes had not been held, he would have seen all along that Kate's instinctive integrity had bereft him of all personal power over her — entirely apart from the fact that he had diminished in her esteem. But his eyes were held and he did not see it, or only saw it as a scruple of propriety that was to be swiftly burned away ; and it was with unfeigned chagrin that he found his heart-tragedy lumped in with his debts and disabilities, and coolly turned over to his successful rival — and by the very woman who had been and was to be chief actress in the great drama ! A slight profaneness might perhaps be excused under the circumstances.

Katherine was profoundly unconscious of her lack of susceptibility. She was entirely unaware of the woful failure she was making. She was only thinking how Walter could be helped out of the Slough of Despond into which he seemed to be sinking, and she referred him to Mr. Glynn from force of habit. The quiet, silent surprise in her eyes brought Mr. Laballe to his manners again — his manners not being entirely the out-growth of himself.

" Excuse me again, Kate, but — but I don't think Mr. Glynn would mend matters exactly."

" You don't know Mr. Glynn's resources per-haps so well as I."

" It is not possible that you — love him ? "

And the manifest sincerity of the question mitigated it a little. But Kate flushed an angry red from brow to chin.

" It is not possible that you could ask such a question — of his wife."

" I know I have no right to — but — Kate — I was so near you once that—I think I might be excused some things. It is a little different from — "

" Were you ever nearer to me than Mr. Glynn is now ? "

" Of course not," he murmured, utterly cowed.

" How I feel towards my husband," said Kate, proudly, " is a matter between him and me. What I think of him the whole world is wel-come to — that he is a man for any woman to thank God for, and to try her whole life long to be worthy of."

Kate was too much in earnest to mind the con-struction of her sentences, but she made herself clearly understood, which is about the best thing, after all, that sentences can do. Mr. Walter La-balle, at any rate, fully understood that he must take his eyes and his woes and his wares generally to some other market. But he came into line handsomely first.

"You are a good woman, Kate," he exclaimed, impulsively.

"Of course I am a good woman," said Kate, relenting after her little flash of passion, and beginning to scold — a sure sign that she was placated. "What did you think I was?"

"Nothing else, of course," he stammered, confused by her unshaded directness. Moreover, her resentment seemed to reveal his meanness to himself. "Heaven knows I think nothing of you but good, and I want nothing of you but good."

"Then say nothing but good. You have been talking very ill indeed."

"I suppose, Kate, I was wild enough to think I might not have lost everything. I must remember that we are wholly two persons, and the past is blotted out."

"Of course there can be nothing else," said Kate, wholesomely. "Why, I am married. That puts a stop to everything — in particular."

Little can be said for Kate's language or her attitude, which were commonplace enough. But at least she was honest and intolerant of sophistry.

"It does not put out the eyes in a man's head. If it did, I should not have made a fool of myself. Kate, I am going away. Don't think any worse of me than I am."

" I won't think ill of you at all if you will not keep saying things that make me. Where are you going ? "

" I don't know. Anywhere, anywhere out of this world."

" But not for a great while yet."

" I suppose not. I shall shuffle along somewhere, like the outcast I am. People don't die because they don't want to live. Good-bye, Kate. Forget that you have seen me. That is the best service you can do me."

" No," said Kate, giving him her hand in most kindly token ; " I shall remember that I have seen you, and that you were a little discouraged and desponding, and therefore a little foolish, but meaning nothing but to behave yourself. And now," — like an experienced matron bidding her eldest son fare forth into life, — " now, Walter, don't give way to discouragement, but be brave and earnest and make a good fight, and I know you have every kind of success lying in store for you yet. O, if you only would, you could!" This last was rather an exclamation to herself than an adjuration to him.

So they parted in friendly guise, neither of them the happier, but both the wiser for the meeting.

And Mr. Glynn, quietly returning home, saw

far off through a vista of open doors the two figures standing in the act of farewell, intent eyes
meeting, hand lingering in hand, the slow, sad
separation ; and turned quickly aside to pursue
in solitude meditations that gave him no pleasure
and boded him no peace.

XVI.

KATHERINE was neither voluble nor minute in giving an account of this visit to her husband. It was a theme she did not gladly dwell on, yet in thought she dwelt on it constantly. She was inwardly shamed — feeling that somehow, unwittingly, she must have betrayed the trust which her husband had — most simply and nobly she felt — confided in her, or Walter could never have spoken to her as he did. And yet, perversely enough, the more discontented she grew with him inwardly, the more she felt as if she must defend him outwardly. Her unusual reticence and silence did not escape Mr. Glynn's notice, and under the circumstances did not add to his content.

"I do not believe," she said, rather abruptly, "that Walter Laballe ever squandered his mother's fortune. He was extremely fond of his mother."

"Who has brought so hard a charge against him?" asked Mr. Glynn.

" There have always been echoes flying about. But I don't imagine any one really knows anything, only that whereas he was rich he is now poor. But he told me that himself, in the first place. He never made any secret of it. It is not a crime to be unsuccessful."

" Certainly not; nor to be successful, either;" with a smile that was a request.

" But everything Dr. Blount has touched, or — or you — has gone right, so you are hard-hearted towards those who fail."

" I ? "

" Well, not you perhaps, but Dr. Blount;" and she repeated, with some softening, what Dr. Blount had said of Mr. Laballe ; adding, " Now do you suppose there is a word of solid truth in this ? "

" Dr. Blount is not a man to speak unadvisedly with his lips."

" He would not make up a wicked story, but he is not infallible."

" Nor am I."

" O, you can tell me what you think ! " cried Kate, a little petulantly, equanimity of temper not being one of her chief charms.

" I have understood that when Mr. Laballe came of age, he came into twenty thousand dollars, and his mother inherited the same. Both fortunes are gone, but it is hardly fair to say that he squandered them. I never heard that he gambled, or was in any way dissipated, but neither he nor she seemed to have the slightest idea that twenty thousand dollars could ever come to an end. But if you never add and constantly subtract, Katy, it inevitably will come to an end, in that most practical of all races, the long run. They travelled and lived at a rate that would not have been extravagant if it had been their income and not their principal, which was twenty thousand dollars. The consequence was that they came to the ground with a thud."

"You know that this is true?"

"I have had a good deal to do with their business affairs."

"And you never told me."

"You never asked me. Besides, Katy, there are many matters of this sort that I should never think of speaking to you about."

"But don't you see, Mr. Glynn," said Kate, feeling a little rebuked, "that it makes — that it shows — that it implies an element of what we call — meanness or — weakness?"

"It does not imply exactly what we call manliness. Not that Laballe is a bad fellow, either — if he only had a guardian."

"But I should think you would have told me."

"I have told you."

"But before this."

"When?"

"Why — why — when I was making up my mind?"

Mr. Glynn smiled. "I don't remember that you confided to me when that time was. Besides, Madame Kitty, it is not a man's way to go to the girl he wants and say, 'Pray take me. The other fellow is a vagabond.' Such a wooing would hardly recommend itself to the girl."

"I think Mr. Laballe is in some special perplexity now."

"I should not wonder. His uncle, who has a considerable family of his own and no more property than the Laballes had, is a little restive under their expenses, and is, in fact, not making it quite comfortable for him."

Kate found that her mortification and chagrin were not to be removed by an appeal to her husband. She experienced for Walter Laballe a whimsical sort of pity, with an admixture of scorn both for him and for herself. While he had been present, pity had rather carried it over scorn; but when he was gone, scorn rather got the upper hand. She had given him so much commiseration on the theory that he had been a sort of big Babe in the Wood hardly dealt with by a hard old uncle; a genius, struggling up into self-expression against adverse circumstances — even at his worst only failing in final endurance, and that partially because of an exquisitely refined if somewhat languid nature. To be sure he had not stated the case in so many words, but certainly from no one else had she or could she have received that impression. Then he had so lived as to seem weak in the eyes of men, and Kate could have as easily forgiven wickedness. And he was not only weak in the original lapse, but there was the unhandsomeness of letting others be unfairly blamed. This was the man she had loved. All her knightly imaginings and her lofty aspirations, her dreams of chivalry and romance — this is where they had led and landed her, said Kate, in fierce spasms of self-disgust. She had gone in and out, weaving her fine web of fancy, holding herself too high for any ordinary lot. Mr. Glynn had been commonplace and Dr. Blount rough, and one and another content with every-day doings. She forsooth must lift her head above the clouds. And her hero of the mighty achievement had achieved a vulgar disaster, and her commonplace fellow-creatures held him in good-natured contempt, and waited and pitied in silence while she had fancied herself dwelling in a palace of dainty delights. What a rare and valuable thing her love must be, indeed! What a delicate and discriminating creature she, with so subtile an instinct for best things! O, Kate did not spare herself! Nothing was too severe and sarcastic to be hurled at that unlucky girl, always known to her friends for a shallow and hollow pre-

tender, but now self-caught in all her high-
sounding and specious charlatanry. And then
Kate relented a little towards herself, not being
naturally hard. After all, she had not the chance
to know the man-side of the man ; and was it
strange that she should have been misled by the
woman-side, which seemed so fair. But, on the
other hand, what made it seem so fair? Certainly it had not seemed fair of late, even before
Dr. Blount wailed his doleful screed. She had
been conscious she had even noted the indefina-
ble change. It was as if a veil had fallen from
his face. What had been interesting, interested
her no more. What had been impressive and to
be studied was common and to be let go. Kate
did not yet know that a stronger nature had
overpowered the weaker, that a finer character
had disenchanted her of the coarser, that a
subtler flavor had rendered the old rank and
insipid. With an earnestness born of the knowledge that life-long peace and life-long grief were
in the question, for weeks and months had Kate
watched a face whose lines had been graven by
no dilettante soul. Were the eyes gray, or blue,
or brown? Even now, Kate could hardly tell.
They were certainly not a languid black. But
as Kate thought and mused she was aware that
behind those eyes somewhere dwelt a soul that
was still a mystery to her. She had neighbored
it for many a year and had never suspected its

existence. It had ministered to her pleasure, it had waited upon her whims; her baby fingers had toyed with its strength, and her maiden grace had unconsciously wrought its gentle pleasance into love, and its love into immortal longing — herself the while unmoved, untouched, unaware. But there came a day when the slighted soul affirmed its existence and asserted its power. In the rush and tumult of that troubled hour had Kate bent her discrowned head, owned allegiance and sworn fealty. Again and again out of the eyes that she had so long looked at and never seen, saw she now the strong and steadfast soul peering with wistful, watchful gaze into her own. From that scrutiny she had not shrunk, not only because she was vestured in the tranquillity of a sincere and simple heart, but because she knew it was the watch of love vigilant to guard, not of severity lurking to ensnare. All the same she had never passed out from under the shadow of its sovereignty. Through all her hours of gay or serious talk, through all her days of careless care, of tender tyranny and playful indulgence, of light-hearted comradeship and the vital solace and succor of faithful friendship, ever and anon would Katherine catch glimpses of this waiting and silent soul — no pallid and pulseless devotee at love's altar, but full of fire as of faith, full of passion as of patience, in its very restraint commanding, absolute in gentleness and in courage.

And how had she responded? What had she returned for all this high worship? Light liking while it was yet unspoken; blank, brusque repulse when it was proffered; and since, the gratitude due for service rendered; while all that she had of love and life to give she had laid at the feet of one who could not discern its value and would not deserve its continuance. Value! value! would then Kate's just wrath against herself cry out. What value could attach to such a love? — a love that was bat-eyed, mole-eyed, owl-eyed, — and if Kate's natural history could have supplied her with any other blind beast she would have marshalled him into line instantly for her own discomfiture — she who had loved love, had adored love as the world's one wealth, had dreamed her bright, high dreams of no such mere habit of love as just stirred the stagnation of dull domestic life, but of a grand, absorbing, heroic passion that should realize the ideals of poetry and recreate the Earth with all the hues of Heaven!

Was it such love as this that had found her out and that she had calmly and curtly rejected? Surely never rode knight to maiden so simply bedight. She had, of course, not expected her lover to come plunging along the fern-bordered, daisy-bedecked, sweetbrier-smelling road, clad in mail, and high-mounted on gold-caparisoned steed — as they dashed down the old ballads and epics — not exactly. Still, she had thought he would be a little out of the common! Certainly she had not dreamed that he had made oak-leaf wreaths and dandelion necklaces for her babyhood, and washed her face with his handkerchief when she fell into a mud-puddle — that in later years he had a bank in town and dropped in occasionally of an evening to talk politics and per cents, or discussed garden seeds and sweet cider across the old gray orchard walls. Who could expect knight in such guise?

And yet, man of money, and notes, and Scotch tweed as he was, what could the love of poetry and romance be that his was not? What could be more stanch, more long-suffering, more unselfish, more slow to grasp, more generous to give? What of fervor or of fineness did this love lack? And O, what use to argue, or question, or justify, since here was the dreadful degrading fact that she had failed to recognize it, had rejected it almost scornfully, had turned aside to a meaner — meaner what? She was not yet sunk so low as to call that love! Kate said to herself, with a little thrill of exultation that even in her low and lost estate there were depths into which she disdained to descend. But it was not Walter that she blamed. Far from it. He simply lived after his kind. He was as he was made. He loved

better than he lived, thought Kate, forgetting
for a moment her self-abasement and reverting
to her original opinions of herself before her
misguided experience had laid her self-respect in
ruins. It was not his fault that there was no
force in him to command either happiness or
prosperity. It was her fault not to have seen his
feebleness, poor dear! to have fancied for a moment that those dark, restless eyes, or even
those dark and languid eyes, could pierce to the
substance of things. But had she done any
better, seen any clearer herself? O, why did
she presume to look down upon Walter Laballe?
He was as good as she. He had blundered no
more than she. It was a fit match for her. A
woman can rise no higher than her love. The
measure of the man she loves is the measure of
her own capacity. Mr. Glynn should have stood
aside and left her to plod along the valley lands
to which she was born. She was not good
enough for him. She was altogether too trivial
and insensate, altogether shallow and frivolous.
But then he loved *her!* That was the worst
thing she knew about him. Why had he pinned
his faith to such a broken reed? asked Kate,
forgetful of the decorum due to metaphors.
Yet, except for that fatal feebleness, how noble
had his trust been, how magnanimous! Why,
said Kate, feeling about for adequate expression,
he is — he is the best man I ever knew!

XVII.

KATRINA, I think it is time for you to come to moorings," broke in a cheerful voice, the voice of the best man she ever knew, upon one of her numerous mental diatribes. She had been pacing back and forth through the twilight parlors with an energy of abstraction, and Mr. Glynn had been noting her for the last few moments through the open door of the library across the hall. Kate went in to him instantly, glad to be diverted from her own unsatisfactory thoughts. "I am sure you must have got to the sixth act of your tragedy by this time."

"It *is* a kind of tragedy," said Kate.

"What is?"

"O!" cried Kate, with barefaced and instantly detected fraud, but frightened at the possibility of being forced into an explanation, and catching the sudden sparkle of stars through the broad bay-window, — "O, I feel dislodged and discouraged. I always thought we had the stars to go to as a last resort. And it was so sociable to look at them and send up friendly thoughts to our unknown kinfolk. And now they are all turned into suns, and the sun is a great roaring hurricane of flaming gas, and there is no living with him, and I feel lonesome."

"I would not mind it, Katy. Perhaps they are a salamander-folk, and like that kind of thing."

"But that new invention has felt out and found that the worlds are made of the same stuff we are, — iron, and magnesium, and such, — so of course the people must be like us too."

"Not certainly, if you are bent on company. Fishes are made of the same 'stuff' we are, but you can't live in the water, Mrs. Katy, and a trout can as long as you will let him, and that is a good while for all your hook harms him. You can't slip up into the air either, when the whim takes you, but the thrush can. Depends on how you mix things, don't you see?"

"It is not I that mix things. I had it all nicely arranged long ago. I knew just how the world was made, and the whole universe running. But now everything is unsettled, and we do not really know anything."

"Then of course we don't know that people cannot live at a white heat, so it is as broad as it is long."

"Only the analogy is against it instead of for

it. Everything ought to tend one way when you never can get exact proof."

"Well, you can get some comfort out of your analogies if you must have it. Suppose the sun is not inhabitable, and the stars are all suns. We know that one sun has planets swinging around it, and the only one of those planets whose condition we certainly know is inhabited by a thousand millions of souls, as we facetiously call them, and the sun keeps them in fuel and board and clothing. Now why not suppose that the other suns also have their little families to support? We do not see them, but it is the instinct and charm of domestic life to seclude itself. The suns stalk through the skies, carrying on their business, seen of men; but the homes of heaven are hidden."

"Why, yes; I think I like that."

"Of course. When you are in trouble, come to me. I shall never allow a few little universes to stand in the way of your peace of mind."

"That is what the Bible says, too. 'Canst thou guide Arcturus with his sons?' His sons of course are his planets, that are dependent upon him."

"That is right, Katy; back me up with good Scriptural authority."

"Only I don't feel quite so sure of the planets as I did. I did not mind giving up the moon."

"No? Now I always felt rather attached to the moon myself. Our next-door neighbor."

" Yes ; and it is quite desolate to think of tho bleak, cold, dark silence up there. But you can remember that it was once a pleasant, peopled, possible world. But the other planets don't keep faith. Look at Jupiter yonder — so splendid he looks, and when you get to him he is only a great, gloomy swash of warm water."

" I would not go, Katy. Give it all up. Nothing is so unpleasant as to be living in hot water all the time."

" You have got to live in hot water. if you depend on the stars. Now if there was anything I was sure of, it was ' Saturn seven and two broad rings,' for I learned it when I was a speck of a girl."

" I hope you are not laying up any grudge against Saturn. I have special interest there."

" Only that he is fickle like all the rest of them. His two broad rings are three rings, then they are many rings, then they are whole systems of rings, and suddenly everything is rings."

" Exactly, Kate. That is why you must keep the peace with Saturn. We can't afford to lose him, for there is where Nature is caught in the act of world-making."

" What do you mean ? "

"Well, dear, I am not so well up in my astronomy as you seem to be."

"O, I was always devoted to the stars; but two or three days ago I came across that big book with the pictures, and I have been reading it ever since; but what do you mean by Saturn?"

"Is not the last guess at creation a waltz? The gas whirled itself into rings, and the whirling rings break up into suns, and the suns keep at it and whirl off other rings which presently break up into planets, and the planets whirl off other rings which break up into moons. For proof, Saturn got a little behindhand, so we caught him before his jig was up, rings and all."

"Do you suppose Saturn's rings are on the way to be broken?"

"Should not wonder. There seems to be a good deal of uncertainty in real estate up there."

"If the rings are not solid, but little bits of separate bodies dancing around close together and keeping time, I don't see why they should ever break rank."

"They must keep time in order to keep up. If the rings did not wabble but spun around stiff, they would come down thump! on Saturn at the slightest provocation. Accordingly they wabble. But there seems to be a new one putting in an appearance, and does not somebody say the old ones are widening at the rate of thirty miles a day, or so? That is 'made land' worth talking about. What are your 'back bay,' or Zuyder Zee, compared with such operations in civil-engineering?"

"And of course if they keep widening, they must touch in time."

"And when they do touch, won't the fur fly?"

"Is it not dizzying just to think of it?"

"Well, these fellows have a long way to go. They can't afford to let the grass grow under their feet. On the whole, it is rather encouraging to us slow coaches that though our friend at the end of the lane is whizzing along totally regardless of his wind, it takes him a hundred and sixty-five years to lumber around the sun once."

"And it is such a poor little sun for him to lumber round, too. I should not think it would answer."

"Suppose he should come to the conclusion that it did not answer, what could he do about it? Go it alone? Smash himself up into broken crockery like the asteroids? Would not you like to live on one of those little pocket-planets pirouetting about among the steady old stars? Just think of it, you could make the tour of the world in a day and come home to early tea."

" But there is another reasonable little theory gone ; for your big book says they are not broken crockery, but were made so. What could be nicer than to have one world surely broken up and flying around in pieces?"

" I should say a world flying around whole. I think I like that way best myself."

" Not for a theory. The worlds have got to come to some kind of an end."

" Don't be impatient ; the sun may get out of fuel any day and grab us."

" But if you are glad to see a world making, like Saturn, why should you not be glad to see a world breaking up? It corresponds. I did not object to your Saturn. You ought to come to the defence of my asteroids."

" I will, Katy. I am ready to testify that I saw the pieces. Seeing is believing."

" Not even that. For we have seen the stars burning up and going out. But now the big book says no — they are not burning stars at all, but variable stars probably, and will be just as bright again presently."

" This fable teaches that what with telescope and spectroscope, and imaginative scope, Astronomy has made great strides in ignorance since you and I were young."

" Sometimes it makes me faint-hearted to think of it all. Does it seem as if this great, glowing, rushing universe could have taken such an eternity to form, and then we little insignificant creatures be made and stuck on the outside?"

"Think we grew up out of the iron and magnesium, do you?"

"Well, it looks just as if simple matter kept growing more and more complex till it became us. If I did not know I was alive, I should not think I could be. I should think I was a sort of animated weed—just Tennyson's Talking Oak."

"But there, Kate, you have hit on the vital point—consciousness. There comes in something wholly new. No gas whirls that off."

"But it seems to come up slowly out of the dust through flies, and canaries, and dogs, and horses, to us."

"No, Katy. I should say that the shadow, the symbol of it, comes up slowly out of matter till it reaches us, and the divine afflatus comes down lowly, out of mind, till it reaches us; but betwixt the two there is a great gulf fixed. Matter becomes ever finer, more delicately organized, more exquisitely sensitive, till it is fit to receive the breath of the higher life; but I see no sign whatever that this higher life is evolved out of the organism."

"And if the gas does whirl itself into worlds, something must have set it spinning in the first place, and our little spark of life came from that. I hate to think I just grew up like a toadstool."

"A toadstool has a long life compared with you, my Katy, if this is all. But if Nature runs the firm economically as she pretends, I cannot think she would be so extravagant as to destroy mental force, which is a far more difficult production, so to speak, than physical force."

" And better worth preserving, I hope Nature thinks."

"So she should. What is the use in your talking about insignificance, Katy? We are not as big as Jupiter, if that is what you mean ; but we would knock Jupiter into a cocked hat any day to save the life of one man. What is twenty-five thousand miles of granite and iron and trap-rock, compared to five feet of sweet little feminine flesh and fire?"

" Five feet two," said Kate, demurely.

" Is that so? Certainly. Science should be exact."

" What you mean is, that the worlds were made for us, not we for the worlds."

" Exactly. There never was, to my thinking, anything more intrinsically absurd than the notion that matter is eternal and mind ephemeral. A lot of great lumpish globes, that never knew they existed, and take up more room than all their generations of men, streaking around in space forever, and the living beings who alone make these globes of the smallest value perish in a day!   You can't make me believe Nature is such a blockhead."

"I like to hear you say that, because that means future life."

"I hope so."

"And that God made the world."

"I think so."

"Can't you say you know so?"

"I think there must be, behind all worlds and all existences, a great First Cause, but as I look around, all that I see is man."

"Mr. Glynn, what are you?"

"*Homo sum.*"

"But you are not a real born Orthodox, though of course you go to that church — I suppose because there is no other."

"Happens, Katy, a born Orthodox is just what I am.   Being reared under Orthodoxy, I naturally saw its objectionable points more clearly; too clearly, perhaps, to be Orthodox by adoption."

"O, no!   I was born there too, and I never want to be born again."

"That must be Kitty's Sixth Point of Calvinism.   I don't recognize it as one of the original Five."

"Just as good.   I don't believe in leaving your own religion, whatever it is.   I go for my country, right or wrong; 'when right to be kept right, when wrong to be put right.'"

" An admirable sentiment! And Orthodoxy is an admirable creed to sharpen its teeth on."

" You don't hate Orthodoxy, I hope."

" O, no! it was the faith of my fathers; but it is a grim faith, my dear, and it requires a good deal of ingenuity to get the hatefulness out of it. I think you could do it if any one could. I think even a free-thinker could stand a dose of Orthodoxy dissolved in Katherine."

" Do you mean future punishment? "

" I don't really know that Orthodoxy is any more menaced by future punishment than by the sin and suffering that are visibly rampaging through this world."

" And you can't think it all comes from Adam's sin, and that we suffer for what we never did, thousands of years before we were born? "

" Well, my Katy, with you sitting here by me, I feel so certain that in Adam's case I should have eaten too, that I have not the heart to be hard upon him; and I must say I think it was rather plucky and patriotic for those old divines to stand up like a man and a brother and divide the responsibility.

'In Adam's fall,
We sinned all.'

No shirking there. That is true Catholicism ! "

" You can't be a Unitarian, then."

" I don't know that I want to be; but if I did, what's to hinder? The Unitarians make the

least possible ado about it. Any one who has
no creed at all, but merely believes he ought to
be decent, is allowed to call himself a Unitarian.
I think I could come in on that count."

" You would have to give up your total de-
pravity, then."

" It would be no great sacrifice. I don't set
such store by it as you Orthodox do, though
your belief in it is very much mitigated by your
unbelief."

" Why, I believe in it. Don't you ? "

" Well, I shut myself up sometimes on Sundays, and think over what few sins I am guilty
of, but somehow I can't make them fill the bill ;
and as I look around on my townsmen, I think
they are a pretty clever set of fellows. They
are generally honest and civil, and they bear
each other's burdens most of the time, though
they may occasionally set them down and swear·
at them."

" I am afraid that is not the right kind of sin-
ning exactly."

" Perhaps not. In fact, I don't think I know
what a sinner is. A villain I know, and a
drunkard I know, and a liar I know ; but a sinner is an elusive sort of scamp ; now you see
him and now you don't. On the whole, Katy,
let us stick to what we know. Why should a
man crawl before his Creator any more than before his neighbor? It can be no God who is

pleased with abjectness. I like to see a man stand up cheerful and hearty, and say, 'Here I am, Lord, as upright as I know how to be, strong and healthy, and ready to put my shoulder to the wheel.'"

"And yet one does despise one's self sometimes," said Kate, with fresh memory of her late mental castigations.

"One despises one's self for definite folly, or treachery, or badness of some sort; not in a general way, as a work of art. We must not be too hard upon ourselves, lest we thereby reflect upon our Creator."

"But," said Katherine, softly, hesitatingly, "we must have needed Christ — some way."

"If we needed him, he came."

"But he did come. Surely you do believe that?"

"Would it grieve you if I did not?" he smiled down upon her.

"It would sadden me inexpressibly," said Kate, with no smile in her earnestness. "I am not good: it is not that; I know that I am not a good Christian at all. You are infinitely better than I am : it is not that. You must not think of judging by me. You will never think that I think I am better than you because I belong to the church? But I should like —"

"I shall never think anything of you that is not sweet and good. You may be sure of that.

But, my darling, if there is a God who made the world, he meant well by the world he made. You may be sure of that, too. The Christ of history came a long while ago, and I confess the evidence is not quite clear to me, and the philosophy of it is wholly obscure."

"But you are willing to believe?"

"Perfectly. A God would certainly save his world somehow. If by a Christ, then so; if not, then some other way. But he would certainly save it. Otherwise he would not be God. Whatever his way, I accept it as the best possible. But I don't feel sure of the way. Does that distress you, Katy?"

"O, I am sure you yourself must be right, whatever you believe. I wish you could be more certain, because then I could be. It would be dreadful to lose out of this life the certain faith in another."

"It would be very confusing. Unless there is another, this certainly is wholly illogical, and its Creator has a good deal to answer for. We are limited in every direction, and we can afford to wait for full understanding. As at present advised, I do not understand, and I cannot afford to say that I do."

"Do you not like to think of the other world? Don't you think that just the possibility of Heaven is a great comfort and consolation?"

"Do you not think we shall both of us feel more at home down here than we shall there?"

"O, no, indeed. I think that is the real home, where we shall never feel strange or out of place. If I am only good enough to go, or if I am somehow let in without being very good, — as I am afraid I shall have to be if I get in at all, — that will be enough. How can it be that you do not care for it?"

"My dear, what can there possibly be in that land that I care for?"

"Why, everything."

"Yes, only I take no especial pleasure in everything. I want something. That future is wholly indefinite. Ministers either follow St. John into his revelations about four and twenty elders, and beasts with seven heads and ten horns, which mean absolutely nothing to me, or else they leave the blessed where novelists leave their heroes and heroines, — at the very entrance of Paradise."

"That I suppose is inevitable, because we cannot now comprehend that world. The blind have no conception of light or color, yet light and color exist."

"But if I can have no conception of Heaven, how can it be real to me?"

"Can't you think how nice it would be never to be afraid, never to make mistakes, or do anything wicked? To see all the people who are there — our own, and all the people we could never see in this world? Think of St. Paul telling you all about his coming to Great Britain! I should not wonder if he would like to do it. And Boadicea perhaps sitting by, and putting in a word now and then, poor thing!"

"Yes; and I might find Abraham interesting in the way of early history; and Moses would be good authority in law. Cain, the leading agriculturist of his race, might or might not be of my company. You may chat with Paul, if you please; but I consider his style rather too logical and hard for light conversation. But, my Katy, the world beyond would look pleasanter to me if, instead of sitting and talking with Moses and the Prophets, I could be sure of you."

"O," said Kate, softly, "but I feel sure of those we love."

"How 'sure'? I look at you, and see you fresh and changing. I hear you, and your voice is clear and cordial. I take your hand, and the touch is sweet to me. How shall I come at you when the only medium by which now we meet is gone back into the dust whence it came?"

"It sounds very dreary," said Kate, with filling eyes.

"It is not dreary, my darling — or only dreary when we try to reason it out — to pass from the indefinite to the definite. I am not anxious or despairing about the future. I have a very great hope that the same Power which set us in this world will give us a large life beyond. But I can do nothing to bring that about. What I know is that it is good for this world to be honest and kind, and I do not think it can be bad for any world. I cannot see that it is worth while to trouble ourselves with preparations for a world of which we know so little; but it is in the highest degree worth while to make the most of the one world we are sure of. God, if He exist at all, is just as much the God of this world as of any other, and we can never be any more in His presence than we are every moment of our lives. There is nothing better than brightness and goodness and love within the limits of my imagination. Is there in yours, Katy?"

"Nothing can be better."

"And that we can do, be, have, and enjoy here. I hope," he added, more lightly, and with a half-smile, — "I hope there is a world where my little Katy will find it in her heart to love me; but I own I should feel more sure of her if she could love me a little here."

Kate flashed upon him a glance of sudden, eager inquiry. "Do you care for me still?" she asked, obeying some swift, strange impulse.

"Do I *care* for you! — "

"Would you care for me if you knew — if I

were — if you knew — everything?" and in uncontrollable agony of shyness and shame, Kate sank at his feet and buried her face in his hands.

"My darling! my dearest!" he cried, shocked by this unlooked-for and seemingly uncaused outburst. Unmindful of pledge or pact, he drew her into his arms and clasped her and kissed her, and strove to soothe and reassure her with every endearing word and fond caress. "Tell me everything, little Katy. Nothing is so bad as that you should not trust me wholly. I am sure you are disquieting yourself in vain. Tell me what it is that troubles you, darling. There is not a thought in your heart that you need be afraid to show me. I will smooth it all away; only trust me." For still his fatuous mind went meandering about after some offence that Kate imagined herself to have perpetrated by a lingering love for the old lover so lately met, so lothly left, as his own eyes had seen. Kate did not answer him, but she clung to him with unheeding energy; and when he fain would have got a glimpse into her eyes she wedged and wormed her tousled little head in among his various coat-collars with such desperate vehemence to hide her burning face, that presently even into his dull, slow, stolid, commonplace, banking-house brain penetrated some faint glimmer of the eternal truth of things.

And then, of course, he had it all his own way.

XVIII.

KATE'S troubles were over, and my story is
told. It is not so much of a story as it
would have been if Kate had not had a way of
slipping out of every situation provided for her,
by virtue of a simple but sturdy, native honesty.
Several times in her life had circumstances so
arranged themselves around her as to need but
her helping hand to produce an excellent tragedy,
and Kate walked straight out of them every time.
She had not head enough to perceive their capabilities, but she had heart enough to discern their
duties. She was no poet, artist, saint, or genius
of any kind ; she had only her common sense,
such as it was, and her rectitude — both in the
blood. She knew nothing of fate, or temperament, or temptation ; she only tried heartily and
humbly to be good — cheerful, and helpful, and
true — in whatever position she found herself,
even though it were a position not at all to her
mind, and in entire opposition to her efforts.
How can you make a tragedy with such mate-

rial? Only by fibbing, of course; and I have permanently alienated two of my best friends by firmly refusing to do just that. "O," says my friend, the Woman, seeing Katherine ruthlessly married to her body-snatcher, "there you have a strong situation for tragedy, for of course her love for that little whipper-snapper is not going to last, and she will fall in love with the Great Unknown." That is Woman's way out, — is it? "Now," says my friend, the Man, at a little earlier stage of Katherine's life, "you must have a tragedy here. Make her, out of sheer pity and sympathy, almost compromise herself with one, and the other come to the rescue and overpower her with his generosity." So that is the Man's way out, — is it? Get thee behind me, Satan. I will have neither my Katherine's honor nor her dignity sacrificed to the exigencies of your pitiless High Art. Slay your own friends, if you will, with the sword of your evil spirit, but Kate shall not be laid on your altar. Lie under the boundary-wall of morality, and dream your sweet dreams of forbidden fruit beyond, but I will stand by the facts. And if a hot, spiced, high-seasoned world finds the flavor but insipid, the world must make shift to bear it alone; they shall have no help from Kate. For, as I said, Kate's troubles were over. I do not mean that she was miraculously or exceptionally exempt from the disturbances and perplexities of earth ; but the centre of her life was transferred to another, to a strong, noble, self-restrained nature ; and whatever of sorrow came to her was softened, and whatever of joy was sweetened by the sympathy, the confidence, the love which wrapped her around like an atmosphere. It was long before she understood what had happened to her. Brooding over her own heart alone, she had involved herself in a tangle of doubt and dread. She had failed to justify herself to herself. Deploring alike her love and her lack of love, she mistrusted even her power to love. She did not know what her feeling was towards her husband, and she had even questioned whether he could himself care what it was, or set a value on so uncertain and variable a possession. She was in danger of becoming morbid, introspective, unhappy. The network in which she had ensnared herself was not the less hampering or calamitous because it was impalpable. But the one moment which caught her off guard revealed her weakness — or was it her strength ? — and she passed out of her own keeping forever. Her husband, who was perhaps over-cautious, or it might be over-chivalrous, in not levelling her defences, was not slow to take possession when once she had left the gates ajar. But what became of all her misgivings and fears, Kate never could divine. All those inconsistencies and mortifications and humiliations that had enmeshed her seemed to have simply disappeared. She knew only that whereas she had been wholly doubtful and apprehensive, and whereas nothing had been explained or denied or refuted — here she was in a haven and heaven of peace. All the mist of subtilties and gloom of forebodings were dispelled in the fervid sunshine of a great, manly, generous love. When she tried to bring forward her self-accusations for formal sentence, that she might be wholly frank, she found that she had nothing to say. Her strongest criminations served only to point a jest. Happiness carried all before it.

"My love is not worth anything," would Kate say, shame-faced, after some over-lavishment, and artfully but vainly trying to temper present weal with past woe.

"Then you will have no excuse for hoarding it," would her husband reply, with the most cheerful acquiescence.

"Watch me closely," she warned him with a frown, when she had grown more confident and careless. "I am a variable function. I shall fall in love with the newspaper agent or the lightning-rod man."

"I will see you don't!" was the succinct reply of the unterrified.

Kate was never tired of her own love-story. In fact, it rather seemed to grow in interest for her; and had it not been for that inexplicable folly of love which makes one particular woman charming, and everything which she says and does charming in the eyes of one particular man, Kate, I fear, would have bored her husband sadly with her inexhaustible chatter. As it was, the best sermons that were preached by the ablest divines, the most exhaustive pleas of the most distinguished lawyers, the most learned financial or political discussions of statesmen and economists, did not give to this man of college-breeding, and travel, and large monetary responsibilities, half so lively a pleasure as the saucy, sophistical, contradictory, and imperious love-talk of this one useless and ignorant little woman. A scientific and earnest world, bent on philanthropy and the march of intellect, would not believe me if I should say how long this contemplative idiot would sit, listening to her airy nothings, toying with her bright hair, watching her flitting color, marvelling at her little shells of ears, admiring even her modest gowns, and thinking — and not always careful to refrain from saying — that never was such a wonderful, winsome, and altogether delightful creature as this — just as if ten thousand of them were not all around him, with eyes and ears and gowns to match — if he would only think so!

"All our story is an underground story," would Kate suggest, slyly turning over the hundredth new leaf of her own cherished romance. "Just on the outside it has a bad look, — has it not?"

"It did have at one time."

"Ah! but now. Look at it. It is a two-story story with a basement."

"But the abasement was all on my part. You never lowered your colors."

"O, don't frivolize into wit. It always interrupts to have you — levitous — when I am serious. And the abasement was on my part, too. But on the outside there was no story at all. You and I were just two old neighbors, and we married."

"No thanks to you."

"At any rate we married, and there is no help for it. That is the first story, the chambers. But below that, a poor young man was engaged to an ambitious young woman who dismissed him, though she — well — did not like to, and married a rich man whom she did not love. That sounds well, — does it not?"

"Moral: Always discard a poor man you love for a rich man you don't, eh?"

"Why, it looks like that certainly. It shows how delusive appearances are. Well, that is the second story, and an ugly old story it is."

"But the cream of the joke is not there."

"No. All the best part of it is underground. The first is commonplace, the second is mercenary ; but the real romance, the life of life, is where you and I, under the rose, were slowly feeling our way along towards each other."

"Not a bit of it! I found my way to you on the double-quick, and then had to wait in the cold, while you went chirping and fluttering and twittering around Robin Hood's barn forever and a day."

"O," said Kate, with a wry face, "that is what I never can like to think of."

"I should imagine not."

"You don't seem to care about it half so much as I."

"I have not time to go prowling about in the prehistoric ages for a grievance."

"It is the one bitter drop in my cup."

"I will take the taste out of your mouth ;" which he would do effectually for the time being.

But presently up would come Katherine again, fresh with her whimsical regrets.

"I think there ought to be a law passed that a girl should never be engaged to any one but the man she marries."

"Move an amendment to the Constitution of the girls, then, Katy, or give me the pick of the man."

"I wish, O, I sorely wish," — hiding her face in the ample provision made for such contingencies, — "I had never kissed — any one — but you."

"Constructively you never did, you know. You could carry it up on a writ of error."

"Really, I never did.　Really, myself."

"Passive voice?"

"Entirely."

"But Saul was consenting?"

"Well — not to say violently — opposing.　I wish I had it not to remember."

"Much, Katy?"

"O dear!　It seemed much then, but — circumstances have arisen since — so that — now it does not.　Still, I wish it had not been at all. You don't care?"

"Bless your dear heart!"

"I am not sure it would not be more complimentary to me if you did care."

Or, in more humble mood, Kate would break out, "I never, never, never can make up to you all that time I wasted."

"You can try, though.　It will keep you in a healthy frame of mind towards me."

"I can't think of any way to make it even between us but for you to stop loving me a year or two, and so give me a chance to catch up."

"All right.　Only you give the word when I am to begin."

"Richard Glynn!" towering aloft with indignation, "if I ever hear you dare to dream that

you will stop loving me on any pretext whatever! It was your own self did it. You just
bounced upon me out of a clear sky," — Kate
was ever reckless in tropes, — "and would
have ruined us both if I had not intervened. I
never saw any one act so entirely without intelligence."

" Bounced! I wonder what form of fixity you
would call slowness! I courted you steadily from
the time you were two years old."

" O, two-year-old courting does not count. It
is just as I said. I was all ready to love you.
You were just the kind of man I had made up
my mind for. But instead of letting me know
it, you kept on digging potatoes, and one day,
in course of conversation, rolled up your eyes,
bang! bang! bang! I am in love with you,
Miss Katherine! bang! bang! bang! Naturally I thought you were a lunatic. Any well-
brought-up girl would!"

" But I got you, Katy! There was method
in my madness," said Mr. Glynn, laughing
heartily at Kate's condensed novel.

" By the skin of my teeth. And that was
just as bad. What a horrible risk you ran!
Suppose you had happened not to be you, but
an indifferent sort of person, and the real you
were somebody else outside?"

" Should not care a farthing, Kitty, so long as
you were inside."

"Ricardo;" coaxingly, and striving with an abstracted air to bring his beard and hair into conjunction upon the bridge of his nose, — an operation which could not have been comfortable to the subject of it, and which was certainly unbecoming, but against which, in his reduced state of mind, he offered no further protest than occasional growls and sputterings when breathing was too seriously tampered with, — "Ricardo, *am* I as nice as you thought I should be?"

"O Lord!"

"Sweet must not swear."

"That isn't swear; it's prayer."

"Amen, then."

"Ah! but, Katy, weren't you hard to woo?"

"You need not fling it up at me if I was. I did not force you into it, you know."

"Yes, you did. ' 'Twas the same love that spread the feast, that sweetly forced me in;' and when I was in, did I not have a time taking the kinks out of you? — a good time too?"

"There never were any kinks in me, and they are all in still. But it was a horrible risk. I wonder you dared. If you had not happened to be just what you are, there is no telling what might not have happened. Suppose, instead of loving you, I had come to hate you!"

"O, you could not. I would not have let you. Think I did not know that before I began?"

"*I* did not."

"It was not necessary. I was engineering this thing."

"What I have always admired in you was your modesty. I fear now that you are losing it. Lo! the conquering hero comes in the tone of your last remarks."

"Comes to make his blessings known, not hide them under a bushel. You are just learning the *a b c* of love, Katy. When you get up into the Differential Calculus, say alongside where I am now, you will learn that love knows as well as feels ; knows its own, and will make sure of it with half a chance."

"I don't think you have anything to boast of in that line. You never made anything of your chance till you lost it."

"And gave you no peace till I got it again."

"And not much then. But I was not bad after everything was settled ; was I ? Give me so much credit."

"O, you were jolly ! We have a good deal to congratulate ourselves on, Katy-did. If I had been a knave, and you had been a fool, or *vice versa*, instead of being what we are, a half decent sort of chap and a wholly delicious sort of chit — why, we might have come to grief. Instead of which ! "

"But you did have a sad time with me. It was cruel."

"But I never let go, you see. You held out, but I held on."

"I am so glad you did. Fancy what it would be not to have you!"

"Better try and put up with having me."

"I will tell you what I have decided on as an infallible rule for the right conduct of life : We must never both be cross at the same time."

"Excellent. We will turn and turn about."

"Yes; only that as I can never be sure how much you love me, or whether you are not getting tired of me, if you are cross I shall fear it means something, and be unhappy. But I shall always know that I love you, and that if I am cross it is merely superficial and insignificant; so I make Rule Second : That you are never to be cross to me ; but if I am to you, you are not to mind it."

"I understand : Never be cross at the same time, and Katy to occupy all the time. Agreed."

And it must be said for Katherine that she rarely abused her privilege. The best of men call into exercise a good deal of patience, and patience was not Katherine's strong point. Luckily her husband was large-natured, and if Katherine was sometimes over-earnest with her Brutus, he never took it to heart. He took her to his heart instead, and was so frankly sorry for the forgetfulness or the inconsiderateness that had annoyed her, and so frankly desirous to make amends, that Kate usually went into spasms of self-abasement over her vile impatience, and into grotesque adulation of the tempter who had wrought her fall, and would work it again with the same bland and blithe unconsciousness.

There was one thing that always moved Katherine to violent, and far be it from me to say unrighteous, wrath, and that was the philosophical assumption that conjugal love must by its own weight subside into "tender friendship." "'Tender friendship!' O, yes; I know what that means. It is love gone to seed!" would Kate cry sarcastically, her bucolic antecedents ever reappearing in metaphor and simile. "Richard Glynn, if you love me, say so; if you don't — don't! But as for your 'tender friendship,' let it not be so much as named between us!"

And it never was. Whether it were the shoals and breakers of their early voyage, or some inborn quality of their own, their love never seemed to tone down into that "practical and possible" domestic convenience which is the accredited heir-at-law of love, but kept always something of its honey-moon, holiday nature. Nay, but how fiercely would my Kate resent such a statement! Rather as the happy weeks sped into happy months, and the months into happy years, it seemed to Kate that with each fresh year she was freshly learning love's real, regal meaning. Her husband never became to her uninteresting.

Not only did his society never cease to be agreeable, it never ceased to be exhilarating. His intellect, trained to more careful observation and more tranquil judgment, stimulated hers, which in turn lent color and glow to his. And neither was separated from the other without a conscious lack, or met without a conscious gladness. In his love, strong, unfailing, free from everything petty, full of trust and help and cheer, and building itself into nobler proportions as each succeeding year laid broader and firmer foundations, Katherine dwelt secure, content, rejoicing, nor refrained ever and anon from breaking forth into exultant thanksgiving. All the little rootlets of her daily life thrust out boldly into the inexhaustible riches of his unselfishness, and drew thence sustenance and strength, and in the sunshine of his gentleness every shy bud was won to its perfect blossoming. So Kate grew in grace daily.

What was her ministry of grace to him, the angels desire to look into — and perhaps they do. But what they see of Divine purpose toward the world in the sweet and austere mysteries of feminine service, it is not given mortal lips to declare.

And yet it would not have been Kate if her bright days had not been freaked with fantastic woes. In spite of her Orthodox church-membership, she was a little heathen at heart, and constantly strove with peace-offerings to placate the hostile deities and avert fancied disasters.

> " Meanwhile the best way to escape his ire
> Is not to seem too happy," —

was the real attitude which this little feminine and Christian Caliban would occasionally assume towards her Setebos. As her own happiness brightened out of the gray twilight into the rosy dawn and the brilliant morning, she was fain to cast about her for danger that menaced or gloom to gladden. Walter's fate proved for some time a very satisfying source of uneasiness, and precluded the necessity of other search. Mr. Glynn could never be brought to take a serious view of the subject, and treated Walter's woes with a cavalier indifference, not to say gayety, which Kate could not pronounce anything but heartless. While himself professing the greatest delight in Katherine's society, he firmly maintained that Mr. Laballe would never be very rash or very wretched at being deprived of it, and steadfastly refused to pay his wife the compliment of fearing in the least degree that her early lover would ever become a Blighted Being on her account. And the event proved him right. Mr. Laballe did not marry. The death of a distant relative gave him a small share in a large fortune; not enough to give him any wide sweep in life, but enough to insure personal comfort in a small way. He held his law-office, but was never slave to briefs and pleas, and was never called on to waste his time and talents in the preparation and presentation of difficult cases. This left him leisure for the cultivation of his mind and the acquisition of liberal, un-partisan views, in which he was so successful that in any emergency he could always be relied on for deploring and even denouncing the savagery of American manners, the poverty of American literature, and the corruption of American politics, — and so became a valuable member of society.

All of which did not hinder Kate from indulging now and then in the luxury of woe. She was happy : that, with the best will in the world, she could not deny ; but she had always the one grievance to fall back on, that she was happy at the expense of a shattered ideal ! One love — first, last, and always, to live for and to die with — that had been the dream of her girlhood, her inexorable demand. Anything less was fickleness, shallowness, unworthy to be named by the sacred name. And here she was, climbing up the heights of one love on the ruins of another ! Pitiless and haughty was her self-disdain — till in an unlucky moment even this last fortress of whimsical discontent was wrested from her by a visitor who pointed the moral of a bit of neighborhood gossip with the very sentiment which had been the burden of Kate's life-song. Kate could lecture herself with great volubility, but she bridled instantly when the same lesson, however innocently, was enforced upon her from a foreign source. Mr. Glynn watched Kate's chagrin with great amusement. He even took occasion, rather wickedly, to draw out the offending visitor upon the objectionable topic, after whom no sooner was the door closed than Kate, with great sacrifice of matronly dignity, shook her fist at the retreating silk. "'First love is best,' — is it ?" repeating her guest's departing words. " O, yes, first love *is* best ! and this," — turning upon her husband in final surrender, and endangering his life through impeded respiration — yet he seemed to like it, — "this, *this*, THIS is first love !"

20

NEW AND POPULAR NOVELS.

SLAVES OF THE RING. By F. W. ROBINSON, author of "Second Cousin Sarah," "Little Kate Kirby," "For Her Sake," "Poor Humanity," "Her Face was her Fortune," "True to Herself," "A Woman's Ransom," &c. 1 vol. 8vo. Cloth, $1.25; Paper, 75 cts.

*** "'Slaves of the Ring' is a remarkably interesting romance. The story is well written, the characters are well drawn, and racy sketches of rural life are pleasantly interwoven with the action of the narrative." — *Boston Transcript.*

A WOMAN'S RANSOM. By F. W. ROBINSON, author of "Slaves of the Ring," "Little Kate Kirby," "For Her Sake," &c. 1 vol. 8vo. Cloth, $1.25; Paper, 75 cts.

*** "The new novel, by the author of the ' Slaves of the Ring,' is alive with incident; it is ingeniously constructed, and there is a cleverness in incident and management of the story which cannot be denied; the interest is kept up with singular vividness, and without the extravagant expedients to which popular novelists often resort." — *Press.*

TOO MUCH ALONE. By Mrs. J. H. RIDDELL, author of "A Life's Assize," "Phemie Keller," "George Geith," "Above Suspicion," &c. 1 vol. 8vo. Cloth, $1.25; Paper, 75 cts.

*** "The story is deeply interesting. It is one of the very best of recent fictions." — *Worcester Spy.*

ABOVE SUSPICION. By arrangement with Mrs. J. H. RIDDELL, author of "Too Much Alone," "A Life's Assize," &c. 1 vol. 8vo. Cloth, $1.25; Paper, 75 cts.

A TANGLED SKEIN. By ALBANY DE FONBLANQUE, JR., an author who has inherited genius of an uncommon order. 1 vol. 8vo. Cloth, $1.25; Paper, 75 cts.

*** "This novel captivates the reader when he first opens it, and holds him in strong and agreeable chains to its closing page." — *Boston Traveller.*

"It is so well written that, having once taken up the book, it will be impossible to lay it down until the end." — *Press.*

A FAMILY TREE. By ALBANY DE FONBLANQUE, JR., author of "Cut Adrift," "A Tangled Skein." 1 vol. 8vo. Cloth, $1.25; Paper, 75 cts.

*** "It is a well-conceived story, and is presented in a manner to interest. — *Toledo Commercial.*

THE WIDOW LEROUGE. By EMILE GABORIAU, author of "The Mystery of Orcival," "File No. 113," "The Clique of Gold," "Other People's Money." 1 vol. 8vo. Cloth, $1.25; Paper, 75 cts.

*** "A novel of much power." — *Journal.*

"Gaboriau is an author whose works are appreciated for their originality and ingenuity." — *Messenger.*

THE MYSTERY OF ORCIVAL. By EMILE GABORIAU, author of "File No. 113," &c. 1 vol. 8vo. Cloth, $1.25; Paper, 75 cts.

"Admirably written, each character finely drawn. It will be read with sorrow, with pleasure, and profit. Read it, and then we have no doubt you will add it to your collection of choice novels with as much pleasure as we do." — *Lawrence American.*

THE CLIQUE OF GOLD. Translated from the French of EMILE GABORIAU, author of "File No. 113," "Other People's Money," "Within an Inch of His Life," "The Widow Lerouge," "The Mystery of Orcival," &c. 1 vol. 8vo. Cloth, $1.25; Paper, 75 cts.

*** "It is strongly sensational, but the materials are managed with so strong a dramatic insight that one has not time or inclination to think of improbabilities. M. GABORIAU is without a peer in this particular style of story." — *Boston Gazette.*

"Gaboriau's novels increase in power as we become familiar with his style." — *Transcript.*

OTHER PEOPLE'S MONEY. From the French of EMILE GABORIAU, author of "File No. 113," "The Clique of Gold," "Within an Inch of His Life." 1 vol. 8vo. Cloth, $1.25; Paper, 75 cts.

*** "Exciting throughout, the story appeals to refined tastes, and should be read widely, as its merit is sterling." — *Traveller.*

WITHIN AN INCH OF HIS LIFE. From the French of EMILE GABORIAU, author of "The Widow Lerouge," "The Mystery of Orcival," "File No. 113." 1 vol. 8vo. Cloth, $1.25; Paper, 75 cts.

*** "An exciting and entertaining novel, full of dramatic incident and well-figured character-pictures." — *Commercial Advertiser.*

FILE No. 113. By EMILE GABORIAU, author of "The Clique of Gold," "Other People's Money," "Within an Inch of His Life," "The Widow Lerouge," "The Mystery of Orcival." 1 vol. 8vo. Cloth, $1.25; Paper, 75 cts.

*** "As good as Gaboriau's stories of French life and character uniformly are, we think this one surpasses all his former efforts." — *Journal.*

"'File No. 113' has created a sensation wherever it has appeared." — *Critic.*

For Sale at all the Bookstores and Depots, and sent, postpaid, to any part of the World, on receipt of Price, by ESTES & LAURIAT, 301 Washington Street, Boston.

WOVEN OF MANY THREADS. By C. V. HAMILTON, author of "Ropes of Sand," "Crown from the Spear." 1 vol. 8vo. Cloth, $1.25; Paper, 50 cts.

*** "As at present advised, we may venture to say that this 'first novel of the season,' from the pen of an American lady, will meet with acceptance from the readers of fiction. The style is free and glowing, and the author, locating her story in Italy, finds opportunities to show familiarity with the land of song and art, of which she makes incidental use to heighten the interest of the tale." — *Boston Transcript.*

ROPES OF SAND. By C. V. HAMILTON, author of "Woven of Many Threads," "Crown from the Spear." 1 vol. 8vo. Cloth, $1.25; Paper, 75 cts.

*** "A work woven as well as this in plot, character, general finish, and execution, deserves to have its writer publicly heralded upon the title-page." — *Times.*

CROWN FROM THE SPEAR. By C. V. HAMILTON, author of "Woven of Many Threads," "Ropes of Sand." 1 vol. 8vo. Cloth, $1.25; Paper, 75 cts.

*** "It is a story of French domestic life and character, full of interest, and written in attractive style. The moral of the story is that the crown of happiness may be won after long struggle and suffering." — *Herald.*

"Coming from the pen of the author of 'Woven of Many Threads,' this story is sure of a warm welcome. In some respects it is an improvement upon its predecessor, having a more compact and artistic form, and more powerful interest." — *Phil. Inquirer.*

KATE BEAUMONT. By J. W. DE FOREST, author of "Overland," "Miss Ravenel's Conversion," "Playing the Mischief." 1 vol. 8vo. Illustrated. Cloth, $1.25; Paper, 75 cts.

*** "He has written a novel that is very readable, and he has given proof of being able to do more and better work. His painstaking, his careful observation and sprightliness, are qualities which will certainly achieve a more than partial success." — *Nation.*

"This is one of the best American novels we have ever read. It is written with a vigorous pen that never flags till the last word is written and the last scene closed." — *People, Concord.*

VINETA. From the German of E. WERNER, author of "Good Luck," &c. 1 vol. 8vo. Cloth, $1.25; Paper, 75 cts.

BROKEN CHAINS. Translated by FRANCES A. SHAW, from the German of E. WERNER, author of "Good Luck," &c. 1 vol. 8vo. Cloth, $1.25; Paper, 75 cts.

. "It has spirit and action, united with power and depth of feeling." — *Transcript.*

"The plot is highly interesting, and is well developed, while an art atmosphere pervades the work, that shows both refinement and æsthetic appreciation on the part of the writer. The style is strong and vigorous, and contains scenes of great power." — *Gazette.*

GOOD LUCK. By the author of "Broken Chains." 1 vol. 8vo. Cloth, $1.25; Paper, 75 cents.

. "An attractive and fascinating volume, with highly dramatic characters, clearly drawn and well sustained throughout, and containing many pages of absorbing interest. The translation is graceful and natural, one of the happy kind that makes us forget that the story was first written in a foreign tongue." — *Enquirer.*

"I began to read the proof-sheets last evening, and was compelled by the interest of the story to read into the small hours." — *L. C. M.*

NOT EASILY JEALOUS. 1 vol. 8vo. Cloth, $1.25; Paper, 75 cts.

. "This 'Not Easily Jealous,' has some bright and sparkling characters in it. There is not much plot or incident in it; but the interest is well-sustained, and it is written in such a taking sort of style as to make it very fascinating." — *People.*

EXPIATED. By the author of "Six Months Hence," and "Behind the Veil." 1 vol. 8vo. Cloth, $1.25; Paper, 75 cts.

. "The author shows power of invention, felicity in the management of details, and a keen insight into the mysteries of life." — *Boston Globe.*

SIX MONTHS HENCE. By the author of "Behind the Veil," "Expiated." Cloth, $1.25; Paper, 75 cts.

. "This remarkably well written story comes to us characterized by a most skilful arrangement. 'Behind the Veil' gave promise of considerable ability in the field of design. 'Six Months Hence' has fully realized this promise." — *Philadelphia Age.*

"It is of absorbing interest; and whoever takes it up will not readily put it down till the last scene is enacted, and the curtain falls." — *People* (Concord).

For Sale at all the Bookstores and Depots, and sent, postpaid, to any part of the World, on receipt of Price, by ESTES & LAURIAT, 301 Washington Street, Boston.

CHECKMATE. By J. S. Le Fanu, author of "A Lost Name," "Tenants of Malory," &c. 1 vol. 8vo. Cloth, $1.25; Paper, 75 cts.

₊ "Full of startling surprises, and written with great power."—*N. B. Mercury.*

"A powerfully written story, with an excellent plot, well carried out."—*Farmer.*

"A work of fiction with a plot as deep as Wilkie Collins's 'Woman in White.'"—*Herald.*

OPEN SESAME. By Florence Marryat, author of "Love's Conflict," "Prey of the Gods," "Her Lord and Master." With Illustrations. 1 vol. 8vo. Cloth, $1.25; Paper, 75 cents.

₊ "The plot of this story is deeply laid."—*Register.*

"A story of much love."—*Herald.*

DEEP WATERS. By Anna H. Drury, author of "Misrepresentation," &c., &c. 1 vol. 8vo. Cloth, $1.25; Paper, 75 cts.

₊ "A novel full of melancholy and pathos."—*Democrat.*

"The story opens in one of those old English homes which have been highly respectable and wealthy, and is well worth reading."—*Commercial, Toledo.*

WOMAN'S LOVE; or, Like and Unlike. By J. F. Smith, author of "Lady Ashleigh," "Marion Burnard," &c. 1 vol. 8vo. Cloth, $1.25; Paper, 75 cts.

₊ "This novel will satisfy the most exacting readers of the old style of romance."—*Albany Journal.*

STRETTON. By Henry Kingsley, author of "Ravenshoe," "Geoffrey Hamlyn," "Hetty," &c., &c. With Illustrations. 1 vol. 8vo. Cloth, $1.25; Paper, 75 cts.

₊ "A charming, bright, and sparkling novel for the tourist."—*Bangor Whig.*

"Henry Kingsley has done more to cultivate a correct taste among readers of modern novels, than any other author of the day."—*Times, New Orleans.*

JETTATRICE. From the French of Madame Augustus Craven, author of "Fleurange," "A Sister's Story," &c. 1 vol. 8vo. Cloth, $1.25; Paper, 75 cts.

₊ "A tale of rare purity and nobility."—*Press.*

"The scene is laid at Messina, and runs through Naples and Italy."—*Courier.*

JOCELYN'S MISTAKE. By Mrs. J. K. SPENDER, author of "Her Own Fault," "Brothers in Law," &c. 1 vol. 8vo. Cloth, $1.25; Paper, 75 cts.

**** "Mrs. Spender's English is unusually good, and she has learned the art of working her opinions of men and things into the web of her story, instead of merely intercalating homilies. . . . The Jocelyn of the book is very skilfully drawn. . . . It rises in type and diction far above the ephemeral stories of the season." — *Academy.*

THE LOST DESPATCH. Translated from the German of FRIEDRICH FRIEDRICH, by L. A. WILLIAMS. 1 vol. 8vo. Cloth, $1.25; Paper, 50 cts.

**** "Lovers of pen-pictures and florid writing will not find any of their favorite style. There is no padding, no burning sensation, no bigamy, nor divorce. But there is a well constructed story, well-told, and also some finely-drawn characters. The interest, too, is well sustained. 'The Lost Despatch' will serve to pass a couple of hours pleasantly enough; and what is more to the purpose, in these days of filthy novels, it may be read by all without fear or hesitation." — *N. Y. Globe.*

CHOISY. By JAMES P. STORY. 1 vol. 8vo. Cloth, $1.25; Paper, 75 cts.

**** "We recommend the book for a pleasant companion on listless August days. While shedding a tear of sympathy over the fate of Nina Choisy, its salutary lesson cannot fail to produce lasting results." — *Transcript.*

"It is full of interesting and thrilling incidents from beginning to end." — *Press.*

NOBODY'S FORTUNE. By EDMUND YATES, author of "Black Sheep," "The Yellow Flag." vol. 8vo. Cloth, $1.25; Paper, 75 cts.

**** "The fact that Dickens was connected, even thus indirectly, with the work, will give it additional value in the estimation of most readers." — *Cleveland Herald.*

"The best of his productions." — *Boston Post.*

THE YELLOW FLAG. By EDMUND YATES, author of "Nobody's Fortune," "Black Sheep." 1 vol. 8vo. Cloth, $1.25; Paper, 75 cts.

**** "The story is dramatic from opening to close, keeping the reader constantly attent, and each moment giving a gratification." — *New Bedford Mercury.*

For Sale at all the Bookstores and Depots, and sent, postpaid, to any part of the World, on receipt of Price, by ESTES & LAURIAT, 301 Washington Street, Boston.

ELENA: AN ITALIAN TALE. By L. N. COMYN, author of "Atherstone Priory," "Ellice," &c. 1 vol. Cloth, $1.25; Paper, 75 cts.

*** "'Elena,' in character and plot, is excellent." — *Traveller* (Boston).

"An Italian story of great power and beauty; sure to live." — *Leeds Mercury.*

"The most elegant and interesting fiction of the season." — *London Messenger.*

"A very pleasing and touching story. It is sure to be read." — *London Daily News.*

ATHERSTONE PRIORY. By L. N. COMYN, author of "Elena," "Ellice," &c. 1 vol. Cloth, $1.25; Paper, 75 cts.

*** "A quiet, charming, English romance of real life. The scenes are life-like, and the story interesting. The heroine at once wins the sympathy of the reader, which deepens into admiration, and an intense interest in her fortunes and misfortunes." — *Examiner.*

ETHEL MILDMAY'S FOLLIES. By the author of "Petites Romance." 1 vol. 8vo. Cloth, $1.25; Paper, 75 cts.

*** "A story which we do not hesitate to recommend." — *Spectator.*

"A taste would be difficult to please which could not find amusement in following the fortunes of the actors developed in this story." — *Transcript.*

MAUD OR NINA — Like Cures Like. By G. J. WHYTE-MELVILLE, author of "Katerfelto," "Digby Grand," &c., &c. 1 vol. 8vo. Cloth, $1.25; Paper, 75 cts.

*** "Sprightly and sensational." — *Vox Populi.*

"The most fastidious may read Maud and Nina." — *Journal.*

ZELDA'S FORTUNE. By R. E. FRANCILLON, author of "Earl Dean," "Pearl and Emerald." 1 vol. 8vo. Illustrated. Cloth, $1.25; Paper, 75 cts.

*** "This book shows as much power as Bulwer's early novels did." — *Springfield Republican.*

"Charles G. Leland and Louise Chandler Moulton speak of it in very flattering terms." — *Public.*

THE WICKED WOODS OF TOBEREEVIL. By Miss MUL-HOLLAND, author of "Hester History." 1 vol. 8vo. Cloth, $1.25; Paper, 75 cts.

*** "A tale of Irish life, legend and humor, sketched with vivacity, and replete with racy incident, stirring adventures, and well-depicted feeling." — *Inter-Ocean.*

For Sale at all the Bookstores and Depots, and sent, postpaid, to any part of the World, on receipt of Price, by ESTES & LAURIAT, 301 Washington Street, Boston.

THE FOE IN THE HOUSEHOLD. By CAROLINE CHESEBRO'. 1 vol. 8vo. Cloth, $1.25; Paper, 75 cts.

*** "It is purely domestic in its character, instructive in its moral teachings, and possesses a subtle interest more absorbing than that which attaches to the conventional style of modern romances." — *Press.*

CAN THE OLD LOVE. By ZADEL BARNES BUDDINGTON. 1 vol. 8vo. Illustrated. Cloth, $1.25; Paper, 75 cts.

*** "The most unique and original portion exhibits a married man of sixty-three years of age, who falls in love with the child of his friend, on her return from boarding-school." — *Philadelphia Age.*

RUTH MAXWELL. By Lady BLAKE, author of "Claude," "Lady of Lyndon." 1 vol. 8vo. Cloth, $1.25; Paper, 75 cts.

*** "This story is told with a quiet charm, and contains thoroughly good and pleasant reading." — *Morning Post.*

"It is a gracefully written story, full of interest, and distinguished by some capital character drawings. The tone is healthy, and the style bright and spirited. The heroine is a charming conception, and is developed with rare skill and effect. We can conscientiously recommend the book as one thoroughly pure in its morality, and peculiarly adapted to summer reading." — *Globe.*

LADY OF LYNDON. By Lady BLAKE, author of "Claude," "Ruth Maxwell." 1 vol. 8vo. Cloth, $1.25; Paper, 75 cts.

*** "There is nothing sensational in its plot; the moral it inculcates is pure, healthy, and instructive, while its literary qualifications cannot be gainsaid." — *New York Albion.*

A ROSE IN JUNE. By Mrs. OLIPHANT, author of "Story of Valentine and his Brother," "Squire Arden," "For Love and Life," "Innocent." 1 vol. 8vo. Illustrated. Cloth, $1.25; Paper, 50 cts.

*** "In 'A Rose in June' Mrs. Oliphant is at her very best again. The book is full of character, drawn with the most delicate of touches." — *Athenæum.*

"A pleasant novel, agreeably told. Mrs. Oliphant is accomplished in her art; her knowledge of the instrument with which she has to deal, and of the audience for whom she plays upon it, was never more thoroughly exhibited than in her latest work, 'A Rose in June.'" — *Observer.*

"One of the sweetest, most charming, and most natural stories which that popular writer has given us." — *Boston Journal.*

For Sale at all the Bookstores and Depots, and sent, postpaid, to any part of the World, on receipt of Price, by ESTES & LAURIAT, 301 Washington Street, Boston.

MISS ROVEL. From the French of VICTOR CHERBULIEZ, author of the "Romance of an Honest Woman," &c. Translated by FRANCES A. SHAW. 1 vol. 8vo. Cloth, $1.25; Paper, 50 cts.

⁎ "This translation of one of the popular French novels is a thorough love story; it is alive with incident, and the interest is kept up with singular vividness, and without the extravagant expedients to which popular novelists often resort." — *Gazette.*

"The story is very strong in plot, and the translation is excellent." — *Commercial.*

BUFFETS. By CHARLES H. DOE. 1 vol. 8vo. Cloth, $1.25; Paper, 75 cts.

⁎ "It is very spicy and thoroughly modern." — *Chicago Journal.*

"There is a great deal of pleasant humor in this novel." — *Albany Journal.*

"This novel shows much skill and some delicacy of touch, in which our novelists generally are most wanting." — *Springfield Republican.*

INA. By KATHERINE VALERIO. 1 vol. 8vo. Cloth, $1.25; Paper, 75 cts.

⁎ "In the construction of the story, we find proof of considerable inventive power, a lively and brilliant imagination, and a certain fluency of expression." — *N. Y. Tribune.*

"There is a freshness in this that is attractive." — *Messenger.*

"A charming Italian love-story, as mellow, genial, and pure as an Italian sun."

"A cleverly written story of Italian life, pure in tone." — *Transcript.*

ONLY THREE WEEKS. 1 vol. 8vo. Cloth, $1.25; Paper, 50 cts.

⁎ "Just the kind of a story for reading leisurely on a summer day." — *Advertiser.*

"The book is a good one, full of powerful situations, excellent delineations of character, and capital writing." — *Gazette.*

"A sparkling, racy novel." — *People (Concord).*

"Charming little story." — *N. Y. Tribune.*

A COMEDY OF TERRORS. By JAMES DE MILLE, author of "American Baron," "Cryptogram," "Dodge Club." 1 vol. 8vo. Cloth, $1.25; Paper, 75 cts.

⁎ "Every chapter is full of mirth. DE MILLE is a rare genius with the pen." — *Press (Providence).*

"It is in many respects the most ingenious of this fertile novelist's books." — *Boston Journal.*

For Sale at all the Bookstores and Depots, and sent, postpaid, to any part of the World, on receipt of Price, by ESTES & LAURIAT, 301 Washington Street, Boston.

EPOCHS OF ENGLISH HISTORY.

A SERIES OF BOOKS NARRATING THE

HISTORY OF ENGLAND AT SUCCESSIVE EPOCHS.

EDITED BY

The Rev. M. CREIGHTON, M. A.,

Late Fellow and Tutor of Merton College, Oxford.

The object of this Series is to supply an Elementary History of England, which shall be sound and trustworthy as well as inexpensive. English History conveniently divides itself into eight Periods. By the adoption of this division a more intelligible and more interesting view of the course of English History may be obtained, while the advantage of cheapness will be secured by the separate sale of the several divisions.

Early England up to the Norman Conquest. By FREDERICK YORK-POWELL, M. A., Law Lecturer Ch. Ch. Oxford; Historical Lecturer Trin. Coll. Oxford. With 4 Maps. 1 vol. 16mo. 50 cts.

England a Continental Power, from the Conquest to Magna Charta, 1066–1216. By LOUISE CREIGHTON. With a Colored Map of the Dominions of the Angevin Kings. 1 vol. 16mo. Cloth. 50 cts.

The Rise of the People, and Growth of Parliament, from the Great Charter to the Accession of Henry VII. (1215–1485. By JAMES ROWLEY, M. A. Professor of Modern History and Literature, University College, Bristol. With 4 Maps. 1 vol. 16mo. Cloth. 50 cts.

The Tudors and the Reformation. (1485–1603.) By the Rev. MANDELL CREIGHTON, M. A., Late Fellow and Tutor of Merton College, Oxford; Editor of the Series. With 3 Maps. 1 vol. 16mo. Cloth. 50 cts.

The Struggle against Absolute Monarchy, from 1603 to 1688. By B. MERITON CORDERY, author of "King and Commonwealth." With 2 Maps. 1 vol. 16mo. Cloth. 50 cts.

The Settlement of the Constitution, from 1688 to 1778. By JAMES ROWLEY, M. A., Professor of Modern History and Literature, University College, Bristol. 1 vol. 16mo. Cloth. 50 cts.

England during the American and European Wars, from 1778 to 1820. By O. W. TANCOCK, M. A., Assistant-Master, King's School, Sherborne, Dorset. 1 vol. 16mo. Cloth. 50 cts.

Modern England from 1820 to 1875. By T. ARNOLD, M. A., author of "A History of English Literature," &c. 1 vol. 16mo. Cloth. 50 cts.

For Sale at all the Bookstores and Depots, and sent, postpaid, to any part of the World, on receipt of Price, by ESTES & LAURIAT, 301 Washington Street, Boston.

EPOCHS OF ANCIENT HISTORY.

A series of books narrating the History of Greece and Rome, and of their relations to other countries, at successive Epochs. Edited by the Rev. G. W. Cox, M. A., author of the "Aryan Mythology," and jointly by Charles Sankey, M. A., late Scholar of Queen's College, Oxford; Assistant Master, Marlborough College. Uniform with "Epochs of Modern History."

The Greeks and the Persians. By the Rev. Geo. W. Cox, M. A., late Scholar of Trinity College, Oxford, Joint Editor of the Series. With 4 colored Maps. 1 vol. 16mo. Cloth. $1.00.

The Early Empire. By the Rev. W. Wolfe Capes, M. A., Reader of Ancient History in the University of Oxford. With 2 colored Maps. 1 vol. 16mo. Cloth. $1.00.

Early Rome, from the Foundation of the City to its Destruction by the Gauls. By Wilhelm Ihne, author of "History of Rome." With 1 colored Map. 1 vol. 16mo. Cloth. $1.00.

The Athenian Empire, from the Flight of Xerxes to the Fall of Athens. By the Rev. G. W. Cox, M. A., late Scholar of Trinity College, Oxford, Joint Editor of the Series. With 5 colored Maps. 1 vol. 16mo. Cloth. $1.00.

The Roman Triumvirates. By the Very Rev. Charles Merrivale, D. D., Dean of Ely. With 1 colored Map. 1 vol. 16mo. Cloth. $1.00.

The Age of the Antonines; or, the Roman Empire of the 2d Century. By the Rev. Wolfe Capes, M. A., Reader of Ancient History in the University of Oxford. With 2 colored Maps. 1 vol. 16mo. Cloth. $1.00.

Macedonian Empire, its Rise and Culmination to the Death of Alexander the Great. By A. M. Curteis, M. A., Assistant Master, Sherborne School. With 8 colored Maps. 1 vol. 16mo. Cloth. $1.00.

The Gracchi, Marius, and Sulla. By A. H. Beesly, M. A., Assistant Master, Marlborough College. 1 vol. 16mo. Cloth. $1.00.

Rome and Carthage, the Punic Wars. By R. Bosworth Smith, M. A., Assistant Master, Harrow School. 1 vol. 16mo. Cloth. $1.00.

Spartan and Theban Supremacy. By Charles Sankey, M. A., late Scholar of Queen's College, Oxford; Assistant Master, Marlborough College; Joint Editor of the Series. 1 vol. 16mo. Cloth. $1.00.

For Sale at all the Bookstores and Depots, and sent, postpaid, to any part of the World, on receipt of Price, by ESTES & LAURIAT, 301 Washington Street, Boston.

NATURAL HISTORY AND SCIENCE.

HALF-HOURS WITH INSECTS. A Popular Account of their Habits, Modes of Life, &c.; which are beneficial, and which are injurious to vegetation. By A. S. PACKARD, JR., of the Peabody Academy of Science. The subjects treated of are: Insects of the Garden; Relations of Insects to Man; Insects of the Plant-House; Edible Insects; Insects of the Pond and Stream; the Population of an Apple-Tree; Insects of the Field; Insects of the Forest; Insects as Mimics; Insects as Architects; Social Life of Insects and Mental Powers of Insects. The volume contains colored plate, 260 wood-cut illustrations and 392 pages, bound in one volume. Crown 8vo., cloth. $2.50.

OUR COMMON INSECTS. A Popular Account of the more common Insects of our Country, embracing Chapters on Bees and their Parasites, Moths, Flies, Mosquitos, Beetles, &c.; while a Calendar will give a general account of the more common Injurious and Beneficial Insects, and their Time of Appearance, Habits, &c. 200 pp. Profusely Illustrated. 1 vol., 12mo., cloth. Price $2.50.

SAY'S ENTOMOLOGY. A Description of the Insects of North America. By THOMAS SAY. With 54 full-page steel-plate Illustrations, engraved and colored from nature. Edited by J. L. LECONTE. With a Memoir by GEORGE ORD. 2 vols., 8vo., cloth, $15.00; half-calf, $20.00.

*** This standard work is now out of print, the plates having been destroyed. We offer the balance of the edition at the above prices. It will soon become scarce, and command a very much higher price.

FIELD ORNITHOLOGY. A Manual of Instruction on Collecting, Preparing, and Preserving Birds. By ELLIOTT COUES. With which is issued a Check-List of North American Birds. 1 vol. 8vo., cloth. $2.50.

KEY TO NORTH AMERICAN BIRDS. By ELLIOTT COUES, M. D. 369 imperial octavo pages. Illustrated by 6 Steel Plates, and 238 Wood-Cuts. A Manual or Text-Book of the Birds of North America; containing a Synopsis of Living and Fossil Birds, and Descriptions of every North American Species known to this Time. 1 vol., royal 8vo., cloth. Price, $7.00.

PACKARD'S GUIDE TO THE STUDY OF INSECTS. Being a Popular Introduction to the Study of Entomology, and a Treatise on Injurious and Beneficial Insects; with Descriptions and Accounts of the Habits of Insects, their Transformations, Development, and Classification. 15 full-page Plates, and 670 Cuts in the Text, embracing 1260 Figures of American Insects. Sixth edition. 1 vol., 8vo. Price reduced to $5.00.

*** This book is now acknowledged to be *the standard*, and is used in the leading universities and institutions of Europe and America.

For Sale at all the Bookstores and Depots, and sent, postpaid, to any part of the World, on receipt of Price, by ESTES & LAURIAT, 301 Washington Street, Boston.

Natural History and Science continued.

LAND AND GAME. The Land and Game Birds of New England. With Descriptions of the Birds, their Nests and Eggs, their Habits and Notes. An entirely new and accurate work, which no sportsman or collector can afford to be without. 1 vol. 8vo. Cloth, $3.00.

TYLOR (E. B.). PRIMITIVE CULTURE. Researches into the Development of Mythology, Philosophy, Religion, Art, and Custom. 2 vols., 8vo cloth, $5.00.

*** "Scanty justice can be done to Mr. Tylor's admirable discussion of animism. It is in the skill and sagacity with which such illustrations are introduced that one principal charm of Mr. Tylor's book consists. The author asks us to admit nothing on *a priori* evidence, for which irrefragable inductive proof cannot also be cited, and at every step he halts to take his bearings, minutely scrutinizing the whole visible field. In tracking the wilderness of primeval speculation, he is a guide no less safe than delightful." — JOHN FISKE, *in the North American Review.*

LIFE HISTORIES OF ANIMALS, INCLUDING MAN; or, Outlines of Comparative Embryology. With numerous Illustrations. 1 vol. 8vo. Cloth, $2.50.

*** "An ample work of reference for advanced students." — *Tribune.*

THE UNITY OF NATURAL PHENOMENA. An Introduction to the Study of the Forces of Nature. Being a popular Explanation of the Latest Discoveries in the Domain of Natural Science, including the Correlation of Forces, Mode of Motion, Force of Gravity, and Mutual Convertibility of the Forces of Nature. From the French of EMILE SAIGEY. With Notes and an Introduction by Prof. T. MOSES, of Urbana University. 1 vol. Crown 8vo. $1.50.

A HAND-BOOK OF HARDY TREES, SHRUBS, and Herbaceous Plants. Containing Descriptions, Native Countries, &c., of the best species in cultivation; together with cultural details, comparative hardiness, suitability for particular positions, &c., based on the French work of DECAISNE and NAUDIN, of the Institute of France. By W. B. HEMSLEY; with an Introduction by EDWARD S. RAND, JR. 300 fine Illustrations. 1 vol. 8vo. 700 pp. $7.50.

TYLOR (E. B.). THE EARLY HISTORY OF MANKIND, and Development of Civilization. By EDWARD B. TYLOR, author of "Primitive Culture," "Mexico and the Mexicans," &c. 1 vol, 8vo. $2.50.

WHAT YOUNG PEOPLE SHOULD KNOW. Being the Anatomy, Physiology, and Hygiene of the Human Reproductive Organs. By Prof. BURT G. WILDER, of Cornell University. 12mo. $1.50.

*** A careful and straightforward essay upon this important subject, by this distinguished naturalist, and one which is sure to attract great attention.

HALF-HOUR RECREATIONS

In Popular Science. Vol. II.

Twelve Parts. 25 Cts. each. Twelve Consecutive Numbers, making a Complete Volume, will be sent, postpaid, as issued, on receipt of $2.50.

We annex a list of some of the papers which appear in Vol. II. of the series:

The Transmission of Sound by the Atmosphere. By JOHN TYNDALL, F. R. S. —— **Gigantic Cuttle-Fish.** By W. SAVILLE KENT, F. L. S., of the Natural History Department of the British Museum.

The Glacial Epoch of our Globe. By ALEX. BRAUN.

The Sun and the Earth. By Prof. BALFOUR STEWART, F. R. S. —— **Force Electrically Exhibited.** By J. W. Phelps.

The Ice Age in Britain. By Prof. A. GEIKIE, F. R. S. —— **Causes of the Degeneracy of the Teeth.** By Prof. HENRY S. CHASE. —— **The Great Pyramid of Egypt.** —— **Photography.**

Plant Life in the Sea. By L. KNY. —— **The Illumination of Beacons and Buoys.**

Brain and Mind. By Prof. BURT G. WILDER, of Cornell University, author of "What Young People Should Know."

SPECTRUM ANALYSIS EXPLAINED. An explanation of this wonderful discovery, and its uses to science, including the received Theory of Sound, Heat, Light, and Color: with chapters on the Sun, Stars, Nebulæ, Comets, and Meteoric Showers. Abridged from the works of Schellen, Roscoe, Huggins, Lockyer, Young, and others, by the editor of "Half-Hour Recreations in Popular Science." With 2 Colored Plates and 20 Illustrations. 1 vol. 12mo. Cloth, $1.50.

NORTH AMERICAN SYLVA; or, A Description of the Forest Trees of the United States, Canada, and Nova Scotia. Containing all the Trees discovered in the Rocky Mountains, in Oregon, down to the shores of the Pacific, and into the confines of California, as well as in various parts of the United States. Considered with respect to their use in the Arts and their introduction into Commerce. By F. ANDREW MICHAUX and THOMAS NUTTALL. Illustrated with 277 beautifully colored Plates. 5 vols. Half morocco, gilt edge. Price $75.00.

STRUTT'S SYLVA BRITANNICA AND SCOTICA; or, Portraits of Forest Trees distinguished for their Antiquity, Magnitude, or Beauty. Drawn from Nature and Etched by JACOB GEORGE STRUTT. Imperial folio, comprising 50 very large and highly finished Etchings. Half bound, morocco, extra, gilt edges. $45.00.

For Sale at all the Bookstores and Depots, and sent, postpaid, to any part of the World, on receipt of Price, by ESTES & LAURIAT, 301 Washington Street, Boston.

HISTORICAL BIOGRAPHY, &c.

**CAMPBELL'S LIVES OF THE CHIEF JUSTICES OF ENG-
LAND.** Illustrated with Views of Westminster Hall, and Portraits of
the Justices. A new edition, printed on fine tinted paper, and bound
in bevel boards.

    Cloth. lettered, 6 vols., 8vo $21 00
    Law sheep,   "   " 26 00
    Half calf. marbled edges, 6 vols., 8vo 36 00
    New edition, cloth, 4 vols., 12mo 8 00

MEMORIES OF WESTMINSTER HALL. A Collection of Interesting Incidents, Anecdotes, and Historical Sketches, relating to Westminster Hall, its famous Judges and Lawyers, and its Great Trials.
With an Historical Introduction by EDWARD FOSS, F. R. S., author of
the "Lives of the Judges of England," &c. Handsomely Illustrated.
Superbly printed on tinted paper, and elegantly bound with bevelled
boards, uniform with the 8vo edition of Campbell's Chief Justices.
2 vols. 8vo. Cloth, $7.00.

ADVENTURES OF AN ATTORNEY in Search of Practice. By
Sir GEORGE STEPHEN. An amusing account of the mishaps, adventures, and difficulties experienced by a young attorney who made his
way in the world. 1 vol. Crown 8vo. Cloth, $2.25.

CAMPBELL'S LIVES OF THE LORD CHANCELLORS and
Keepers of the Great Seal of England. From the Earliest Times till
the Reign of Victoria, including the Lives of Lords Lyndhurst and
Brougham. Laid paper. Fully Illustrated. Bound uniform with the
8vo edition of the Lord Chief Justices. By the same author.

    Cloth, bevelled, 10 vols. $35 00
    Law sheep,   "   " 45 00
    Half calf, extra 60 00

FAMOUS CASES OF CIRCUMSTANTIAL EVIDENCE. With
an Introduction on the Theory of Presumptive Proof. By S. M. PHIL-
LIPS, author of "Phillips on Evidence." Second edition, revised and
greatly enlarged. 1 vol. 8vo. Cloth, $3.00.

ERSKINE'S SPEECHES. The Speeches of Lord Erskine, while at
the Bar. Reprinted from the 5-volume 8vo edition of 1810. With a
Memoir and Notes. By EDWARD WALFORD, M. A. 2 vols. 8vo.
Portrait. Cloth, $7.50.

MEMOIR OF THOMAS, FIRST LORD DENMAN, formerly
Lord Chief Justice of England. By Sir JOSEPH ARNOULD, late
Judge of the High Court of Bombay. Published uniform with
Campbell's Lives of the Chief Justices, and making volumes five and
six of the Series.

    2 volumes, 8vo, tinted paper, cloth, bevelled . . . $7 00
    "   "   "   sheep 9 00
    "   "   "   half calf 12 00

MISCELLANEOUS.

ROBINSON CRUSOE, Life and Adventures of. With a Biographical Account of DE FOE. Illustrated with 12 characteristic Engravings. Uniform with "Pilgrim's Progress" and "Swiss Family Robinson." 1 vol. Crown 8vo. Cloth, $1.50.

SWISS FAMILY ROBINSON; or, Adventures on a Desert Island. Uniform with "Robinson Crusoe" and "Pilgrim's Progress." With Illustrations. 1 vol. Crown 8vo. Cloth, $1.50.

PILGRIM'S PROGRESS. Large Type, with fine Illustrations by Dalziel Brothers. Uniform with "Swiss Family Robinson," "Robinson Crusoe," "Arabian Nights." 1 vol. Crown 8vo. Cloth, $1.50.

ARABIAN NIGHTS' ENTERTAINMENT; or, The Thousand and One Nights. Uniform with "Pilgrim's Progress," "Robinson Crusoe," "Swiss Family Robinson." 1 vol. Crown 8vo. Cloth, $1.50.

THE AMERICAN STATE AND AMERICAN STATESMEN. By WILLIAM GILES DIX. 1 vol. 12mo. Cloth, $1.50.

*** Consisting of Essays on the following subjects: Charles Sumner; Senators and States; The British Parliament; The American Congress; Christianity the Inspirer of Nations; Materialism the Curse of America; America a Christian Power; Abraham Lincoln; Origin of the Empire of North America; National Unity the Source of Authority; National Sovereignty; Are the United States a Nation?

CURRAN'S SPEECHES. The Speeches of John Philpot Curran, while at the Bar. With a Portrait, Memoir, and Introductory Notes. Edited by J. A. L. WHITTIER, Esq. 1 vol. 8vo. Tinted paper. Cloth, $3.50.

PASSAGES FROM THE LIFE OF CHARLES KNIGHT, Publisher, Author, and Leader in the Work of Popular Education; Editor of the "Penny Encyclopædia," "The Libraries of Useful and Entertaining Knowledge," and "The Popular History of England." Revised and slightly abridged from the English edition. Large 12mo. 500 pp. Cloth extra, $2.50.

For Sale at all the Bookstores and Depots, and sent, postpaid, to any part of the World, on receipt of Price, by **ESTES & LAURIAT, 301 Washington Street, Boston.**

NOVELS.

THACKERAY (W. M.) WORKS. The Kensington Edition. Complete in Twelve volumes. Crown 8 vo. Cloth, $24.00.

1. **Vanity Fair.**
2. **The History of Pendennis.**
3. **The Newcomes.**
4. **Esmond and Barry Lyndon.**
5. **The Virginians.**
6. **The Adventures of Philip.** To which is prefixed a SHABBY GENTEEL STORY.

7. **Paris, Irish, and Eastern Sketches.**

Paris Sketch Book.	Irish Sketch Book.	Cornhill to Cairo.

8. **Hogarty Diamomd, Yellowplush Papers, and Burlesques.**

The Great Hogarty Diamond.	A Legend of the Rhine.
Yellowplush Papers.	Rebecca and Rowena.
Novels by Eminent Hands.	The History of the next French
Jeames's Diary.	Cox's Diary. [Revolution.
Adventures of Major Gahagan.	The Fatal Boots.

9. **The Book of Snobs,** and Sketches of Life and Character.

The Book of Snobs.	Men's Wives.
Sketches and Travels in London.	The Fitzboodle Papers.
Character Sketches.	The Bedford Row Conspiracy.

A Little Dinner at Timmins's.

10. **Roundabout Papers and Lectures.**

Roundabout Papers.	The English Humorists of the
The Four Georges.	Eighteenth Century.

The Second Funeral of Napoleon.

11. **Catherine, &c.**

Catherine.	Dennis Duval.	The Wolves and the Lamb.
Lovel, the Widower.	Ballads.	Critical Reviews.
	Little Travels.	

12. **Christmas Books.**

Mrs. Perkins's Ball.	Our Street.
Dr. Birch.	The Kickleburys on the Rhine.

The Rose and the Ring.

For Sale at all the Bookstores and Depots, and sent, postpaid, to any part of the World, on receipt of Price, by ESTES & LAURIAT, 301 Washington Street, Boston.

NEW EDITIONS.

NORMANDY PICTURESQUE. By HENRY BLACKBURN. Illustrated.

ARTISTS AND ARABS. By HENRY BLACKBURN. Illustrated.

WORDS OF WASHINGTON. By JAMES PARTON.

FAMILIAR LETTERS FROM EUROPE. By C. C. FELTON.

HAMILTON'S (GAIL) WORKS. 16mo.

> **Country Living and Country Thinking.**
> **Gala Days.**
> **Stumbling-Blocks.**
> **A New Atmosphere.**
> **Skirmishes and Sketches.**
> **Summer Rest.**
> **Wool-Gathering.**
> **Woman's Wrongs.**
> **Sermons to the Clergy.**
> **First Love is Best.**

THE FOLK-LORE OF ROME. Collected by Word of Mouth from the People. By R. H. BUSK, author of "Patrañsas," "Sagas from the Far East," &c. With Index. 1 vol. Crown 8vo. $2.50.

MEETING THE SUN. A Journey all Around the World, through Egypt, China, Japan, and California, including an account of the Marriage Ceremonies of the Emperor of China. By WILLIAM SIMPSON, F. R. G. S., Member of Soc. Bib. Archæology. With about 50 Heliotypes and Illustrations engraved on Wood, from Original Drawings by the author. 1 vol. 8vo. Cloth, $4.50.

SUBSCRIPTION BOOKS.

—

GUIZOT'S
POPULAR
HISTORY OF ENGLAND,

From the Earliest Times to the Reign of Victoria.

BY M. GUIZOT,

Author of "A History of Civilization," "Popular History of France,"
&c., &c.

TRANSLATED BY F. MOY THOMAS,

And magnificently Illustrated with Steel Plates and Woodcuts, by

A. DE NEUVILLE,	EMILE BAYARD,	LEYENDECKER,
SIR JOHN GILBERT,	RIOU,	WEBER,
A. MARIE,	STAAL,	AND OTHERS.

☞ To be published uniform with the "Popular History of France."

Thirty-six Parts, paper cover		$18 00
Four vols., cloth extra, gilt side		22 00
" " full library sheep, marbled edges		26 00
" " half calf, gilt extra, marbled edges		30 00
" " half morocco extra, marbled edges		30 00
" " full morocco, gilt edges		40 00
" " full tree calf, gilt edges		40 00

*** The publishers offer this work confidently believing that it will acquire the position attained by the "History of France," by the same author, and be acknowledged as

The Standard History of England.

The well-known eminence and impartiality of the great historian, and the sumptuous style in which the work will be produced, will insure it a welcome by all lovers of good literature and art.

For Sale to Subscribers only, and sent, postpaid, to any part of the World, on receipt of Price, by ESTES & LAURIAT, No. 301 Washington Street, Boston.

THE GLOBE ENCYCLOPÆDIA

OF UNIVERSAL INFORMATION.

EDITED BY

JOHN M. ROSS, LL.D.,

Senior Master of English Literature, High School of Edinburgh; formerly Assistant Editor of "Chambers' Encyclopædia;" with a numerous and able Staff of Contributors.

*** (1.) The Globe Encyclopædia will contain articles on a greater number and variety of subjects than any previous work of the same character.

(2.) Though these articles will, in general, be very condensed, every particular essential to a proper understanding of the subject will be given; and where space is absolutely required, the new Encyclopædia will be as complete in treatment as much larger works.

(3.) In all the more important departments of knowledge, the Globe Encyclopædia will not only furnish the results of the most exact and solid research, but it will also seek to carry out more thoroughly than any of its predecessors the practice of referring to the best authorities on the subjects discussed or described.

(4.) The meaning of names of places, &c., always interesting and often suggestive, will be given with a fulness, and, it is believed, with an accuracy, not hitherto attempted.

(5.) Special attention will be bestowed upon the language, literature, and history of the English Nation, its Colonies and Dependencies.

(6.) The most recent statistics regarding the population, agriculture, commerce, and social condition of foreign countries, will be given, so that the Globe Encyclopædia, as the latest work of the kind, will necessarily prove of the most useful.

(7.) The articles in the scientific departments — e. g., Medicine, Chemistry, Natural History, and Botany — will be in accordance with the best and latest teaching on these subjects.

Forty-eight Parts, paper covers	. . . .	$24 00
Six volumes, quarto, cloth	. . . .	30 00
" " " full library, sheep	. . . .	36 00
" " " half morocco, extra	. . . .	42 00
" " " calf	. . . .	42 00

For Sale to Subscribers only, and sent, postpaid, to any part of the World, on receipt of Price, by ESTES & LAURIAT, No. 301 Washington Street, Boston.

CHAS. KNIGHT'S POPULAR SHAKSPERE.

(PICTORIAL EDITION.)

Illustrated with 340 Woodcuts and 36 Full-Page Plates.

By Sir *JOHN GILBERT*, A. R. A.

Together with Illustrations on Steel, from Pictures by

C. W. COPE, R. A.,   E. M. WARD, R. A.,
W. P. FRITH, R. A.,   C. CLINT, A. R. A.,
LESLIE, R. A.,   H. S. MARKS, A. R. A.,
MACLISE, R. A.,   W. Q. ORCHARDSON, A. R. A.,
And Others.

*** The text adopted in the present edition is that recently revised by Mr. CHARLES KNIGHT, who, thirty years ago, issued the first number of his Pictorial Edition of Shakspere. As a "Labor of Love," the work grew under his hands, and on its completion, in England and America, it was universally admitted to be the best edition of the works of Shakspere, and one of the noblest contributions to the literature of the day. Thoroughly familiar with all that has been added to our knowledge of the poet's writings, Mr. Knight undertook a revision of his original work. By a collation of the early editions of the separate plays which are in various public and private collections, he has been enabled to produce

The Most Accurate Text of Shakspere Extant.

The size of this edition, being two volumes Royal Octavo, will keep it within the range of the bookcase, as well as render it a handsome addition to books for the drawing-room table, and it is believed to be *the cheapest finely illustrated edition ever offered the public.*

In addition to the carefully edited text, and beautiful illustrations, it will contain a full GLOSSARIAL INDEX, and

Charles Knight's Complete Notes,

reprinted from the last London edition, *without alteration* or *abridgment*, thus making it invaluable to the student, as well as an ornament to the library.

The work will be published in thirty-six serial parts, at 50 cts. each.

For Sale to Subscribers only, and sent, postpaid, to any part of the World, on receipt of Price, by ESTES & LAURIAT, No. 301 Washington Street, Boston.